Time to Talk

STORIES FROM THE HEART OF IRELAND

Michael Healy-Rae

Gill Books

I dedicate this book firstly to the two people that brought me into this world, Jackie Healy-Rae and Julie Healy-Rae. I also want to dedicate this book to my family, friends and supporters, who have stuck by me in every way.

Introduction

As I'm writing this introduction, I'm sitting in the passenger seat of my car. My son Jackie Jr is driving me and I don't know what route he's taking me at all, but we're stuck behind a Jeep that has a horsebox attached. The horse has his head stuck out the side window, his long mane blowing in the breeze, and he has the biggest smile on his face. If I had hair like his, wouldn't I be doing the same thing? My head out the passenger window with one fierce-lookin' smile on my face. But sure isn't that what we all want? To be happy, content, and to go through life smiling? Granted, that isn't always possible, but sure look, if you do happen to be going through a difficult time at the moment, well then I hope the stories in this book will entertain you enough to distract you from your troubles for a bit. Above all, I hope the distraction lasts long enough to carry you through to the dawn of a new day, so you can start again and start afresh.

I say this because there was one person I didn't carry through to a new day, and that regret will stay with me for the rest of my life. To this day, I wish I had gone to his house and talked the ears off him. Had I done that, he might not have chosen to take his own life that night following our phone call. Had I handled things differently – well, okay, his problems would still be there, but he would have lived to have seen another day, and who knows but that day might have brought with it a new perspective on his struggle.

There's great power in talking, but there's greater power in laughing. Even the best doctor in the world would be hard pushed to find a treatment with better medicinal properties than a good laugh. This is why you can't beat old Irish stories and the wit in which they're wrapped. This is also why this book is not a political one or a memoir. Instead it is a book filled with stories about various incidents that occurred throughout my parents' lives and my own. Some are humorous, some are poignant, some are heartbreaking, but each one of them is the God's honest truth. I've always said the best stories are the ones that actually happened. From the story of my father driving a car into the village with a coffin on the roof, and the dead man still inside it, to him canvassing a person in the bath, nothing but suds covering their bit of modesty, and let's not forget the brain surgery that was carried out in a pub in Kilgarvan . . . sure look, there are things that happened back then that you wouldn't ever see happening today. Rather than let these memories stay in my head, I decided to put them down on paper for others to enjoy, and I honestly hope that each and every story either entertains you or moves you. The one thing my mother always used to say about my father was 'you'd never find him boring'. I hope you say the same about this book.

Michael Healy-Rae

Time to Talk

Not Right in the Head

Even before I was born, I was very 'lively', you could say.

Wait 'til I explain.

When my mother was heavily pregnant with me – a week or two away from giving birth – she was inside in the house getting the dinner ready when she went to get milk from the fridge. What she didn't realise was that the fridge was live, and when she put her hand on the door, didn't she get a strong electric shock that jolted her right to the ground. She wasn't hurt, thankfully, but she always used to make out that the reason she survived being electrocuted that day was because I had taken the brunt of the electricity. She would joke that I was always very 'lively' as a result. One of her famous lines was, 'Ara sure Michael, you were never right in the head anyway because of the electric shock you got that time!'

She was a deeply intelligent woman, my mother; so articulate and well-read. I remember when I was a child, Mrs Shine would only ever sell two copies of *The Irish Times* in her shop each day. One copy was to the local priest, the other was to my mother. She was always so knowledgeable when it came to world affairs. In fact, before meeting my father and moving to Ireland, she had worked for the Syrian Consulate and was based in New York's Empire State Building. She spoke seven languages fluently and could read and write Arabic. You would think after she moved to Kerry she would lose the languages through lack of use – not much need for Arabic around here – but she never did.

The funny thing is, when I was a young lad, I had dyslexia, so I couldn't read or write until I was nearly a teenager. I always used to think it was mad that my mother had all these exotic languages under her belt, and here was her own son who couldn't read or write so much as his own name in the one language he was born with.

My mother was an absolute lady, but a gas woman at the same time. She was never overly religious, but you know how people would give up different things for Lent? Well, my mother used to do things for Lent; things that she hated. She saw it as a type of penance. Her most memorable one involved Guinness. Now, my mother absolutely despised the taste of Guinness, but as her Lenten penance she would buy a bottle of it and then try to drink it over the course of two nights. To make it a little more bearable, she would even mix it with some milk. I'd see her trying to drink it, and I used to think it was hilarious altogether the way she'd crease up her face in disgust with each sip of her milky Guinness. She hated the stuff, but she saw it as a necessary evil, and sure she was a typical Healy woman; once she got an idea into her head and committed to it, there was no talking her out of it.

I was very lucky that I grew up around strong people. The women were very resilient characters, both mentally and physically. My grandmother on my father's side – I actually had six grandmothers in total, but I'll tell you more about that later – was a great woman known as Nana Rae. The one thing I remember about Nana Rae is that her two hands were like shovels. She had hands bigger than any man. She would be out cutting turf barefoot in the bog and it was a well-known fact that if you needed someone to help you with the work, you would be better off having Nana Rae by your side than any pile of men.

One lasting memory I have of Nana Rae is of her washing clothes outside the front door of the old house. She would have this timber wash board – if you were to see it today you'd think it was a very primitive-looking device altogether – but it was on this board that she would rub the clothes vigorously to get them clean. If you think about it now, people back then had to invest a serious amount of physical effort in washing their clothes, but yet when they were going somewhere like Mass, they were always so clean and smartly dressed. People made do with very little back then, but they always, without fail, took pride in their appearance. These days, if people don't have it easy, they won't have it at all.

Whenever anyone called to the house, Nana Rae would always insist on them having something to eat. Even if you weren't hungry, if Nana told you to eat, you'd eat. In the kitchen, there would be a big open fire, over which would always hang a big black pot for boiling spuds. It was on this open fire that Nana also used to bake the most fabulous of apple tarts. There has never, nor will there ever be, an apple tart made in Ireland that could compare to those made by my grandmother. Now, you might ask what was so special about them. Well, the pastry had a lovely buttery taste to it, while around the edge there'd be this delicious hard crust of syrup that you'd have to crack with your teeth. Even the way my grandmother used to place the slices of apple inside the pastry was just different, and each cut of apple was always so juicy and sweet. The top of the pastry would then have this mouth-watering sugary coating, and if you bit into a slice of the tart while it was still hot from the fire, you'd almost feel the sugar melting on your tongue.

Maybe it's just me, but fruit also tasted fresher and sweeter back then. During the summer months, we used to head out picking blackberries and wild strawberries. You wouldn't see wild strawberries in as many places these days, but when we were children, we would head out into the fields and pick an absolute pile of them. When we'd return home that evening, the lot of us would sit down and enjoy this big bowl of sweet fresh fruit. Then in the autumn, we would pick hazelnuts. You can buy a nutcracker now, but back then we didn't have anything of the sort, so what you'd have to do was go looking for a stone that would be small enough to hold with one hand but still heavy enough to crack the hazelnut. You'd put the hazelnut on the ground, try to keep it from rolling, and then land the stone down on top of it, but only with enough force to crack the shell. You didn't want to go crushing it entirely or you'd make bits of the hazelnut inside in the shell. It just wasn't as enjoyable when it wasn't in one piece.

Autumn was a great time for things like that, but, funnily enough, we didn't really do the Hallowe'en thing of dressing up in costumes. Although, come to think of it, no one did it that time. Dressing up for Hallowe'en was more of an American thing. What I remember most about Hallowe'en as a child is the games we'd play. Snap Apple was the main one. This was where you'd put a coin in an apple, hang it from the ceiling, and then you'd have to try and bite the coin from the apple. The nose would be nearly gone from you by the time you'd get the coin. Another game we'd always play didn't have a name, but it involved putting a coin in a pan of water and then whoever got the coin out with their mouth got to keep it. The innocence of it all! Hallowe'en for us was about the games and the barmbrack. Barmbrack was an awful novelty that time because it wasn't every day you'd have a brack in the house. It was such a luxury item.

One treat we were lucky to have all year round, and it was something I absolutely loved, was the brown bread my godmother Eileen used to make. Every Sunday night, without fail, she and her husband, John, would call over to the house with the brown bread, and it still piping hot. I used to love nothing more than cutting that first slice. Straight away you'd see the blade of the knife steam up with the heat as you'd glide it through the bread. I'd then smother a slice in butter and sure the butter would barely be on the bread a few seconds when it'd be melting into every pore. I'd follow it then with a bit of jam on top, and you know, you wouldn't call the queen your aunt when you'd be having it. The brown bread would be in one hand, and a massive cup of tea would be in the other, and I'd savour every last bite and every last drop.

Another long-standing tradition of Eileen's involved making a massive Christmas cake every December. Even though my birthday was on 9 January, you could say it fell under the Christmas umbrella, so when she would be bringing over the cake, she would also have with her a jumper she had knitted for my birthday. She was an expert knitter, so she would usually make me an Aran jumper. It would be the real deal too, with its big brown buttons and traditional báinín-coloured cable-knit pattern. I'd knock sparks out of the jumper for the whole year, wearing it here and there until it was nearly threadbare, but sure by that stage I'd be ready for the next one she had knitted for me.

Eileen's husband, John Galvin, God be good to him, was always known as Whitey. Where I'm from, everyone has a nickname. In a place where there could be ten families with the same surname, and many with the same first names as well, nicknames were the only way to distinguish one from the other. In those days we didn't have Eircodes, so if you were sending a letter to someone in Kerry, and you wanted to be sure the right person got it, all you'd have to do was put down their nickname and the postman would know exactly who it was for. Sometimes you wouldn't even need to put in their address. Just writing their nickname and something like 'South Kerry' would do just fine. Your nickname could come about in the most random of ways too. Before my time, a good few of the locals were involved in a play in Kilgarvan and didn't the names of the characters each of them played become their nicknames afterwards. It was actually from that play that Whitey got his nickname.

When Whitey died suddenly at a young age, Eileen found herself the sole breadwinner, and with a young family to take care of, she decided to take on a part-time earner known as 'home work'. Home work was what we called home employment. A good few companies would have offered it back then, and a lot of families in Kilgarvan would have availed of it in order to bring a few extra pound into the house. Eileen's home work involved making those white ring-binder stickers that you would place on the punctured holes of your copy sheets to prevent them tearing. She would have made tens of thousands of them, I'd say. Other families then would have been responsible for making things like net bags for fruit and vegetables. In our house, we made hair rollers, or curlers, as they were known at that time. Myself, my mother and my sister Rosemary used to sit around the kitchen table making hundreds, if not thousands, of them for the curler factory in Kenmare. Every spare bit of time we'd have, we'd spend putting them together and packing them up.

Would you believe I can still remember every single part of the process? You would start with a round bar on a base, and then you would pull what we called 'the sock' down over the bar. You would put the spring up on top, and then pull the sock up over the spring. Then you would cut it, before pushing in both sides. You would then take a brush from another box and push that in through the spring so that the bristles would cock out through the curler. That was one curler made. You would make three of them and then place a rubber band around the three. You'd have to arrange them in the box in a certain way, so they'd sit evenly. In one box alone, there would be two hundred and forty dozen curlers, and for that you would be paid three pounds and sixty pence. I've always thought it funny that a follicly challenged man could know so much about hair rollers.

Six Grandmothers

Technically speaking, I had six grandmothers.

And you might wonder how someone could have six grandmothers, but I'm telling you, I did. My grandfather on my father's side, Danny, well, he had two wives. After the first wife died, he married again. He had twelve children in total, six with each wife; my father was the eldest of the second family. My mother, on the other hand, was born in Wilmington, Delaware. When her biological mother passed away, she was still a child, so she was sent to live with her uncle, Daniel Stephen, and his wife, Hannah, who were living in New York. From that day forward, she looked on Daniel Stephen as her father and Hannah as her mother, and they likewise doted on her as a daughter. Her birth father, Jerry, meanwhile, had three wives over the course of his life, so strictly speaking, they could be counted as my grandmothers also. And there you have it, the six grandmothers I had. We'll call the first four 'the originals'. The main two grandmothers, however, were Nana Rae, who I already told you about, and Hannah, Daniel Stephen's wife.

Daniel Stephen was fierce interesting. I know that he fought in the First World War, but the God's honest truth of the matter is that I couldn't tell you anything about what it was like for him because he never talked about it. People who came back from war that time never talked about what they saw or what they went through. They just parked it and got on with their lives. Once he was back from fighting in the war, Daniel Stephen worked himself to the bone. He was an extremely hard-working man; awful clean-living as well. He never drank or smoked. Would you believe, he had never so much as set foot inside a pub until he went out and bought one when he came home to Kilgarvan.

Daniel Stephen was also a good man for planning ahead, even if he did so in a more 'Kerry way' than a conventional one. When he was thinking about buying a house on the Port Road in Killarney, the first thing he did was get a rope and tie his two legs together. We call that fettering. If you had a goat, and you wanted to stop it from wandering, you would tie its two front legs together and that would slow it down; you'd fetter them. Well, my grandfather decided to fetter himself. With his two legs tied together, he took off down to the local shop on New Street. Sure, he had no sooner hobbled in the front door when the shop keeper was over to see if he was all right.

'Mother of God, Daniel Stephen, what's wrong with your legs?'

'Not a thing,' replied Daniel Stephen. 'I'm thinking of buying a house down on the Port Road and I just wanted to test something out first.'

'Test what?' asked the shopkeeper, now even more intrigued.

'I wanted to see what the journey to the shop would be like for me in the years ahead when my legs aren't working their best.'

Now, Daniel Stephen was pushing on retirement age at this point, but he was in good health and nowhere near slowing down. Even still, he wasn't going to buy the house until he knew for sure what it would be like to live there in his slightly older and less energetic years. In the country they'd call that 'being cute', and Daniel Stephen, let me tell you, was most definitely cute. When he lived in New York, he would wait until Christmas Eve before he'd buy a Christmas tree, so he could tell the seller what price he wanted to pay for it.

Hannah was also known for her work ethic and her astute ways. She had worked in the kitchen of the Waldorf Astoria, where she oversaw portion control. It was her job to ensure nothing was wasted. They were a good combination, the two of them.

As Daniel Stephen got older, he ended up becoming quite frail, just as he had predicted, so he moved into my mother and father's house and lived out his days there. That's actually the house that I live in to this day. My mother and father built it and not once in my life have I ever lived anywhere else. All the memories are still in the walls. The notches are still there from when we'd each be measuring our height as children, while the indents on the timber doorjambs from throughout the years are all still visible. Every inch of that house has memories attached to it. My brothers and sisters left, my mother and father left, but I never did, and I never will. The day I leave that house is the day my toes will be going out before me.

A Brain Surgery and a Pint of the Black Stuff

The walls of some pubs have seen all sorts of carry-on, absolutely all sorts, but how many, do you think, have seen an impromptu brain surgery being carried out? Well, I can tell you there's one that definitely has, and that one is in Kilgarvan.

A long time ago, back in my grandfather's day, there was a local pub owned by a man from another Healy family, the Healy Shines, and at the time the man had been experiencing a problem with his head. I'm not too sure exactly what was wrong with him, but whatever it was, it became very serious very fast, and so it was swiftly decided that only a surgeon had the skills necessary to fix him up and sort him out. There was a surgeon in Cork who was free to perform the operation, but he needed a car to pick him up. Back then, however, there was only one car in Kilgarvan, and if my father's memory served him right, it was owned by a family living above in Sillardane Lodge. Once the emergency was explained to them, the car was duly dispatched to Cork to collect the surgeon, and it wasn't too long before he was in the pub with a medical bag containing everything from scalpels to spatulas. Would you believe there's such a thing as a brain spatula? I'm telling you, there is.

Anyway, the front doors were quickly locked shut and the patient was laid out and administered the anaesthetic. I won't go into the details of the operation, but thankfully, it was a success. Despite the unorthodox setting, it all went off without a hitch. A few hours later as the surgeon was finishing his pint and packing up his stuff, spatulas and all, he gave the strict instruction that the man was to awaken naturally in his own time, and under no circumstances be woken up by noise and the likes. Now, this presented a problem. You see, there was no tarmac on the road back then, so one of the loudest noises you'd frequently hear throughout the village would be the horses' hooves clattering down the stony street.

The great thing about rural villages, however, is that when a family is going through a difficult time, they never have to go through it on their own. Everyone rallies round, helping them in whatever way they can, and that is exactly what the people of Kilgarvan did when this family found themselves faced with this big problem. Straight away, two locals were given the job of sentries and put standing at each side of the village. Their job was to warn any visitors passing through that there was sick man in the locality and that it was important everyone remain as quiet as possible. To tackle the issue of the street noise made by the horses' hooves, the locals set about gathering all the straw and rushes they could find and carefully laying it all down on the road. That way, when any horses were walked through the village, the soft bedding would stifle the noise of their hooves. Sure enough, the plan worked perfectly, and the village remained quiet while the man slept. He woke up naturally and, thanks be to God, went on to make a full recovery. That same pub has sadly since closed its doors but before it did, it had become better known for its fine pints of the black stuff than for brain surgery.

A Makeshift Hearse

Sometimes in life, you have to make the most of any situation, but if you don't have a situation to make the most out of, then you have the make the situation yourself. My father was a great man for putting this into practice. From the time he was a child, he always made the most of what he had, and if he didn't have anything, which was more often than not the case, then he'd make something from nothing.

My father lived on the farm in Rae when he was a child, which was named after the townland in which it was located, Reacaisleach. That's how the 'Rae' in Healy-Rae came about. Before it was part of our name, everyone knew us as 'the Rays'; that was our nickname to distinguish us from the other Healy families in the area, such as the Healy Shines and so on. It was my mother who suggested changing the spelling to Rae and pairing it with the name Healy, so it would become a double-barrelled name. She always said it looked nicer on paper. Anyway, the Rae farmland was home to a number of bogs, so families like the Healy Shines and the Quills would pay my grandfather an annual sum of around thirty shillings for the right to cut turf there for the year.

When my own father was around eight years of age, however, his father was out tipping a load of manure when his legs gave way from underneath him. He was in all kinds of agony, but somehow they managed to get him on the train and bring him to the hospital. They had no idea what was wrong with him, but at the time, there was this belief that being placed in a bath of extremely hot water would cure a person in pain, so the doctor ordered that this practice be carried out on my grandfather. As instructed, he was put sitting in a bath filled with near-boiling water, and sure of course, it did nothing other than make his condition a thousand times worse. My father in later years reckoned it was a slipped disc that had been the cause of the pain.

My grandfather had been a mighty worker right up until that day. When he left hospital, he was never the same again, that's as sure as God. My grandmother, Nana Rae, took over the farm work because from that day forth my grandfather was confined to a chair; he never again walked after that. What he needed was a wheelchair, but getting one at that time was next to impossible, so what did my father go and do, only make one. He got two of the finest bicycle wheels he could find and attached one to each side of an ordinary table chair. He then placed the chair on an axle and secured the lot together. My grandfather had also been suffering an awful lot with his hands around that same time, so my father created makeshift armrests by tying a bit of flat timber to each side of the chair. All his life, my grandfather had worked relentlessly. He would have toiled away in all sorts of weather. As his fingers became painfully gnarled and twisted, it was thought that the cold had crept into his bones and left him with an infection. Knowing what we know now, however, I'd say it was very likely arthritis that the poor man was suffering from. The DIY wheelchair was simple, but wasn't it effective; so much so that my grandfather went on to spend the next two decades of his life in that chair. You'd be hard pushed to get that length of time out of the professionally made ones we have today.

A local man employed my father to work as a hackney driver for him. One day, my father was driving people to Killarney in the man's car when he heard that a Kilgarvan local had passed away.

The family, he was told, had no way of bringing him home. Sure as far as my father was concerned, there was only one thing for it.

They'd have to put the coffin on the roof of his car and he'd drive the deceased back to the village himself. The family had no

A Narrow Escape

Paudie and Timmy Buckley were two bachelor cousins of mine, and probably two of the greatest characters to ever come out of Kilgarvan. I could honest to God write a book on them alone. They worked the farm all their lives, and if ever there were two men who knew how to do things the hard way, it was Paudie and Timmy. If they were knocking a tree, they wouldn't get a man with a chainsaw, they would use a cross-cut; Paudie on one side of the tree, Timmy on the other. It would take them hours and hours to knock the tree, and once it was knocked, it would take them hours to cut it up, but that was how they did things. The hard way.

They also had a large field that Timmy used to mow with a scythe. The field was so big that the only way Timmy could be sure he'd get it all cut in the one day would be to start at around five o'clock in the morning. It would be a grand summer's morning, and there Timmy would be, working away like the hammers with his scythe. He'd stay at it all day until it was done; it was the height of torture. You'd mow that field with a tractor today in the space of a few minutes, five at the most, I'd say, but Timmy used to have to give the whole day to it. Himself and Paudie were actually known for having their dinner fairly late at night because they'd have spent so much of the day out working the farm. It could be nine o'clock at night before they'd start putting down the spuds, and because the spuds would be in a big pot on an open fire, they would take ages to boil, so the two wouldn't sit down to dinner until around eleven o'clock. Their attitude was that they would be so busy during the day, they wouldn't have time to eat any earlier.

Another thing they used to do is manure the field by hand. Outside the door of every cabin was a big dung heap, and in the springtime, that dung heap would have to be brought out into the fields and spread, but what Paudie and Timmy used to do was move the dung up onto the horse and cart, bring it to the field and then start depositing small lumps of it about the place. They'd come along next with their pikes and start trying to shake it and spread it by hand. Awful work altogether.

One morning, anyway, and this now would have been a good few years back, the two set off to check their cattle. At the time, there was a great festival taking place in Kenmare called the Cibeal, but this would have been of no interest to Paudie and Timmy. They liked to be up and out early in the morning, making a start on the farm work. On this one particular morning, they decided to start by checking on their livestock in a field they had rented on the outskirts of Kenmare, known as Master Cousins's field. Now there was one big rock in Master Cousins's field. Paudie, the older man, got out of the van first and made for the gate. Sure what did he see inside in the field, only a man and a woman with not a stitch of clothes on them and they up on this rock. With that, Paudie turned around quick as a flash and stopped Timmy going any further so he wouldn't see what was taking place on top of the rock. 'The cows are all right,' said Paudie, 'everything is fine! Come on away! Come on away!'

That night, the two were having a drink inside in O'Reilly's bar, and while Timmy was chatting to a neighbour, Paudie started talking to Mick Reilly, the proprietor.

'Cripes, man, I had a narrow escape this morning,' he said.

'Why? What happened?' asked Mick.

'Weren't we going into the field and didn't I see a man and a woman up to no good. I managed to stop the young lad in time before he saw anything. Thanks be to God, the young lad saw nothing. He doesn't know a thing in the world about it, but let me tell you, it was a narrow escape!'

The gas thing is, the 'young lad', Timmy, was no teenager. Paudie, the older of the two, was in his seventies, while the 'young lad' he was so worried about was in his sixties.

The Importance of Neighbours

What is a Healy-Rae? A Healy-Rae is the exact same as anyone who started with nothing, but what if you started with less than nothing? That was how my father started. With less than nothing. After my grandfather was confined to the wheelchair, tough times became tougher, but so too did the people who were living them.

Neighbours were so important then. My father used to always tell me about the time they were in an awful way as they had no garden ploughed and set. Having no garden set was a serious situation to find yourself in because it meant the difference between having enough to eat for the winter, and not having anything at all. A diet of bread and potatoes was like the life support of every family back then, so if you had no garden in which to grow potatoes or vegetables, you were facing bleak times, let me tell you. One day, when my father was around ten years of age, he could see their neighbour Jer Donovan tacking a horse way off in the distance. Straight away, he ran into his mother, told her what he had seen, and asked, 'Is there any chance he's coming to us?'

Nana Rae sent him back outside to keep watch on Jer Donovan and see where he was going with the horse. If Jer felt a hole burning in the side of his head, it's because my father didn't once take his eyes off him. Sure enough, Jer crossed the river, went through the field, and made his way closer and closer. Now, while my father is watching all of this, he's giving his mother a blow-by-blow report of where exactly Jer is and what he's doing. Sure enough, in Jer arrives to plough the garden, no questions asked. That simple gesture was like a lifeline to the family. There was no such thing as payment back then, either; sure no one had any money that time. Good deeds were done through sheer good will, by neighbours looking out for each other.

Another neighbour who was responsible for keeping the family ticking over was Mrs Quill. My father always insisted they wouldn't have survived if it hadn't been for her. He never told me the full story himself, but I sat in on an interview he gave Maurice O'Keefe of Irish Life & Lore, and in it, he recalled the incident. He told Maurice of how there came a point when his mother didn't have so much as two pennies to rub together. This was a disaster because it meant she couldn't buy flour. One day, without any notice, Mrs Quill sent Nana Rae the most enormous bag of flour. She left it by the ditch at Rae Cross where my grandmother would get it. How Mrs Quill knew the family needed it, I don't know, because my grandmother never said anything to her, even though the two of them were great friends. Mrs Quill would have known of my grandfather's situation, however, so it's possible that she just decided to send up some flour as a neighbourly way of helping out, without actually realising that she was saving their lives. For the length of time that bag of flour sat in the kitchen, it was minded like it was another child. That's how valuable it was.

Mrs Quill, the Lord have mercy on her, was a lovely woman. Like my grandfather, a trip to the hospital ended up doing her more harm than good. When Nana Rae was hospitalised with gallstones, by sheer coincidence Mrs Quill was in the bed next to her suffering from much the same problem. Mrs Quill had agreed to surgery on her bladder to remove the gallstones, but when the same solution was suggested to my grandmother, she wouldn't hear of it. No way was she going to let anyone put her to sleep so they could go at her with a blade, not a hope in hell of it. The doctor even approached my father at one point to ask him if he could persuade his mother to have the operation.

Mrs Quill went for the operation, and this will show you how cruel fate can be sometimes, didn't she pass away during the surgery. She was the most good-natured lady who never did a thing to hurt anyone, only help them, and yet she lost her life during a routine operation. My grandmother was devastated by the news. It also made her more determined not to have the operation. She begged my father to take her home, and he didn't need to be asked twice. Home they both went. That time, most people would have been afraid to have turned a deaf ear to advice from anyone in authority, especially someone like a doctor, but my grandmother was adamant that she wasn't having the surgery. After she left the hospital with my father that day, what do you think happened her?

She went on to live for four more decades, not a bother in the world to her.

We're Not in Kilgarvan Now, Toto!

When my father was building our house, he built it from scratch, and by 'from scratch' I mean he even made the concrete blocks himself. Rather than buying the blocks, he bought a machine to make them. And do you think he bought the gravel? Not at all. He went straight to the river above in the farm in Rae and took the gravel from there. Sure, wasn't he right? What good was it doing in a river? If you were seen taking gravel from a river today, you'd nearly be looking at a holiday in Mountjoy.

Once he was finished making the blocks for the house, he decided to start making and selling blocks to other people, and once he was done with that, he went and sold the machine and made a few more pound that way. My father was always very industrious by nature. So was my mother, in fact.

When my father started with machinery, he was an expert mechanic, but he had initially started out as a bicycle mechanic. He was offered a job with the Automobile Association (AA), but he realised he couldn't take it because it was above in Ennis. He was the eldest, and with his own father unable to take care of things, he decided it would be best for him to stay put. Now what he did next will give you an idea as to just how easy-going it was at the time. My father went to his good friend, Robert Lyne, who was living just over the road from us, and he said to Robert, 'I'm after getting a job but I can't do it. Will you do it?'

Sure of course Robert said, 'Well, do you know what, Jackie? I'll chance it!'

So off Robert heads to Ennis, but when he landed there he realised he had two problems. When you worked as an AA mechanic that time, you got a motorbike, a set of tools for the motorbike, and a set of clothes. Here was Robert above in Ennis with a company motorbike to mind but nowhere to mind it, and nowhere to store his clothes and tools either. So, Robert pulls into a petrol station and while there he gets chatting to the owner. As he's explaining his predicament to the man, what does the man do only offer him a place to stay. Eventually, Robert started working in the petrol station in his spare time. Fast forward a few years and Robert is still in Ennis, only now he owns the petrol station in question, not to mention a few other petrol stations to boot. He then went on to establish a number of very well-known Ennis businesses that are still there to this day and has amassed a very impressive business and property portfolio. Today Robert is still living in Clare and the Lyne business empire is run by his family.

Isn't it amazing how life turns out, though? Had Robert not taken the chance and headed for Ennis, you'd wonder where his life would have taken him. He'd still be successful, I have no doubt about that. Honest to God, if Robert Lyne had been sent to the moon instead of Ennis that time, he would have set up shop there and still been a success. I always thought it was mad how a simple chat with my father landed Robert above in Ennis and completely changed the course of his life. In saying that, I have always been a great believer in fate. I do believe that certain things happen for a reason because that has always been my own experience of life. I'll never forget, when I was ten years of age, my mother brought myself and my sister Rosemary to New York to visit all our relatives, as well as a childhood friend of hers. My mother had two close friends all her life. One was called Claire Cunningham, the other was a lady called Gloria. Gloria actually finished up in a very high-ranking position in the New York police force. When Pope John Paul II was visiting the city, she oversaw his security.

When we arrived in New York, we went to stay with Claire and her husband, Bob Cunningham, in a place called Bronxville. When you're ten years of age, you wouldn't be long sizing things up, and when I arrived in Bronxville and saw the enormous house, the big garden, the swimming pool, the black Cadillac and all the other bells and whistles, it didn't take long for me to realise that whatever Bob did, he must be good at it. One night shortly after we arrived, Bob said he would take us out for dinner. As he was driving us to the restaurant, he pointed to a big industrial estate, filled with warehouses, between the road and the Hudson River.

'That's my place in there,' he said. 'That's where I go to work.'

Naturally, I strained to see. After what seemed like endless rows of warehouses, suddenly there were yards filled with hundreds of lorries. Each lorry had a distinctive blue, red and white logo on the side accompanied by the words PEPSI COLA. It struck me that we had been driving along at a fairly decent speed, and yet Bob was still saying, 'That's all my place down along here.' The man owned half this side of the Hudson River. Bob, my mother explained to me, was the main distributor for Pepsi Cola in New York state – not the city, mind you, but the state.

When we arrived at the building in which our restaurant was situated, myself and Rosemary took one look at the place and found ourselves in awe. Where had Bob taken us for dinner? Only the Twin Towers. We're not in Kilgarvan now, Toto! The restaurant itself was about three floors from the top, and aptly called Windows on the World. Inside, the place was like nothing we had ever seen before. It was the kind of place where you wouldn't have to light your after-dinner cigarette; the waiter would do it for you. The one thing I will never forget about the place was how one minute you would be able to see out over the whole city, lights flickering all sides; the next, you wouldn't be able to see a thing because the clouds would come along. For a ten-year-old from rural Kerry, it was the most surreal experience.

As we were leaving, Bob went to the counter to pay, and at this point I was eager to suss out as much as I could about this amazing place, so I decided to join him. Right by the till there was a glass bowl, so I reached up and put my hand in, expecting to find sweets, but instead I got a handful of matchboxes. Inside each box, there were eight enormous matches, so I nabbed three or four of the boxes to bring home and show my friends.

Sadly, when the towers fell in 2001, the Windows on the World fell with them, but would you believe, I still have those matchboxes to this day. About five years ago, I gave them to my own young lads, explained the story of how I got them, and warned them to keep them for another forty years, so please God when they have their own young ones, they'll be able to pass a little memento from history on to them.

But back to Bob. I liked Bob, and Bob, I know, liked me. We got on awful well together. When he would go to work during the day, I would clean the swimming pool, cut the grass, wash the cars . . . I was always at something, never idle anyway. Two nights before we were due to fly home, I was summoned into the living room, and who was in the room only Bob and my mother. I knew there had been some quiet talk going on between them throughout our time there, but I didn't have a clue as to what it was about.

After I arrived into the room, Bob started the conversation. 'I have a proposition for you, Michael,' he said.

Now, to a ten-year-old, this all seemed like very serious talk.

'I've been talking to your mother, and I'd like to keep you.'

I looked at him.

'To keep me?' I queried.

'Yes, I'd like for you to stay here,' he explained.

Bob was a real businessman; a tall, strong man, well dressed, big square head on him, and I remember him towering over me as he laid out his plan.

'This would be the deal,' he said. 'I'll keep you here, I'll send you to school, I'll pay for your education and I'll get you educated well. I'll bring you in working in my company, and when you start, I'll put you in at the very bottom. It will be entirely up to you where you'll go after that, but I will give you all the chances. Are you interested?'

Here I was, ten years of age, in this big fancy house in New York, being offered a new life by a man who seemed to own half the city. I looked at Bob, I looked at my mother, I thought about it for, I'd say, barely ten seconds, and then I said, 'Thank you very much Bob, but I'll go home with my mother.'

As I turned and went to walk out the door, Bob called after me. 'Michael?' he said, 'Are you sure?'

The exact answer I gave him was, 'Well I'm not, Bob, but I'm still going to go home with my mother anyway.'

That was the end of that conversation.

It comes back to fate though, and the amazing fact that we are all only one simple decision away from changing our whole lives. My God, the difference it can make. Where would Robert Lyne be if he had said no to Ennis? Where would I be if I had said yes to New York? You never know, I could have ended up somewhere inside in the White House, instead of inside in the Dáil.

Tommy

My cousins, Paudie and Timmy Buckley, had a sister called Mary, and when Mary was thirteen, she was sent off to live with my mother in New York. The reason for sending her to America was quite simple. Her family in Kerry couldn't afford to keep her. Sending children to live with relatives was common practice back then, and not one bit of notice was taken of it.

As the years went by, Mary got married to a lovely man called Dominic and they had a number of children together, including a son named Tommy. He would have been a second cousin of mine. As a young man, Tommy worked as a guard in a New York Prison. Back then, this particular prison had a shocking reputation. If you were sent there, you'd be lucky to come out of it alive. It was a tough job, but he loved it.

When my mother brought myself and Rosemary to America, we stayed in Mary's house for a few days during the trip. I stayed in Tommy's bedroom, and whenever his alarm would go off at 5 a.m., he would be up like a light, no complaints out of him.

One day, anyway, and this would have happened not long after we had headed back to Ireland, Tommy discovered that some prison officers were bringing drugs into the prison and selling them to the prisoners. Now, Tommy was young, probably a bit wet around the ears, and naive about how places like that operated, so he decided the right thing to do would be to report it to prison management. Instead of being grateful for the information, however, top brass gave him a cold reception and sent him on his way.

One morning not long after that, the alarm clock went off at 5 a.m. as usual, and up Tommy jumped to get ready for work. I'd say the poor lad wasn't even five seconds sitting in his car when he realised there was someone hiding in the back seat. The person, who was armed, directed him to drive down to the beach, and it was there Tommy was found later that morning with a bullet to the back of the head. No gun was ever recovered, but what do you think is down on his autopsy report? Suicide. Well I'd say Tommy must be the first person ever in the world to shoot himself in the back of the head, dispose of the gun so carefully that no one would ever find it, and then return to the car to die.

To call a spade a spade, Tommy's death was completely covered up by the authorities at the time. It was a whitewash job. They wanted to get rid of him because he posed a problem – he knew what was going on and wasn't comfortable with it. He thought he was doing the right thing by telling the bosses. Instead he ended up paying for his honesty with his young life.

Tommy's death was devastating for his poor mother, Mary. From the moment she was given the news, she was never the same again. The fact that his death was then filed as suicide when it was so obviously murder – that just tore her asunder. She fought tooth and nail to get justice for Tommy; she campaigned for years, but it never yielded results. Over the passage of time, it became harder and harder for her to fight the powers that be, and when she fell into bad health, sure she didn't have the energy to keep at it. She was up against it, as they'd say.

There are things you'd see happening in movies as a child and you'd think to yourself, my God, that could never happen in real life. Tommy's death would have been one of those things. Back then I would never have thought something like that could happen in real life; not a hope of it. It was such an eye-opener for me as a ten-year-old. My own mother always used to say, 'You can't fight City Hall,' and sure enough, in this case, she was absolutely right.

Awful Scour Talk Altogether

Paudie and Timmy Buckley had great friends who would have been very smart when it come to the modern way of doing things. The brothers would have been more old school in their ways, so one time, a friend of theirs advised that they would be better off having two herd numbers and two flock numbers, and that their pockets would legitimately be all the better for it, if you know what I mean.

Sure the two were only delighted to hear this, so of course they followed their friend's advice and divided the cows, but once they did, they would never refer to each other's half as 'his herd' or 'my herd', they would just say 'him' and 'me'.

One fine spring day weren't Paudie and Timmy sitting inside in Reilly's bar when in walked a few Yanks. After ordering the drinks, one of the visitors turned to Timmy and tried to make small talk. I think he asked him something random like, 'Did you guys have a nice winter?'

'Oh Jesus no,' Timmy replied. 'Sure he got an awful doing altogether with the scour,' he added, nodding at Paudie. 'He was nearly the finish of everything.'

Now, as you can imagine, the Yanks are just standing there looking at each other while they're taking in all this detail. Naturally, they had no idea that Timmy was talking about the calves because Timmy had never once mentioned them.

To put the tin hat on it, he then told them, 'And what's worse . . . didn't I go and get a dose of the scour as well!'

Meeting His Waterloo

When I was growing up, our next-door neighbours were a lovely couple called Jerry and Margaret Donegan. Before they had their daughter Mary, I was like their child. I'd say I was in their house as often as I was in my own, and when I wasn't in either of those, my mother knew she would find me in Nora Quill's house, which was on the other side of Jerry and Margaret's. I idolised Nora, but I couldn't pronounce her name at the time, so I used to always call her Nono. Would you believe, her daughter is Máirín Quill, who went on to become a TD in Cork. I'm telling you, for a small corner in rural Ireland, we produced a fair few TDs.

Anyway, I looked up to Jerry an awful lot. At times, I was like his shadow. He was a forester and whenever he would go to pay the forestry men, he would always take me with him. One night, however, Jerry was nearly shot. And wait 'til I tell you who the trigger man was ... only my own father. It was all over the simplest misunderstanding too. The post office in Kilgarvan had been robbed around that time, and for whatever reason, the robbers decided to drive up the laneway beside Nono's house and count the money there. When Nono found out about this the following day, she was terrified and insisted that my father get a street light installed. Truth be told, the robbery had left him feeling every bit as anxious; it was just a bit too close to home for comfort.

Late one night, not too long after the robbery, didn't my father hear a strange noise outside. He looked out the bedroom window and realised a car had pulled up at the bottom of our road. Even though it was dark, he could make out the shape of a man walking up the road. Well, that was enough; himself went to get the gun. He opened the window and stuck out the gun. By this point, my mother was also up, only she was insisting that he put down the gun. She told him it was likely only Jerry Donegan coming in from playing cards. My father, however, was already taking aim at this 'robber'; he even had his finger on the trigger. I don't know what my mother said to him, or how she talked him out of firing the gun, but he listened to her and put it down. Sure enough, the 'robber' walked up to the front door of Jerry's house, turned the key, and walked in. My mother was right; it was Jerry. It turned out he had stayed out longer than normal playing cards. They were trying to finish the tournament as it was coming up to Christmas. To get to his house, Jerry would have to have driven by Nono's, but he was conscious that he was a good bit later coming home than usual, so rather than drive by Nono's and have her be frightened by the sound of a car pulling up outside late at night, he instead parked his car at the end of the road and walked in. He walked up past Nono's and it was as he was approaching his own house that my father nearly shot him. When he learned the following day of how close he had come to meeting his Waterloo, I'd say he never again parked at the end of that road.

Years later, Jerry and Margaret went on to build a new house. They were only moving a mile away, but as far as I was concerned, it might as well have been Outer Mongolia they were moving to. I can still remember the day they were packing their stuff into the van. I was so upset at the idea of Jerry, Margaret and Mary moving away that you'd swear they were dying. After they moved, I cycled back and over to their new house once a day if not ten times a day. I'd say you'd have had more chance of having Elton John come out and give you a hand with saving the hay than you would have had in keeping me from visiting Jerry, Margaret and Mary.

A Few Drinks Too Many for Santa

My father, being a masterful Director of Elections, was a great organiser by nature. This meant that occasions such as Christmas were a big affair in the Healy-Rae household and would have been carried out with as much military precision as any election campaign. My father had one very strict rule for Christmas morning, though: absolutely no one was allowed down the stairs to see what Santa had brought unless himself and our mother were with us. The door to the sitting room, where Santa would have left the bits and pieces, would even be locked late on Christmas Eve, just in case anyone tried sneaking down during the night to get a first look.

Sure the second we'd wake up and realise it was Christmas morning, we'd tear like mad into my mother and father's bedroom. My mother would lead the way and my father would carry myself and my sister Rosemary on his back down the stairs. We were the youngest of the house, so it became a tradition for him to carry us down to the sitting room that way. My mother would then unlock the door, and whatever about the presents that Santa had left, the big thing for us was to see the absolute state of the room. He would absolutely wreck the place, every single year! There'd be chairs knocked over, a table turned upside down . . . even the bottle of Guinness would be empty and also upside down. We'd always leave out a glass of whiskey as well, and you can be full sure Santa emptied that too before he left! My father always went to great lengths to make it as memorable as possible. If something in the room could be moved, you can be sure it would be turned sideways or upside down. He would tell us that our house was one of the last of the night on Santa's list of deliveries, so by the time Santa had reached us, he'd be after a few drinks too many, and would be staggering around the place. We were convinced that's why the room would always be left in such a mess after Santa had been.

On Christmas Day, the big thing was watching the circus on television. In our kitchen, there was a door into a dining room that was never used except at Christmas. My father would always open the door and turn around the black and white TV, so we could watch the circus while having our Christmas dinner. He used to make such an effort with things like that; every last detail was considered.

Another lasting memory I have of Christmas back then is the sight of a red candle on every window of every house in the village. A big red candle would be placed inside a metal paint tin with a bit of sand in it. The youngest person in the house would light the candles each night on Christmas week. Checking the candles was a big responsibility altogether. Every twenty minutes, you'd hear my mother shout, 'Michael, check the candles.' I'd always be delighted to do this because I loved nothing more than walking into a darkened room that was lit by nothing other than the cosy warm glow of the candle. As I'd be checking the candle, I'd look out the window and see all the other houses with their candles lighting. It was such a big novelty. There was no such thing as flashing Christmas lights or even tinsel back then, it was just the candles. When fairy lights arrived, we thought they were awful smart altogether, the way they sparkled and glittered.

My father was mad for Christmas, he just loved it, but what he enjoyed most was making it as impressive as possible for his children. When my own lot were growing up, I used to keep his traditions alive by doing all the same things he did. I'd carry the two smallest ones down the stairs on my back, and when we'd unlock the door, the first thing they'd see was the room turned upside down. Another thing I used to do was tell the young lads the story about goose's poo. I would explain to them that if a person was going bald, then they should rub some goose's poo all over their head and chest, and that it would give them a mighty blasht of hair. My father always told me that same story when I was a child, but he would tell it in such a convincing way that I never thought to question why he hadn't used this magic cure on himself, considering he had barely a rib of hair on his own head. If my young lads had been smart enough, they would have asked me the same thing.

My father's hair used to get so much attention. Even the American actor from *Married with Children* and *Modern Family*, Ed O'Neill, spoke about his famous hair. He also impersonated him, which was hilarious to listen to. I remember when I was about four years of age, I used to have these Matchbox toy cars. If my father was nearby when I was playing with them, I would insist on standing up on his lap, taking off his cap, and moving his hair out of the way so I could drive these little Matchbox motorcars around his head. I'd call the top of his head the parking space, and I would try to get him to hold his head still so the cars wouldn't fall off. Once the cars were parked up, I would then make a little ditch out of the corner of his hair to stop them falling off the side of his head. He was mad busy at the time, but even when he was rushing, he would always sit there as patient as ever while I turned the top of his head into a car park.

Memories of Happy Schooldays

When I look back on my years in Kilgarvan National School, I remember with great fondness and admiration my principal, Master Hickey. His first name was Dermot but we all only ever addressed him as Master Hickey, even as adults.

Master Hickey was a great man, the finest you could hope to meet, but you wouldn't find a teacher like him in today's schools. For a start, he used to bring his gun into the class with him on occasion and shoot grey crows from out the back window of the classroom. He hated them. As a farmer now myself, I can't say I care too much for them either. Blackguards with wings, they are. No matter how often you'd hear the noise of Master Hickey's shotgun being fired, though, the fright would still lift you every single time. If you were writing, your hand would fly, and so too would the pencil.

Often, I would clean his empty gun for him after class. There's a very specific way to clean a shotgun but Master Hickey taught me how to do it right, and I have to say, I was glad to learn. Even though I was only a child at the time, I still knew it would be an extremely handy skill to have. There was a method to the procedure. First, I'd have to take an auld dry cloth and give the gun the once over to be sure there was no damp inside it. If damp gets into a gun, it's scuppered because rust would be sure to follow, so getting rid of any moisture was one of the most important things I'd have to do first. Then I'd have to dismantle the gun, removing pieces like the barrel and the stock, so I could push the cloth into the smaller crevices. Once that part of the process was complete, I would pour some cleaning oil on a rag and rub it on every inch of the gun, inside and out, to get rid of any dirt build-up. There was also a special type of brush that you would have to spray with oil and then snake through the barrel of the gun, so it could pick up any surface dust. Before you'd finish, you'd then check the barrel to make sure it was absolutely spick and span and that your work was done. Jobs like that, I enjoyed so much. Anything practical was right up my street.

Another job Master Hickey would give me would be to count his money. He would call on me to separate the notes and take account of what was there. I loved counting those notes. The one-pound note was a large green one, and the fivers came in two colours, brown and white, and were almost twice the size of a fifty euro note today. Back then money was money; not like the auld paper we have today. Sure, when I was a child I used to go into what was known as the old post office in Kilgarvan and buy four farthing sweets for a penny. Then I would head over to George Maybury's shop and buy a rake of sweets for a few pence more.

George and Clare Maybury would keep the sweets in tin buckets and if you wanted to buy a few, they would put them into a brown paper bag and place them on a weighing scale which would then determine the price. It's hard to believe it now, but twenty pence would get you some amount of sweets back in those days. The popular sweets back then were the brown cushions and the brown cloves. Brown cushions were the big favourite, though. They were a brown hard-boiled sweet that had a white stripe running through the middle. We also had red clove sweets that were encased in a white hard enamel; I'm nearly certain you can still get them. Once the sweets were bought, I would separate them all out, and then head into school, where I'd sell them off in the yard. I'd not only make my money back, I'd double it. What I would usually try to do, however, was save up a good bit of money so that I could buy an almighty big bag of sweets and then sell them all off in ones, twos, threes, and fours. I learned more from experiences like that than I did from any school book. Even the life lessons I picked up from people like Master Hickey were invaluable. Everyone saw the master as being a teacher with a few businesses, but truth be told, he was a businessman who happened to be a teacher. He owned a hall, a gala ballroom, a petrol pumps, and a butcher shop. He also had a lorry on the road, and through his work as a farmer, he would buy and sell hay and livestock.

We had a roster for our lessons, but on the rare occasion Master Hickey might need help moving cattle on his farm after school, then let me tell you, it was all hands on deck. If he was going selling calves at the mart, some of us would be brought out to help load them onto a lorry after school. If he was going dipping sheep that evening, we'd go out and help him move them into the pen. Sure, we didn't mind one bit what he put us at. We would only be delighted to be out on the farm with him because it meant a few hours of freedom from mundane homework.

Even though he was a very logical man, Master Hickey wasn't above calling on the divine, or in his case the diviners, when he found himself in a spot of bother. I remember one time his car was stolen, and I'd very nearly swear he called the diviners before he called the gardaí. Anyway, he set off to see these two divining brothers in West Cork who were known all over for their skills. Divining, if you're not familiar with it, is an old art in which two metal rods are held up by a diviner. The reaction of the rods can help locate anything from water springs in the ground to missing objects. Anyone can learn how to do it, but there's always those who seem to be born with a knack for it, and the two brothers in Cork were two such people.

Well, Master Hickey went and met with them to see if they could tell him where his car was. Sure enough, they produced the rods and then a map, and in no length of time, they were not only able to tell him that his car was in the county of Cork, they were also able to tell him the name of the street on which it was parked. As you can well imagine, the master was delighted to hear this. Then they said to him, 'You needn't worry one bit about it because there's a garda standing alongside it right this minute looking at it.'

Sure, that was enough to put Master Hickey's mind at ease, so he headed back to Kilgarvan. He was no sooner in the door when Mrs Hickey said to him, 'I have good news!'

'They're after finding my car?' replied the master back to her fairly confidently.

'They are!' she said, a bit taken aback by his response.

'They're after finding it in Cork, over on Harbour Street,' he went on.

Sure, of course, herself was now looking at him in shock. 'They did!' she confirmed, 'But how did you know that?'

'The two diviners told me!'

Mrs Hickey was always a lovely chatty lady, but I'd say that took the talk out of her that evening.

Funnily enough, Mrs Hickey was also our school principal. She had previously been a principal in one of the smaller schools in Kilgarvan, but when that closed, you could say she was centralised to the main school, where her husband was headmaster. Even after the move, however, she retained her position as head-mistress, so we ended up with two principals.

The academic side of schooling was always a struggle for me. As I mentioned earlier, I'm dyslexic, and all throughout primary school I could neither read nor write. Back then, however, there wasn't a name for it, so for years I could never understand why words appeared the way they did. I just knew I didn't like school and that it wasn't for me. I wanted to be out working and doing things, not sitting inside in some classroom. Even on my first day in baby infants in Kilgarvan National School, I remember standing there, taking it all in and thinking to myself, oh Mother of God, what am I doing here?'

I'd say I repeated those words to myself every day I spent there. I would have given anything to have been anywhere else in the world other than inside in that classroom. When I was around twelve, however, things changed. A lovely young nun in Killarney by the name of Sister Regina discovered I was profoundly dyslexic. Only for her, I might not ever have learned to read or write. The timing was tight too. It was the summer before I went to secondary school in Kenmare, and I was at that stage where I had two choices: either continue on into secondary school or stay at home and work. Fortunately, I decided to tackle the problem, and carry on with both school and work.

The first day I met with Sister Regina, she sat me down and explained what was wrong in such a way that it finally started to make sense. I can still remember her exact words too: 'Michael, your head is full of padlocks. What's wrong with your brain is that these locks are there, but there's no key to open each lock, so what I need to do is make a key to open each lock one by one, and eventually we'll get there.'

And that we did.

Sister Regina went on to become a Mother Superior, and I used to be so delighted that this woman I knew, this woman that had helped me so much, was now a Mother Superior. I was awful impressed by that. Thanks to Sister Regina, my time in secondary school turned out to be an entirely different experience compared to that of national school. Once I learned how to read and write, the novelty never wore thin. I always used a fountain pen for my schoolwork, and I was always very particular about my penmanship because it was such a big deal for me to be able to write.

But anyway, to come back to Master Hickey, himself and my father were lifelong friends. As close as brothers, even. They did everything together. They adored music and had played in a band back in their younger years, but what they loved most of all was GAA, in particular hurling. They would have played together in many a hurling match, and the night before each match the two of them would meet to discuss tactics on how they'd go about passing the sliotar to each other. With the master's house being right next door to the family bar, there was barely a day when the two didn't talk. This is why I always maintain that one of the hardest things I've ever had to do was break the news to my father that his friend Master Hickey had passed away.

The day it happened, myself and my brother Danny were out moving a machine with our father, but just as we reached the outskirts of the village of Kilgarvan, didn't the lorry break down. The brakes had gone in it. Myself and Danny left himself with the lorry and we headed back into Kilgarvan to get the piping needed to fix it. Now you must remember, there were no mobile phones back then. If there was news to be known, you heard it by word of mouth; there was no reading it from a little screen. Well, as myself and Danny were going through Kilgarvan, didn't we hear that Master Hickey was after dying, and I'd say neither of us were the better for hearing it. When we got back to the lorry, we were still in shock, but we couldn't tell our father what had happened because we knew it would leave him distraught. He was a proud man; he wouldn't want to be seen upset on the side of the road, so instead we set about fixing the lorry and getting it home. As we were parking it up, all we could do was take a breath and break the news to him that his friend had passed away. He was devastated. I always maintain he felt as though he had lost a brother that day.

Doing the Messages

Back when I was a young lad, if you wanted a bike, you could buy one from Jim Caball, or Jim Caball Himself. Now, I'm not repeating myself when I say Jim Caball Himself. There were two Jim Caballs in Tralee, and both sold bikes, so one was known as Jim Caball, and the other as Jim Caball Himself. It was the only way to distinguish one from the other.

Like most nine-year-olds at the time, I had a decent bike, but once I realised there was an opportunity to make money from it, it became more of a business vehicle. I would call to people who lived outside the village, people that I knew had no means of transport, and I would ask them if they needed me to pick up their messages. 'The messages', as I'm sure you will remember, was the name given to groceries back then. You'd either go out for 'the messages' or 'a few bits', it was usually one or the other. If someone couldn't go out, then I would offer to do it for them. They'd give me the list and sure I'd cycle in and pick up what they had asked for. I had a carrier basket on both the front and back of the bike, so once I had everything carefully packed in, I'd cycle back and give them their messages along with their change. The one thing you wouldn't dare do, however, is ask for money, but let's just say there was a quiet expectation that you would get a few pence, maybe ten or twenty pence. You'd only get thirty pence if you were really lucky.

Along with picking up the messages, I also used to do some odd jobs around the house for a few of the locals; things like cutting grass, carrying in the turf and timber for the fire, a bit of painting, typical odd jobs – you know yourself. Three of my regulars, Mrs Guard O'Connor, Mary Ellen Twomey and Christina Foley, ended up becoming terribly important to me. I spent so much time working for them that I grew to know them extremely well; I absolutely adored all three of them.

I remember when I was working for Mrs Guard O'Connor, I would wheel in the dung for her garden and then spread it out on a small patch of ground where she would grow the most delicious rhubarb. I would keep the fire going for her as well. I should point out that this was another case of a nickname that stuck. Mrs Guard O'Connor was actually Mrs O'Connor, but the reason she became known as Mrs Guard O'Connor was because she was married to a garda. From the second the ring went on the finger, she became known as Mrs Guard O'Connor. It was one sure-fire way to distinguish her from the multiple other Mrs O'Connors in the area at the time. Mrs Guard O'Connor was a lovely woman, a lovely, lovely, woman, and a lady I looked up to so much. She was also very religious. Mary Ellen, my other regular, was also a mighty Mass-goer, but to a slightly lesser extent than Mrs Guard O'Connor. I remember one day Mary Ellen handed me a piece of paper, and on this piece of paper was a prayer. The prayer was for work. That prayer was, and still is, so terribly important to me. I absolutely treasured it from the moment it was handed to me, and not only do I still have it, I still say the prayer every so often. I also passed it on to my children because even though I wouldn't be one for material possessions, I would be very particular about keeping sentimental things like that.

When I think back on it, Mary Ellen had one big obsession. If you were working in her house for a good while, she'd come out and say to you, 'Do you want to pee?' She had this thing in her head – she was convinced that if you needed to pee, you should under no circumstances put off the job. As far as she was concerned, a need to pee was one best heeded immediately. She used to constantly warn me that if I held in my pee, it would come against me in later life and I would suffer no end of health problems. Sure of course, I believed every word of this theory. I was so terrified of what any pent-up pee would do to me in years to come that the second I felt the need to go, I would immediately have to find somewhere. Anywhere would do because I sure as hell wasn't going to carry it around with me for fear it was going to be the cause of my death in later years. No way was I risking an early demise by betraying the gospel according to Mary Ellen.

Needless to say, I was heartbroken when Mary Ellen moved up the country to live with family. She had become a bit too elderly to live on her own, so she sold the house to a lovely lady called Christina Foley. When Christina moved in, I continued doing the same odd jobs for her that I had been doing for Mary Ellen. Women like Mary Ellen and Christina were the people that survived the toughest of times. They were the 'just get on with it' generation. There was no such thing as complaining with them, they just got on with it. They had no money as such, but they still got on with it. Whatever life threw at them, all the different things that happened to them, they just got up and got on with it. Young people today may have so much in terms of technology, but they're still missing out greatly on knowing those kinds of people, I believe.

Anyway, between all the odd jobs I did, and all the messages I picked up for people, I managed to earn a good few pound, but any money I earned from the bike, I always put towards buying a new bike, one that was stronger and faster. It was a big thing back then if you had a bike with two or three gears, but I ended up buying a bike from Jim Caball Himself that had twenty-four gears on it. The height of notions entirely! It cost me £140, which, would you believe, was £100 more expensive than my first car, a MK1 Escort that I bought from John Lyne.

I can't remember what age I was exactly when I bought my first car, but I do remember not having a licence to drive it. Sure I was only using the car to tip about on our own land. To be honest, I don't think I was even old enough to qualify for a licence, so I couldn't get one even if I wanted to. Back then, you were put sitting behind a steering wheel the second you were tall enough to see out the front window. You sat in and you figured out yourself how to drive it on. My father and brothers put me driving when I was around six or thereabouts. It was just the done thing at that time. Sure my own son Kevin told me he was gallivanting around the farm in a car at the age of five. My eldest son, Ian, was the same. My daughter, Rosie, waited until she was that bit older before she followed suit. I think she was the ripe old age of nine when she started. She had her own car up on the farm and she would regularly go up there to drive it around. Mother of God, did she make bits of every ditch she hit, but let me tell you, it made a great driver out of her. Thank God, too, because isn't she now our local postwoman!

I remember the first day I taught my eldest daughter, Juliette, how to drive. We were in an auld jeep on the farm and I was sitting in the passenger seat taking her through the basics. She was about ten or eleven at the time. She had been driving for about five minutes on her own, when she turned to me with a dead serious look on her face, and said, 'Will you show me how to do a handbrake turn now?' I'd say I'd spent longer drinking a cup of tea than she had spent driving, and here she was, looking to do a handbrake turn. I remember thinking to myself, 'my God, that's ambition!'

The Rocking Chair

If I had a spare few pound going handy, I would always save it for special occasions. I remember one time I decided I would splash out and buy a rocking chair for my mother. I had seen a mighty looking rocking chair inside in John R McCarthy's old shop on Kenmare's Main Street. Now John R was a great man. He had a sister living in Kilgarvan and I always used to pluck the turkeys for her every Christmas. I had spotted this rocking chair, anyway, and I saved and saved to buy it for my mother for Christmas. As her birthday was in January, and because it was such a grand purchase, it was also going to be her birthday gift. I was young at the time, but once I had enough saved up, and once I got my mother gone one day, I took her car into Kenmare to pick up the chair.

Carefully, I loaded it into the boot of the car and secured it in place with some baling cord. I made sure to put the cushions into the back seat to keep them from getting dirty in the boot. To protect the handles from any damage, I wrapped them in some old rags I had brought with me. I then covered the rest of the chair in some old clothes, so it wouldn't get scratched or chipped while I was driving. I headed for Kilgarvan nice and careful, afraid for my life that I'd be caught by the gardaí driving my mother's car on the main road and I still only a young lad.

The road between Kilgarvan and Kenmare was very different that time, and God knows I was breaking no speed limit as I was being so careful, but didn't I hit a bad patch at some point along the way. Just as I hit the bad patch, I knew I heard a bit of a thud. It wasn't loud, but it was enough to make me uneasy, so I stopped the car and got out to investigate. Mother of God, there was absolute devastation on the road. Whatever way the baling cord had ripped when I hit the bad patch, didn't the chair fall out and smash into a hundred bits and pieces on the road. I was as shattered as the chair, I was so upset. It wasn't even the kind of damage you could repair. It had gone from being a beautiful chair to firewood. All I could do was throw the bits into the boot and drive the saddest journey home. Apart from the rocking chair cushions that were still in the back seat, I didn't have a thing in the world to give my mother on Christmas Day. I had spent all my money on the chair, too, so I hadn't a bob to buy her anything else either. It had taken months and months to save up the money and for the whole thing to get torn asunder in the middle of the road . . . I don't think I was ever as upset in my life. I envisioned her having that chair for years and years, and instead it never even made it as far as Kilgarvan.

There You Are Now

A lot of memorable things happened in the '70s. In 1974, sure we had the whole commotion with Rose Dugdale and the IRA. I remember my father obsessively following that story. I don't know why but the Montreal Olympics in '76 also stands out. I think it was because I was sent a black cap with 'Montreal' written across the front of it. I wore that cap for years. The Olympics had long finished, and there I was, still going around with the Montreal Olympics cap on my head. Then, of course, in 1977 we lost Elvis Presley. About a year after Elvis died, a set of commemorative stamps were released in America. A relation of mine who was living there sent a few over to me. I still have them, too. Like the Twin Towers matchboxes and Mary Ellen's prayer, it was one of those sentimental treasures I held on to.

Another memory I have from that time was the day our former president, Cearbhall Ó Dálaigh, died. His funeral was being held in Sneem, so we all got the day off school. I remember as I went to leave the house, my mother asked where I was going.

'I'm going to the funeral,' I said.

'What funeral?' she asked.

'Sure, isn't the president dead?' I said, 'So I'm going to his funeral. We'll never see a funeral like this again!'

Thanks be to God, I had a warm coat on me that day because it absolutely poured from the heavens. As I was walking along the road, I put out my hand to thumb a lift. Next thing, this big Mercedes pulled up, so I hopped in and sat between the two seats. I looked out to see who had given me the lift. Sitting in the driver's seat was this man with massive sideburns. They came right down below his nose, nearly reaching his mouth. He had a familiar face and as I was looking at him, he glanced at me in the rear-view mirror and asked, 'Do you know who I am?'

'I most certainly do know,' I replied, as the penny dropped.

'Who am I so?'

'You're Willie O'Brien, the man with the cranes.'

Willie was a famous businessman. When it came to eye-catching marketing ploys, he was one of the originals. He was doing the Michael O'Leary thing before Michael O'Leary was even born. Anyway, when we landed in Sneem, the rain was still pouring. It was so bad, you could almost feel the soaking you were about to get.

When I went down into the graveyard following the Mass, I couldn't see a thing because I was so small and stuck within the middle of such a big crowd. Out of the corner of my eye, I spotted some scaffolding. RTÉ had erected a stand for their cameraman to film the proceedings, so, like a monkey, I pulled myself up from one bar to the next until I reached the crossbar. I held on to that bar for all I was worth. I had to, sure the rain was driving in at this point. At the time, I was wearing a hat that had these flaps down over the ears, and I remember them constantly hitting against my face as the gales blew in. Even from my vantage point, you couldn't see one headstone with all the umbrellas that were up that day. I managed to see the proceedings, though, and I still to this day believe that the only people who saw Cearbhall Ó Dálaigh being buried were the people standing around the graveside, the RTÉ cameraman, and myself.

The following day, the front pages of the newspapers all carried features on the funeral, but one in particular caught my eye.

I turned to my mother. 'Well, there you are now, everyone will know I was at Cearbhall Ó Dálaigh's funeral anyway!'

'Why is that?' she asked.

I showed her the newspaper. There I was on the front page at a state funeral sitting on the crossbar perished with the cold and my mud flaps blowing in the wind.

All My All-Irelands

One thing that not too many people know about me is that I have three All-Ireland Championship medals.

For whistling.

I'm not joking. I won three All-Ireland fleadh's for whistling.

My father was an almighty whistler as well. The knack with whistling is being able to whistle in and out without having to stop to draw breath. You have to have a continuous flow. I had grand plans of taking home a fourth All-Ireland win in a row too, but, unfortunately, my whistling winning streak came to a premature end when I cracked a tooth.

I was on the greasy pole at sports day when I got a belt to the back of the head with a pillow. As my head jerked forward, didn't I hit my tooth off the pole and break it. You can't whistle if you have a cracked tooth, and so I had to say goodbye to my reign as the All-Ireland champion.

That time, there was no such thing as getting a cap for your tooth; you just had to put up with it, so it was left that way for years. Once tooth caps were a thing, however, I had one applied and, sure enough, I could whistle again. I never got that fourth win, but I still say I'm the only Kerryman with three All-Ireland medals and not one of them from the GAA.

Absolutely Twishted

After I'd finish school each day, I used to run down to the pub and get to work. Each one of us served our time behind the counter, and when it was my time, I was always very particular about making sure I'd be behind the bar, ready and organised, for when the forestry and council men would come in that evening. People like Michael Corcoran and Dan Patsy would come in for their few pints after their day's work and chat about all that went on. I remember Michael was working in forestry at the time while Dan was working in the council. Any person who worked in forestry or the council, I looked up to as role models because they would have been out working in all sorts of weather doing what needed to be done.

Another great visitor to the bar was a famous singer called Seán Ó Sé. He used to holiday in our village, and whenever we'd hold the annual Welcome Home festival for people abroad, the likes of Seán would be there singing. I think one of the most memorable singing regulars who graced our bar with his presence was a man known simply as Danno. Now Danno was one of these people who was naturally gifted with an unbelievable sean-nós singing voice, and to this day, I regret that I didn't record him on cassette because the lilt in his voice would have honestly put the hair standing on the back of your neck.

Sadly, for someone who always loved a celebratory occasion, Danno ended up passing away one Christmas Eve. I always hate to hear of that happening, which is why I worry about people living on their own. Some people might find it hard to believe, but there are people living in areas that are so isolated, the only individual they might see from one end of the week to the other would be the postman. I know it's not as common as it might have been before, but those people still exist, and I do worry sometimes that we're all so caught up in our own lives, we forget to check in on those who perhaps might not have the luxury of company. This is why the pub is such an integral part of rural life. For some people, it's the only social interaction they get to enjoy. I remember, for instance, we used to have great storytellers who would have the whole bar enthralled with the interesting tales they'd tell. The stories would always be about things that actually happened, too; they were never fictitious.

After my father opened a singing lounge in the bar, we also had some wonderful professional performers cut their teeth on our stage, people like master musician Dermot O'Brien, the Bards, and the Dublin City Ramblers. One night my father had booked a very famous country singer to perform in the bar. I won't name her, but I will say this, she was a little bit fond of the bottle. Anyway, didn't she disappear not long before she was to go on stage. When we found her, she was on the stairs in our pub, and she was pasted out of her mind. She couldn't sit up and string a sentence together, never mind walk up to the stage and sing. When my father found her, he nearly hit the roof. The lounge was full to capacity, and they were all after coming from far and wide to hear this lady sing. I can still picture her now trying to reason with himself. 'Jackie . . .' she stuttered, 'Jackie, I can't sing, I can't . . .'

My father called her by her name, put his hand on her shoulder, and said, 'Do you know what you're going to do now, my grand girl? You're going to straighten yourself up and you're going to sing like you're a blackbird.'

He got her to neck glass after glass of water until she was semi-sober, and eventually he managed to come around her just enough to convince her she could sing. He then carried her out to the stage, put her sitting on the stool, stuck the microphone in front of her, and not a word of a lie, she gave the absolute performance of her life.

An' she absolutely twishted.

Falling Hatchets

It's an awful thing to say, but when we were children, our ears would perk up when we'd hear the news that a TD from up the country had died. The news bulletin would come on the radio, and next thing you'd hear the sad passing of so-and-so being announced. No sooner would the words have been broadcast over the airwaves than himself would land a bang of his fist on the table. All you'd hear would be the words, 'Thanks be to God! 'Tis a grand time for a by-election!'

My father was a Fianna Fáil councillor at the time, but he was also a superb Director of Elections, so whenever a Fianna Fáil TD passed away, himself would usually be drafted in to fight the by-election. For us, this meant three weeks off school and a trip to some exotic part of the country like Mayo or Meath. We'd be staying in a hotel, and sometimes it might even be a fancy one that had a sink in the corner of the room, but it wouldn't be a holiday for us by any means. Straight away, himself would have us working, hanging up the posters, handing out the leaflets. Anything that needed to be done, we were doing it. No one was idle, I'll put it to you that way.

I remember when Máire Geoghegan-Quinn's father died back in 1975. Off we went to Galway for three weeks. There was Maurice Galvin, Pats Guerin, my father and myself. My father had been drafted in to ensure that Máire Geoghegan-Quinn would win the seat of her late father, which she did. We weren't always successful, though. I remember us losing campaigns, and on those days you didn't hang around for long. You'd bail out of whatever town you were in and hit the road for Kerry as quick as you could. When we were in Galway fighting the by-election, though, I remember John Wilson, the then Minister for Education, was there. He was a great footballer, John. He played with Cavan, his home county. I got to know him well because he would always play football with me in the corridor of whatever hotel we'd be staying in. I was eight at the time we were up in Galway, and I remember thinking to myself, here I am playing football with the Minister for Education while dodging school for three weeks to help fight a by-election. The irony wasn't lost on me at that age.

I remember another time my father was directing the election of '77. At the time he was good friends with the late Neil Blaney, an independent who had earlier been kicked out of Fianna Fáil by Taoiseach Jack Lynch. It was all to do with Haughey and the arms trial. Anyway, one day in 1977, my father was in Dublin and he met Neil for a cup of tea and a chat. Chinese whispers went into overdrive and the story reached Fianna Fáil HQ that their Director of Elections was going to run as an independent. Next thing, word started to filter out that Fianna Fáil were going to expel my father. I'll never forget the headline on the front of the *Kerryman* newspaper that week: 'FF Hatchet to Fall on Healy-Rae'.

According to the article, the party was planning to hold a meeting to discuss getting rid of him. I was in Killarney with him on our way to the election office after this article went out. When we arrived at the office, we were greeted with a bolted door. Someone had locked the election office overnight and put a bolt on the door to keep my father from accessing the campaign office. I was around ten years of age at the time and I'll still never forget his reaction. He looked at the door and then calmly walked away. After about fifteen minutes, less even, he returned with a sledge hammer in tow, and, let's put it this way, he wasn't long removing the obstacles that had been keeping him from going into the campaign office.

The party meeting went ahead as predicted, and there was a vote held over whether he should be kept or sacked. The majority of the members wanted to keep him. I always maintained that the rumours about him leaving to run as an independent were greatly exaggerated. He wasn't intending on doing any such thing. People were too quick to jump to conclusions that time, and sure once the story grew legs, it couldn't be stopped.

Shtone Mad

I always say I got the best education from two groups of people. One was the forestry workers, the other was the council workers. I had a particularly close affinity with people who worked in the forestry, though, and this, as I've mentioned, started back when I used to serve them in the bar after school. To be good behind a bar, you needed to do two things. You needed to keep your mouth shut and your ears open. I did both, so every time the workers would come into the bar each evening, I'd hear all the stories from their day.

Even back then, I always felt the forestry workers were very hard done by. Coillte, or the Department of Forestry as they were known at the time, were awful tough to work for. The working man's pay was docked if it was felt by up on high that he hadn't opened enough drains during the day. His pay was also docked if it was felt that he hadn't planted enough trees. His pay was even docked if it rained. If the forestry worker was sodding all day – this was where he would cut a square in the ground and take out the sod before he'd plant the tree – well, this department man used to come along in the evening and stand a peg in the ground with a piece of string attached to it. He would then walk around in a circle while holding the piece of string and count how many sods were in the circle. If the worker was out by one sod, Mr Department of Forestry would cut his money. If the worker was opening drains all day, his work would be physically measured by the department man. If it fell short of the amount he reckoned the worker should have managed in that day, he was docked. Everything with them was docking. You'd swear 'twas their own money they were spending on wages.

Despite the challenges they faced, the forestry workers would still come into the bar each night and entertain everyone with their stories. They were the finest of people, and you honest to God wouldn't hear a grumble from them. I can remember every single one of them, too, right down to what each of them used to wear. A few of them also had farms, so after having a drink in the bar, they would go home, put down the spuds and get the few jobs done before having the dinner. Some of them would then arrive back into the bar again later that night for a nightcap.

I ended up working in forestry myself for a few years cutting timber, and I saw first-hand just how hard those men had worked to make a living. At the time however, I was doing contract work for the Department of Forestry, so I didn't have a wage at all; I only got paid by the tonne. For a long time I worked with a friend of mine, Dan Casey, but at one point I worked with two men from Fermoy. They were great workers and I know they won't mind me saying this, but they were absolute lunatics. Absolutely shtone mad, they were. Now when I say they were mad, looking back, I was probably in the same category myself.

We worked in the Dark Wood, just outside Killarney, and for about a year we lived in a caravan that was right in the middle of the wood. We used to sleep there from Monday to Friday, and for each of the five days we were there, we would work from the crack of dawn right up until it was too dark to keep going. I remember it was winter at the time and the caravan used to be freezing when we'd get back each night. We wouldn't be cold during the day – we'd be killed out with the heat from cutting heavy timber and stacking it on the side of the road – but at night, we'd be frozen. What we used to do to heat the caravan was boil a big pot of spuds for dinner. The steam from the pot would have the caravan warmed up in no time.

There was another mad fella who also worked with us. Donnacha Twomey was his name, and he was an absolute Trojan worker. He was young and just starting out, so nothing was a bother to him. He used to draw in the timber, and when I say he would work night and day, I literally mean the man rarely stopped to sleep. He might rest for an hour in the cab of his lorry but then he'd be straight back to work.

Donnacha would arrive into the wood in his lorry at two or three o'clock in the morning, and sure of course by that time we'd all be fast asleep, but just as he'd be getting closer to the caravan, he'd start blowing the horn. The noise of it would give you such a jolt from your sleep, you'd jump up with the fright and belt your head off the caravan ceiling. It was an absolute circus in that wood; I don't know how any of us made it out alive.

That said, there was one occasion when a tree fell and nearly knocked the living daylights out of me. As it was being knocked, I was standing right in its path and sure of course it came down on top of me. Thankfully it was the just top section of the tree I was hit by. It wasn't thick enough to do much damage, but it was still enough to give me a fair auld crack on the head. When the lads saw the tree falling on me, they nearly lost their own lives with the panic. To make things worse, they couldn't see me because I was buried under all the branches. Next thing they're all shouting, 'Mike? Are you dead or are you alive?' Even though I was half-smothered by the branches and had a pounding headache from the belt I'd got, there was no silencing the smartass in me.

'Well, I'm alive,' I shouted back. 'Sure I'd hardly be answering ye if I were dead.'

The Old Ways Were the Best

Back when I was a child, every house used to kill pigs. Some houses, however, were more noted for it than others. My cousins, Paudie and Timmy Buckley, were almost famous for it. When the time came for them to kill their pig, it was like a massive social occasion in the area. Different neighbours would come over and everybody who helped out on the night would receive part of the pig to bring home afterwards. Even if it was only a few puddings made from the blood, they all got something as a thank you.

The whole occasion would start at around ten or eleven o'clock at night, because by that time the jobs on the farm would usually be finished. Once the pig had been killed, the water would be boiled for the shaving. It was a big operation, but at the same time it was no trouble because the neighbours were there to help, and each one would be assigned their own job. Once the pig meat was cut into pieces, most of it would be placed into a salted barrel. It would turn a light brown from the salt curing, and what you'd be left with afterwards was the tastiest salty bacon; the nicest part of the pig as far as I was concerned. You wouldn't get anything like it these days.

Homegrown vegetables were another thing that tasted a lot nicer back then. Our neighbour Jerry Donegan had a vegetable garden in which he would grow enormous onions. I haven't seen an onion as big since the day Jerry stopped growing them. He used to have the best of potatoes as well, and I'm telling ye, lads, the food we had back then was a million times tastier than the food we have today. Even the best of restaurants couldn't recreate the kind of earthy flavours we had on our plates back then.

Now this is not me lamenting about the past and painting a romantic picture of that era. Some things were certainly nicer back then, but it wasn't a nicer time overall, especially when you compare it to nowadays, and we here with our luxuries such as central heating and the likes. Back then, the only part of a house that was hot was the spot right beside the open fire. If you weren't sitting in that general region, you were sitting in the cold and that was it.

Having no electricity back then meant people found their entertainment by telling stories in front of the fire, and this in turn led to a pile of superstitions being passed from one generation to the next. I remember hearing stories about the banshees, but one story I heard a lot was about a local family called the McCarthy Moores. We always used to hear a tale that when one of them would die, a cliff at the side of a mountain would open up. Now, I don't know what would happen when this cliff would suddenly open out of nowhere, but I took so little notice of old piseogs even back then that it never occurred to me to inquire.

Funnily enough, being without electricity meant people developed the ability to identify someone in the dark by the sound of their walk. They would know which neighbour it was by the gimp of them as they were going along. Personally, I don't remember the houses not having electricity, but I do remember them not having telephones or televisions. When televisions became more plentiful, our local GP, Dr Boland, and his wife, Nurse Boland, were the first to get a colour television, which was awful fancy entirely back then. Whenever my sister Rosemary would mind the Bolands' children, I would tag along so I could watch the colour television. I'd sit there in awe of it. When I learned how to read and write, however, my main motivation for going to the Bolands' house with my sister was so I could read their Enid Blyton books. They seemed to have an endless supply of Enid Blyton books on their shelves. I soon found out why. Mrs Boland used to nurse Enid Blyton when she was elderly. Would you believe, Dr Boland is in his early eighties and happily he's still a practising GP to this day.

Coming back to the superstitions, though, I still don't believe in them as such, but in saying that, I would have one or two habits that I'd be fairly wary of breaking. If, say, I were to go for a visit to someone's house, I'd have to leave through the same door I walked in. Even if I were with a few people, and they went to leave through a different door, I wouldn't be able to do it. I would have to go out the door I came in. It's just one of those things that I'm very particular about. Then there are the usual things like not walking under a ladder, and sure we've all heard the superstition about how you should hunt away a magpie if there's only one of them in it, but if you see two, then you should beckon them towards you. Don't be trying to picture me racing around the field after a couple of magpies, I wouldn't be going that far. I just beckon them and if they come to me, they come, and if they don't, Goddammit, let them off.

As for piseogs, though, I don't believe in that tripe at all. Years ago, there would be all these warnings and they'd be about the most random of things. One was that you shouldn't put fresh meat into a cart that was being drawn by a mare in foal or you'd land yourself in bad luck. Then there were many superstitions that almost became like traditions in a way. Back in Nana Rae's time, if a person died in the house, immediately the mirrors would have to be covered and the clocks would have to be stopped for an hour afterwards. Although don't ask me how they knew when the hour was up when they had no way of even checking the time.

Being Practical

When it came to school, I always used to love the practical element of different subjects. I remember back in primary school, Master Hickey once showed us how to make a fine pair of oil trousers using nothing more than a fertilizer bag, some baling cord and a scissors. It was almost like the kind of carry-on you'd see on *MacGyver*! All you had to do was cut two holes for the legs, and to hold up the trousers, you'd make a belt out of the cord. It was practical, and to this day if I ever need oil trousers while I'm on the farm, and I don't have a pair handy, well you could be sure there'd always be a fertilizer bag and some cord nearby. Thanks to Master Hickey, I'd have one made in a couple of minutes.

When I was in secondary school in Kenmare, we had a great science teacher called Dermot Kerins. He had a very practical teaching method in that he would take us out on science walks and explain things in a different sort of a way. He was also a horticulturist with his own nurseries, and after I left school he used to give me all his digger work. I ended up working for him for years after that. It was funny, I couldn't for the life of me call him Dermot. We could be having a chat during our ten o'clock tea break and I'd still address him as Mr Kerins. I just couldn't break the habit of how I used to address him when I was in school.

It's funny how things change so much with the times and how certain things that used to happen years back would be unheard of today. We used to have this other great teacher who was always really nice, but if you were blackguarding, he'd take no notice of coming up to you holding up his two fists, saying, 'Well, tell me, fella . . . do you want the left or the right?' You had three choices. You'd either say 'Left', 'Right' or 'God no sir, neither,' and you'd be all apologies because you'd be terrified he'd make the choice for you, and land you with the left or the right one anyway.

Then there was Tom Bambury who was the principal of the school and a very outspoken character. He was a great man for having the students' interests at heart and wanting them to get jobs afterwards. As much as he loved the students, there were certain things that he wouldn't stand for. There was a great bar in Kenmare, the Atlantic. It was owned by a man called Mick, who everyone knows as Mick the Atlantic. No prizes for guessing how he got his nickname. If we were waiting for the bus and it was running late, or if it was raining, we'd head into the Atlantic to play a game of pool. Now, if Tom heard you were in there, he'd go absolutely mental. He'd bring us all into the gym and give us this big lecture about going into pubs. He'd give it to you between the two eyes and he wouldn't spare you either. He'd put the terror of God into you some days. I wouldn't mind, but I worked in a pub, so I'm not too sure why he thought going into the Atlantic for a game of pool was going to lead me astray.

I was always a fairly mannerly student. I did stupid things that young lads do at that age, but I was never a troublemaker by any means. That said, I was persistent when it came to certain matters; I had no problem standing my ground whenever I felt it was necessary. Certainly, the authority of a teacher didn't thwart my perseverance when I wanted to do something. I remember one day, the funeral of a lovely man called Ken Mitchell was taking place and I wanted to go. At the beginning of the class, I explained to the teacher that this funeral was taking place and that I wanted to leave during the lesson, so I could go over to the church to pay my respects. The teacher refused to give me permission to do so. As the class went on, I kept a close eye on the clock. The second it hit 10.50 a.m., well you can be sure I jumped up and swung the school bag over my shoulder. The teacher didn't even blink. He could see the head was down as I was walking towards the door; I was leaving whether or not I had permission. I said straight out to him, 'Look, I'm very sorry, sir, but I'm going to the funeral.' And without even waiting for a response, off I went. There was no way I wasn't going to pay my respects to Ken. I had become good friends with him after he helped me make an aerial for my CB radio. Having this aerial meant I could use the NATO phonetic alphabet code to speak to people in places like Italy and Spain.

That time, you would have a CB radio for a car, but if you got a transformer you could use the house electricity to work the radio, and if you got a certain type of aerial, you could use it to talk to people in other countries. It was a big fad at the time. The idea that you could be sitting at home talking to someone driving along the road in Italy was a huge novelty. It was very interesting too because you got to find out what was happening far away; you got to hear bits of news from other countries and it gave you an insight into all the goings-on outside Kerry. It was like a primitive form of Skype, you could say. The first time I tried it, I spoke to a lorry driver in Italy. He had good enough English, so we were able to have a right chat. I explained where I was, and he explained where he was, and I remember thinking it was gas craic altogether that here I was in a village where it was pouring rain, talking to someone who was roasted out of it in southern Italy while they were driving along delivering bananas.

It's funny, I can literally remember the price of everything I bought back then because everything was so hard earned. My first CB radio cost me £30 exactly. If you asked me about something I bought today, sure I wouldn't have a clue. As a child, I had an appreciation for every pound earned. I remember when I started fourth year in Kenmare Secondary School, I was only a month into it when I decided enough was enough, school was a waste of my time and I wanted to be out earning a wage. At the time, I had been working in the piggery for the summer, and, luckily, I was able to return. I did the Inter Cert, but I did no more than that.

Pigs Don't Know It's Christmas

I remember when I applied for the job in the piggery the first time ever, Christy Hussey was the manager; he's still there to this day. He was a great man to work for, but he was as tough as iron. When I went to him looking for a job, I'll never forget his first question.

'What age are you?'

I was fourteen, but I didn't want to tell him a blatant lie, so instead I said, 'Well, Christy, I'm around sixteen.'

He probably knew I was younger.

The employment laws weren't what they are today, so even though he probably guessed I had been exaggerating the detail regarding my age, he still gave me part-time work, summertime work, and even Christmas work, which was a big earner. Working on Christmas Day was great because you always got paid extra. Sure the pigs didn't know it was Christmas; things had to continue regardless, and I was happy to do them if it meant I got well paid. I used to like working in the piggery. Pigs are a lovely animal, very clean, so I enjoyed working with them. There's a type of work with pigs, however, that people might call unsavoury. Young lads today would turn their noses up at it, but back then if you wanted to earn your wage, you had no choice but to do what the generation before you did, and just get on with it.

When I wasn't working in the piggery, I'd be doing all sorts of work everywhere else. I remember my father used to rent a farm in Aghadoe and this was where he'd bale hay. Back then, the summers were hot ones but sure there was no such thing as sunscreen then, and during the first couple of days of loading the bales into the lorry and bringing them the twenty miles to Kilgarvan, you'd get absolutely roasted. When you'd go to bed at night, you'd have to lie on your belly because your back would be scalded from the sun. There would even be blisters coming out. Once you got one right good burning, though, you were sound after that. You toughened up to it. There'd be outrage over that today because of all the health messages, but that was just the way it was done back then. We didn't have a care in the world only to be out working while the weather was fine.

Pallaskenry

The year I should have been doing my Leaving Cert was the year I went to Pallaskenry, an agricultural college. There were one hundred and four of us in the class, one hundred lads and four women. As you can imagine, the hundred lads were all very interested in the four women. Every day I was at Pallaskenry, I adored it. It was honestly one of the best years of my life. Everything about the place, even the food, was just brilliant. It was like being in the army, and every bit as strict too. The highlight of our week would be a Thursday evening when the *Farmers Journal* would arrive in. Every one of us would get our own *Farmers Journal.* I'd start at the front page and read every single word on every single page until I got to the end. We weren't allowed radios and we certainly didn't have any phones or TVs, so the only way you'd know what was happening in the outside world was through the *Farmers Journal.*

Debating was another thing we did to pass the time. The college used to enter a debating competition, but they'd never win, so they put me in charge of the team, and didn't we debate our way around Ireland. By the time we were finished, we ended up winning the overall prize in the national debating competition.

Whenever I was going to Pallaskenry, myself and my friend Billy Connor used to thumb our way to and from. By doing this, we actually made some great friends along the way because it was often the same people who would stop to give us a lift. One morning, just outside Newcastle West, we were standing on the roadside, thumbing in the rain. We happened to be outside a house at the time. Out comes this lovely elderly woman and invites us in out of the rain. The woman, what do you think she said to us? 'Lads, are ye hungry?' Sure, we were starved. After we had a bite to eat, I asked her if there was anything we could do for her in return, so she asked us if we would split some timber for the fire, which we did. After that, we used to stop at her house whenever we'd be passing to see if she was all right and if she wanted anything done, but truth be told, the real reason we would stop by was because she always used to feed us. We would be delighted to see her, and she equally delighted to see us.

I continued working weekends in the piggery while I was attending Pallaskenry, but I quickly found another way to supplement my income. It was a surprising niche in the market that I quickly realised existed when we started going through Rathkeale on our way to the college. Even back then, Rathkeale was populated by members of the Travelling community. These were the people with the enormous houses and the caravans outside each one. I got on with every single one of them; they were the finest of people, but there was one thing they were stone mad for. Now, I'm not talking about teenagers here, I'm talking about the older generation of Travellers; they were stone mad for one thing that they couldn't get.

Poitín.

And who do you think had access to poitín but myself? I'd buy it, bottle it, wrap it and bag it. Instead of carrying a big bag of clothes to Pallaskenry, I'd carry a bag of poitín and get rid of it in Rathkeale along the way.

I wouldn't have been a drinker of it. I think the only time I drank it was when I was sick and it was mixed in with some punch. Even the Pallaskenry students who used to take it from me for their fathers and grandparents, no way in the world would any one of them think of tasting it themselves. To my knowledge, the tradition of poitín-making in Kerry no longer exists. Even back in my Pallaskenry days, the poitín I bought would have come from Cork. Those great makers have all since gone to their eternal reward, and their stills gone silent, so I'm not sure where you'd get it now.

The thing with poitín is that people didn't drink it to get drunk, they drank it to get warm. They'd be perished after their day out working, so when they came in at night, they'd pour a drop of poitín in a glass of hot water and add a bit of lemon and a few cloves. After a few sips by the open fire, they would be warmed right up. It probably saved many a man from pneumonia. When you see all the filthy things going on today, drugs and whatnot, really there was nothing in the world wrong with a person enjoying a small glass of poitín, especially when it was made right and was of good quality.

Back in 2008, I appeared on the television programme *The Restaurant*, and I'd say I caused one of the biggest production difficulties they ever had. As part of my menu, I brought along a small bag of poitín bottles with me so that when my dessert was handed out, it would be accompanied by a taster of Ireland's finest. I also gave some to everyone on the team. This was the real stuff now, mind, the best quality you could get.

Unfortunately, word came down from above that there couldn't be any references made to poitín as it was illegal. The thing is, the filming of the show had already been completed. I think I used it when I was making bread and butter pudding, and then when everyone in the restaurant got their poitín at the end of the night, they were filmed taking a sip of it. Some of the people there had never tasted it before, so it made for mighty viewing, but as far as I'm aware, it all had to be edited out. It was a logistical nightmare because they had to try to insert other sounds over any mentions of the word poitín. It also had to be done without it being too obvious. To this day I don't know how they managed to do it as well as they did, but I'd say they needed a stiff drink of the stuff by the time they were finished all the editing.

What's a Lesbian?

The world we used to live in was very innocent. It's actually baffling when you think about it now. For instance, my sister Joan used to teach in Dunloe up in Donegal. She would have taught Packie Bonner and Daniel O'Donnell. When she finished teaching on a Friday evening, she would thumb her way from Dunloe all the way down to Kilgarvan in Kerry. She'd spend the weekend at home and then, on a Sunday evening, my mother would drop her off at Hickey's Hall, where Joan would start thumbing her way back up to Dunloe.

Thumbing was the big thing that time. There wasn't the same element of danger attached to it as there would be nowadays. It was how we got around. I remember myself and my friends, John and Eamon Sweeney, always used to thumb our way to FCA training on a Friday night. We used to call the FCA the Free Clothing Association because after you'd sign up, you'd get these fine warm coats, socks, hats and boots. You'd be walking around like you were the bee's knees in your new get up.

If we had enough money, on the way home from training we'd go into a chip shop in town that was run by two ladies, and we'd buy ourselves some chips and burgers. One night, however, we were in there having some food when a drunk man walked in. Landing his fists on the table, he remarked to the two behind the counter, 'And how are the lesbians?'

I'll never forget, one of them all but somersaulted over the counter, grabbed the man by the neck, gave him a fist to the face and quite literally bate him out the door. Myself and my friend John were sitting there taking all of this in, and once the man was outside on the street, and the woman back inside the counter, I turned to John, and in all innocence, asked, 'What's a lesbian?'

'I'm not quite sure, Mike,' he said, 'but is there any fear that it's a woman who likes women more than she likes men?' I remember thinking to myself, cripes, that's awful confusing.

It was one of those things that was a bit too complicated, but I also figured it was none of my business what anyone else was into, so I parked it and didn't give it a second thought. That will tell you the innocence of the time. We were old enough to be in FCA training, but too young to know what a lesbian was.

Eileen

We were always brought up to believe that two women should never live under the one roof. There could only ever be one lady of the house. Well, the Healy-Rae house was very much the exception to that rule. From the first time my mother met my now-wife Eileen, they got on mighty. They just hit it off altogether. When Eileen later moved into my home house, where I lived, herself and my mother became even greater friends. If one of them wanted to get around me for something, you know, they'd almost gang up and take me on together.

The day Eileen made her 'in sickness and in health' wedding vows, well, she wasn't just making them to me, she was making them to my mother also. She was always by her side and looking out for her whatever the circumstances, and that was something that really meant a lot to me. I remember one particular night when my mother took ill. Straight away, Eileen had the doctor around at the house. After examining her, he decided she was an ambulance case and he asked the family if they wanted to send her to Tralee or Cork Hospital. I had been at a meeting in Dublin and was on my way home when I got the call from Eileen. She explained the crisis and put the doctor on to me. I told him my mother would have to be sent to a certain hospital in Dublin. She had been admitted there not long before that, and I felt it was only right that in an emergency she would be sent to the hospital where they knew her as a patient and would have all her files. The doctor was adamant it couldn't happen; it had to be Tralee or Cork as no ambulance would be able to bring her to Dublin. 'You leave it to me,' I said to him. 'I'll be the ambulance.'

A short while later, I landed at my mother's house. We placed her in the back of the car. Eileen sat beside her to keep a watchful eye the whole way up and to ensure she was as comfortable as possible. Sure enough we made it to Dublin, and the following day, my mother had an operation that gave her a few more years of life, thank God.

My mother never spoke too much about that night, but she was very matter-of-fact and firmly believed that she would have died had she been sent to a hospital where they didn't know her history. The first Christmas following that operation, she gave myself and Eileen a card. In it, she had wished us a happy Christmas and thanked us for saving her life.

Eileen was also very close to my father. She trusted him to such an extent that she even let him perform a minor operation on her. As I already mentioned, my father was one of those people who could turn his hand to anything. He could repair anything that was put in front of him, and on one occasion, it was Eileen that needed his skills when her wedding ring became almost welded to her finger. She was pregnant at the time and once her fingers started swelling, she couldn't remove the ring. It caused her a massive amount of distress and discomfort. My father examined it and decided there was only one thing for it.

He went out to the boot of his car and started rummaging around for the tools he needed. He was an amazing man for carrying the most unusual things in the boot, on the off chance that he might need them in an emergency. I remember he always had a small chainsaw, just in case he was driving along and came upon a fallen tree blocking the road. (Now, I should point out, he didn't use the chainsaw to remove Eileen's wedding ring.) He also used to carry a baby vice grips in his inside pocket. I'd say he was the only man walking around the Dáil with a vice grips in his pocket.

Once my father had everything he needed, he came back into the house, took a towel from the hot press, and told Eileen to straighten her fingers. He then placed a lump of the towel in the palm of her hand, and what do you think he produced next? Only a junior hacksaw. 'I'll get that ring off,' he said with a wink.

I swear, her fingers had swollen up around the ring to such an extent you could barely even see it, never mind get at it with a hacksaw. But my father simply put on his glasses and began cutting in the expert way that only he could. He clinically sawed through the ring without so much as touching the skin or drawing an ounce of blood. And off it came.

When he went outside to put the hacksaw back into the boot of his car, I followed him out. 'How in the name of God did you do that?' I asked. He showed me the blade. He had used a brand new one. 'You should always have a great edge,' he said. He was talking about blades, but the advice stayed with me. When you think about it, doesn't it apply to us also? Sure if you don't have a bit of edge to your character, you'll go nowhere in life.

Here Come the Healy-Raes

D'you know the way you'd have to do a pre-marriage course before your wedding? Well, when myself and Eileen took the course, I remember one of the subjects you had to cover was all about household finance and how to budget. The volunteer whose role it was to teach couples about this sort of thing was a lovely gentleman by the name of Brian McCarthy. He was shocking knowledgeable and an absolute pleasure to deal with on what I'd normally have found to be an awful boring subject.

Fast forward a few years, I was watching the nine o'clock news when this man appeared on screen talking about his burgeoning company. I was sitting there watching this and thinking, I know you to see. Who was it, only Brian. Turns out he owned a relatively new company called Fexco. Little did I know at the time of our pre-marriage course that the man sitting in front of us teaching us all about household finance was in fact a pioneering entrepreneur. As I watched the news report, I remember thinking, that man will definitely go far. Anyone who takes the time to teach others about something as important as finance, despite having nothing to gain from it themselves, well, that struck a chord with me. I was right about Brian going far. Today Fexco employs thousands.

When it came to our wedding, Eileen and myself went with a very simple affair in New York. Neither of us likes fuss. I'm telling you, there weren't even six people inside in the church when we said our vows. We couldn't have had the wedding at home in Kerry, sure where would we have started with the invites? Not even the INEC in Killarney would be big enough to hold the size of the crowd we'd have to bring. The priest who married us was a cousin of mine and an awful interesting man. Back before he was wearing the collar, and living in America, he was unfortunately shot twice in the chest.

Following the shooting, my cousin was dying in hospital when a priest visited him. He was in and out of consciousness but during a moment of lucidity, didn't he promise that if he survived he would devote his life to God. Now, this man was supposed to die; his time was up, there was no doubt about it. The account we received back home was that he didn't have long left. I don't know if God decided he needed a new recruit here on Earth and so he kindly orchestrated some sort of divine intervention, but either way my cousin lived. Sure enough, he kept true to his promise and became a priest. When myself and Eileen were getting married, he was the only person we wanted to have marry us, and thankfully he was alive to do the job!

Milk for the Tea

When I was on the *Tommy Tiernan Show*, Tommy joked about creating an independent Republic of Kerry by finding the money to dynamite the county off the map. Little did Tommy know, but that very nearly happened some years back.

Back when Johnny Randles ran the garage that I now own, he had some oxygen canisters on the premises. I'm not too sure exactly what went wrong, but something happened the hose pipe that was attached to the canisters and sure didn't it go on fire. If the flame had reached the gas, the explosion would have blown Kilgarvan out to sea.

Just as the fire started, a local bachelor called Petie Hagerty was passing the garage on his bike. Petie had a cow that he used to milk every day and, on this particular day, he was on his way home with the milk. Whatever way Johnny happened to look out on to the street, didn't he see Petie cycling by with the bucket of milk on the handlebars. Over he runs to Petie, and without saying a word, grabs the bucket and throws the milk on the fire. With fresh cow's milk being so thick and heavy, sure it smothered the fire instantly. 'Twas better than any fire extinguisher, let me tell you. In a matter of seconds, it had stopped the garage from going up in flames, it had stopped the village from being annihilated, and it had saved us all from an awful calamity altogether.

But what do you think was Petie's main concern?

'Ara, Jesus, where am I going to get milk for my tea now?'

Party in Healy-Rae Ward

Would you believe, a few of my toes don't work? I swear, there isn't a budge out of them, but then, considering their ability to move was killed by the same thing that very nearly killed me altogether, well sure look, a few lazy toes are a small price to pay. It all goes back to a very bad road accident I was involved in nearly thirty years ago. I was coming down by the Kilcoran Lodge in Tipperary. I was carrying a digger and a rock breaker, so I was going fairly slow because of all the weight that was on. Unfortunately for me, a tired lorry driver was also on the road at the same time, and when he came up behind me, didn't he momentarily lose his concentration and smash right into the back of me. At first, they couldn't find me because the impact had thrown me to the side of the road, but they got me in the end. Sure they knew I had to be somewhere.

The day before the crash, my wife Eileen had given birth to our first daughter, Juliette. For the first few weeks of Juliette's life, I didn't get to see her at all, which was very tough. I was in a full body cast, so there was no chance of being able to hold her either. Financially, it was extremely difficult. I had loans to pay and jobs to do, and the idea of not being able to stay on top of those commitments meant the stress felt every bit as torturous as the injuries themselves. In the end, I had to take nine months off work to recover. Once the body cast was off, the only way I could get around was by using a walking frame. I was then on crutches for over four years; then I was fitted with leg callipers, which I had to wear for five years. Physically, the injuries from that crash still affect me to this very day. One of my legs is different, and sure I've already told you about the toes. I trained myself to hide it, though; you genuinely wouldn't notice anything wrong with my leg unless I pointed it out to you.

When I was in hospital after the crash, by pure chance my good friend Maurice O'Donoghue was also in there at the same time. Maurice used to head out during the day and then come back in the evening when the nurses would be looking for him. Whenever Maurice would come back, he'd usually bring a drop of whiskey with him. I was already plastered thanks to the full body cast on me, so in order to get me properly plastered, Maurice would almost have to spoon feed the whiskey into me. My room used to be like a circus. There were a few doctors and nurses who would run up from A&E, dying for a quick cigarette, and the only place they could sneak one was in my room, where we'd already be smoking. Word soon got around, and sure a few more staff joined in. In the middle of the night, you could walk into my room and find twelve patients from the corridor and nearby rooms, around five doctors and nurses, Maurice, and then myself inside in the bed. If you opened to the door to the room, you'd have hardly seen a thing with the cloud of cigarette smoke. I remember a few of the doctors there were from other countries as well, and sure they thought this was great craic altogether. I'd say they thought this was how all hospitals were run in Ireland.

Maurice and myself had been friends for years. In fact, Maurice's mother, Sheila, and my own mother were also great friends. I only ever called Sheila Mrs O'Donoghue and so too did my mother, funnily enough. At the time, exactly sixty years ago, the O'Donoghues ran a popular venue outside Killarney, which they extended over the years. Today, that little venue, would you believe, is now the famous Gleneagle Hotel and INEC. Years back, whenever a dance would be held in a hall, you'd usually only get tea, coffee or minerals served there. The Gleneagle, however, held a dance at which they served alcohol. The following Sunday at Mass, the priest took to the pulpit, furious at the idea that this place was serving alcohol. He warned the congregation that nobody was to go to this new place called the Gleneagle. Sure the following weekend, the crowds nearly knocked the walls of the place trying to get in.

Another story I always remember about Mrs O'Donoghue, and one I told at her funeral too, was from back when my mother decided to stop driving at night. She was in her seventies at the time and driving at night made her awful anxious. The thing is, she liked to head off to various places each night, so during the day, I'd ring her and ask her what her plans were and if she needed a lift. The response I would usually get would be, 'Oh, I'm heading off out to play bridge, but I'm all right because Mrs O'Donoghue is driving.' The thing is, Mrs O'Donoghue was in her mid-nineties! I always thought it was gas that my mother was in her seventies and too anxious to drive at night, so she relied on her friend who was nearly a century old to drive them both.

But anyway, I've gone off point. Being in a full body cast and not being able to move nearly cracked me up mentally. As quick as I could get back to work, I did. I wasn't able to walk, so a great friend of mine, Cathal Sullivan, who was working with me at the time, used to hoist me up on to his back and carry me to and from the digger every day so I could work. The nature of my injuries meant that I often had to travel to London to see specialists. Another lifelong friend of mine, Patrick Sean, would always accompany me on these trips because he had worked in England and knew a lot about the place. He was a great companion to have, an awful funny man altogether.

One time, we had to go to London to see a doctor called Dr Birch, whose surgery was on Wimpole Street, a stone's throw from Harley Street. My mother had read a newspaper article about this man and decided that he would be a big help in my recovery as he was an expert in the type of injuries that I had sustained. Now, before I go any further, what you need to know here is that Ireland had just suffered a very bad winter. Sheep everywhere were starving, and farmers were incurring great losses as a result of the cold snap. Anyway, early one morning, myself and Patrick Sean were sitting inside in Dr Birch's waiting room. We were the only two people there. Next thing, we heard some racket start up on the street outside, but we took no real notice of it until this big square man opened the door and gave myself and Patrick Sean a bit of a suspicious look. He went away, and maybe a minute later, he came back and stuck his head around the door again. No sooner had he left when in walked this grand-looking gentleman. I knew I recognised him from somewhere, but I couldn't put my finger on it.

Anyway, the polite British gent was sitting there looking at myself and Patrick Sean, so in a bid to break the silence, God love him, he decided to attempt some small talk.

'Oh my goodness,' he starts. 'Isn't the weather atrocious?'

'Ah, for God's sake, man, you know nothing about it,' says Patrick Sean back to him. 'Everything that we have at home is starved, and what's not starved is either dead or half-dead.'

Unfortunately, what Patrick Sean failed to mention is that he was talking about sheep. While Patrick Sean carried on lamenting about how bad things were at home, the man just stared at him in horror at what he was hearing. I'd say he thought we were from some famine-torn country. Next thing, the receptionist entered the room and said, 'Sir Geoffrey? Dr Birch will see you now.'

With that the gentleman got up, said goodbye to us, and left the room. I went over and looked out the window. The street had been completely closed off. There were now two black Jaguars outside the door and all these policemen standing around. I turned to Patrick Sean.

'Do you know who that man is?'

'I don't,' says Patrick Sean, 'But I'll tell you one thing about him, he knows feck all about sheep.'

I started laughing as it dawned on me who we had just been talking to. 'Patrick, that was Sir Geoffrey Howe. He wouldn't have time to know anything about sheep. Sure isn't he too busy being Maggie Thatcher's Chancellor of the Exchequer?'

When we arrived in Stansted Airport to catch our flight home, there was a bit of a delay, so we took a seat and I lit up a cigarette. In Britain at the time, they had a 'no smoking' rule for certain areas, but I wasn't aware of this, so I lit up right there in the middle of the airport and started smoking away. Next thing, this nice young man comes over, taps me on the shoulder. Now, Patrick Sean, who was sitting beside me at the time, is the most kind-hearted person I have ever had the privilege of knowing; he'd give you the shirt off his back, but my God don't go annoying him or you'll see an awful blunt side to him.

'What's wrong with you, man?' says Patrick Sean back to him, gruff as could be.

Very politely, the lad replies, 'I'm very sorry, sir, but you realise you can't smoke in here?'

Sure neither of us had never heard of any such nonsense about not being allowed to smoke in a public place, so Patrick Sean, who was intimidatingly big and strong, immediately took to his feet and started to square up to this young man. I'd say he put the fear of God into him.

'I'll tell you now,' Patrick Sean starts. 'This man will smoke wherever he wants to smoke, and you'd better walk away ... while you're still able to walk.' Sure enough, the poor young lad turned and scarpered, and that was the end of all attempts to stop us from smoking.

I said to Patrick Sean, 'I'd better quench this quick. If the poor man says I can't smoke here, I should put it out.'

All I got was a sour look from Patrick Sean followed by the order, 'You finish your fag, and no more about it.' I wasn't long putting the head down and finishing the cigarette as quick as I could. I didn't want to go drawing him on me either.

Whenever myself and Patrick Sean went to England, we never used to stay in a hotel. He always thought it was the height of stupidity to go staying in a hotel when the city was filled with perfectly fine lodging houses. These houses would have always been known for renting their rooms to Irish workers, so whenever we'd stay in them, we'd usually have great craic because we'd almost always end up chatting to some Irish lads.

I remember one time, myself and Patrick Sean were staying in a room with a big crowd of lads and I was starting to feel a little claustrophobic; I was on crutches at the time, but I just wanted to get up and get out, even if only for a bit of fresh air. I knew there was a chipper nearby, so I said to Patrick Sean, 'I'm going for chips.'

Next thing Patrick Sean jumps up. 'Well isn't this awful rubbish now?' he announces to the lads in the room. 'I'll have to go with him.'

'Will you stay there!' I said back to him. 'Amn't I perfectly capable of going by myself and getting my own chips?'

Anyway, he insisted on going with me, so we headed off to the chipper and got something to eat. As we were sitting on a window eating the chips, didn't this crowd of young fellas come along. They knew by the cut of us that we were Irish, so they started passing some smart remarks about Irish people. There was a fairly big crowd of them; they were almost like a small gang. Anyway, things got out of hand and sure didn't a row ensue, ending with Patrick Sean giving one of the gurriers a particularly hard clip around the ear.

'Off you go now and gather whatever crowd you like,' he shouted at them. 'Come back to me then, and Goddammit, I'll take ye all on! Every single one of ye!'

I never saw a crowd to leave an area as quick. And they didn't come back either. I only know this because Patrick Sean insisted we wait for them.

Travelling the World

When the proprietor of Reilly's bar, Mick Reilly, passed away, my cousin Paudie Buckley (he of the Paudie and Timmy duo) was lamenting in the bar about his late great friend.

In the middle of the reminiscing, he said to the crowd: 'By God, Mick Reilly . . . sure he was a great man. We travelled the whole world with him. The whole world.' In all seriousness, he then added, 'Sure we even went as far as Bandon one time . . .'

Now, Bandon would be about fifty miles from where they were standing. On a good day, sure you'd cycle it no bother, but in Paudie's mind, 'twas almost like you'd need a passport to go there. Timmy, on the other hand, was a bit more adventurous. In the early 1980s, his curiosity got the better of him. He had heard so much about New York and America that he decided it was time to throw caution to the wind and go see it for himself. I suppose the young lad saw his chance and probably said to himself, 'By God, this is it, I'll make a break for it!'

For Timmy to go to America, well, it was a serious operation because it took military-level organisation. For a start, he wouldn't go on his own, so a local tradesman by the name of Small Mickey went with him.

Anyway, Small Mickey had been to America before, so he seemed like the best person to go with Timmy. That was only one part of the operation, though. The other part was figuring out who would stay with Paudie while Timmy was away. Paudie had never been on his own in the house before, so they asked me if I would move in with him for the two weeks Timmy was gone.

Living with Paudie was exactly how I'd expected it to be in that everything had to be done the awkward way, the slow way, the hard way, because that was Paudie's way, but I didn't mind, I adapted. In the meantime, Timmy was over in America, taking it all in. He was like a sponge; he was years telling stories about what he had seen in America. One thing about Timmy is that he always had a great head for retention. All the cousins he met over there, he was able to remember every detail about each and every one of them. It was his first time ever being anywhere like America. When he first arrived in New York, he couldn't get over how built-up the place was, and sure the height of the buildings nearly knocked him with shock entirely.

Paudie was never interested in going anywhere like that. America was too far away for him and, at that stage of his life, he had become too set in his ways to even want to go. He had also formed the opinion that New York was full of thugs and thieves. Paudie and Timmy's sister, Mary, had a holiday home in the Catskills in New York. Mary Buckley, you might remember from earlier in the book, was the mother of the young prison guard who was shot dead on the beach. Well, at one point, word came through that someone had broken into the holiday house belonging to Mary and her husband Dominic. The intruder then stayed there for a week or two, only to set fire to it before leaving. The same person had done this to a number of houses. Unfortunately, he burned Mary and Dominic's house during a very cold spell, and when the firemen arrived out to quench it, the water in the hydrant was completely frozen. Without the water supply, they couldn't save the house. This was always one of Paudie's stories when he would be talking about the type of blackguards that were in America.

'Not only do they break into your house and shtay there,' he'd say, 'but when they've finished, they burn the damn thing to the ground! Blackgards, they are.'

I Hear You're Getting Married Soon, Petie?

There was a mighty man who used to come into our bar, and cripes was he some character. Petie was his name. He lived in a house known as the 'Red Restaurant'.

Petie, well, he was like an institution. I mentioned him earlier in the book. He was the man who complained about having no milk for the tea after Johnny Randles used what he'd taken from the cow to quench a potential explosion. Everyone knew Petie, and everyone loved him. He was a great conversationalist too. He'd never drink, though; he stuck to his 7Up or his Lucozade. The gas thing was, he always had this notion about getting married. Every time he'd meet you, he'd be dead serious when talking about his upcoming wedding. The only thing is, it'd be a different woman each time.

'Did you hear I'm getting married soon?' he'd say.

And sure of course, we'd always say back, 'Ah sure Petie . . . when is the wedding?'

We always used to have great craic with him when he'd start telling us stories about who he'd be going marrying that week. He'd be telling you all about the wedding plans, and then next thing he'd be telling you about how women were mad after him, wanting to get married, and how one would be fighting with the other one because she'd want to marry him as well. Petie ended up never getting married, but d'you know something, I suppose he had more sense!

Great Characters

We had two more absolute characters in Kilgarvan – John and Ken Mitchell. John is a motor mechanic and big into his vintage cars. He loves restoring them, but he is also a great mechanic locally. Ken sadly died very young from pneumonia. No more than my grandfather, he was always out working in all weather. John is still alive, thank God, and not only does he still have a garage, which is now run by his sons, he also has a fine vintage motor museum near the village. If you like your vintage cars, 'twould be well worth your while calling to Kilgarvan to see it.

But back in the day, John and his wife Joan owned a garage, which they later went on to sell to Johnny Randles. Johnny held on to the garage for fifteen or so years before he decided to sell it. At the time, I was around nineteen, and had really wanted to buy the business. We did the deal, but at the last minute didn't Johnny change his mind, which in fairness he was entitled to do. I ended up having to wait another couple of years before I could get it, and unfortunately by the time it came on the market again, the price had gone up. I was determined to buy it, though, so when the opportunity arose a second time, I borrowed the money I needed and got the garage I wanted.

From age seventeen to this present day, I have never known what it is like to be debt-free, but then, who isn't in that situation? My father was the same way. He had to borrow when he first started out and it wasn't easy then either. I can still remember my first time going into the bank to ask for a loan. There was a great man in Killarney by the name of Denis Cronin and he was the manager of the AIB bank there. Denis brought me upstairs to his office and as we were walking up, I remember thinking to myself that I hadn't a hope of getting the money. Anyway, Denis sat me down and asked me what I wanted. I needed money to buy machinery and diggers, and the likes, so I outlined my plans and explained what I wanted to do.

I was winging it the entire time I was sitting in front of him, so much so that I started asking him questions. I asked him things like how much interest he was going to charge me and what was the best rate of interest I could get. I wanted to give him the impression that I could possibly get the loan on better terms somewhere else. Sure, I hadn't a hope in hell of getting so much as a cent anywhere else, but I think I concentrated so much on what he was going to be charging me in interest that my line of questioning somehow gave him the impression I knew what I was talking about. It won him over. To be fair to him, though, he was also a nice man and even though I was just seventeen at the time, he believed in my plans for the machinery business I wanted to set up.

He told me what the monthly repayments were going to be and asked if I would be able to commit to them.

'Denis,' I said, 'I will have no problem in the world paying them because of this . . .'

'What's "this"?' he asked.

I stood up and shook his hand. He had my word.

'That means I'll pay you,' I told him. 'I'll always pay you, and I'll never fail to pay you.'

My God, it used to be difficult. I'd never spend anything less than twelve hours each day driving the digger. I'd start at half seven in the morning and I'd finish at half seven in the evening. I was always worrying about the repayments because it was such a big responsibility on my shoulders. When I ended up buying the garage from Johnny, the pressure doubled because I still had the machinery business as well. To make matters worse, interest rates had gone through the roof. I'll never forget doing the sums on the money I had borrowed for the garage. The interest worked out at £150 a month more than I had bargained for. At that time £150 was a savage week's pay, so it meant that I had to find an extra week's pay out of nowhere. I did this by employing a great man called Eoin Brendan O'Sullivan. His family nickname was 'the Downs'. You remember when I was telling you about how my mother, Rosemary and myself would make the hair curlers? Well when the Downs were young, they would make net bags.

Every one of the Downs family was extremely intelligent. They were also ridiculously talented with their hands. They could do anything, they could make anything, they could plaster, they could plumb, they could block lay; they were probably the most talented family I ever knew. When Eoin Brendan started with me in the garage, I could honestly say I wouldn't have got going at the time if it weren't for him. He was such a hard worker and he really helped build up the garage and get it going with me. Granted, even with Eoin Brendan's help, there would still be times when, during the few hours I would set aside for sleep, I would lie awake genuinely worried about the loan repayments. Sometimes you'd feel as though all you're doing is working day and night, and then handing the money over to the bank. That's what I signed up for, though, and sure look, it made things interesting because if I hadn't been loaned the money in the first place, I wouldn't have been able to have done the things I wanted to. In the end, it was worth it, because I still have the garage and the machinery business today. The garage is now a grocery shop, run by my wife, Eileen, and my daughter, Juliette, while the machinery business is run by my son Ian.

When the crash happened, I was in the same boat as everyone else, except I didn't have just the one mortgage. Cripes, I don't even want to think back on how many I had at the time. We all bit off more than we could chew. Every single solitary person made mistakes. I don't know anyone who didn't. All I could do was adopt the mentality that helped my father's generation survive the hard times . . . I got up and I got on with it.

The Bishop and the Playboy

It's amazing how you'd hear two different stories about the same event. I would hear a version of a story from my mother and then I'd hear another version of the same story from my father, and you know, it would be like hearing about two totally different scenarios altogether. I remember one night there was a dinner being held in a hotel in Glenbeigh for a very small group of people, and my mother and father were among those invited. Bishop Eamonn Casey was also one of the dinner guests. Years later, when my mother told me about that night, she mentioned that Bishop Casey had attended the dinner with a woman he introduced as his cousin. Annie Murphy was her name.

My mother sensed that there was more to this supposed family duo than what met the eye, so she told me how in the car on the way home, she mentioned to my father that there might be something untoward going on between Annie and the bishop. Straight away, my father blessed himself; he was shocked at her even thinking that Bishop Casey would do such a thing! Not a hope of it!

Now, I was very good at keeping my counsel, and whatever I'd be told by one, I wouldn't say to the other. The information would go into my head where I'd analyse it but never tell a soul, and to this day, I'd be very slow to tell my left hand what my right hand is doing. I find it's a better policy in the long run, so with that in mind, I never relayed to my father what my mother had told me about their conversation in the car that night.

Fast forward to Annie Murphy's appearance on *The Late Late Show*. Myself and my father are sitting there listening to her tell Gaybo all about the goings on that occurred within in the parochial house. Next thing my father turns to me.

'Ara sure I knew all along that that was going on,' he says.

'Did you now?' I smiled.

'Ara yeah, but sure what harm was it?'

He was dead right. There was nothing wrong with it. Bishop Casey and Annie had been living in a place called Red Cliff House – I pass it on a regular basis when I'm on my way to clinics in Dingle – and you know, 'tis an auld wintry, desolate spot. To think that a consenting man in his perfect health was living inside in this house with a consenting woman who was also in her perfect health, and the two of them strictly prohibited from a bit of this 'n' that and whatnot, well isn't it crazy? As my father said, what harm was it? When you think of the horrific acts committed by others in that profession, sure Eamon and Annie did nothing out of the way by comparison.

I want the Catholic Church to continue for generations to come. Now people needn't be breaking their legs running to confession, but a quick visit every few years never did anyone any harm. Unless you're out committing serious crimes altogether, then the frequent visits aren't necessary. In years gone by, it was overdone. Sure, there was a time when a fella would only have to think about eyeing up a girl and he'd feel inclined to go running to the confessional, blessing himself along the way for good measure, doing what he could to counteract the sin. I would, however, like to see us keep the Catholic traditions. It's sad that the number of men entering the priesthood has decreased to a minuscule number. We have so many priests who do great work, but they're being run into the ground with the workload. Some are juggling two or more parishes; they're rushing from weddings to funerals, while trying to visit the sick in their homes and in hospitals.

That reminds me of when a very good friend of mine was in hospital in Cork. I can't say his name, but for the purpose of the story, I'll call him Paddy. A mutual friend of ours came into my shop one day and told me he was going to be heading into the hospital that evening to visit Paddy. At the time I was working behind the counter, so I came out from behind it and went around the shop putting together some bits and pieces for the man to bring in; a sort of care package, if you will. I picked up some newspapers like the *Farmers Journal* and the *Cork Examiner*, as it was known as the time, but didn't I look up a bit higher on the shelf and what did I see only *Playboy* magazine, so I threw it in with the rest. Might as well include all the necessities. I handed my friend the bag and asked him to pass it on Paddy from me.

That evening, our friend arrived into the ward and gave Paddy the bag. After he left, Paddy decided to have a look through the contents I had sent in to him. Of all the things that were in the bag – the Lucozade, the cream crackers, the fruit, the *Farmers Journal*, the *Cork Examiner* and so on – what do you think he put his hand on first but *Playboy* magazine. Well, he started looking at it from all angles . . . sideways, upside down . . . Next thing, he spots this man walking towards him. Now Paddy had no idea who the man was, not a clue, so he quickly put the magazine face down on the bed, so only the back cover was visible. The back cover of *Playboy*, in case you didn't know, was usually something inconspicuous like an ad for a cigarette brand. Basically, the subject on the back cover would give nothing away as to the subject on the front.

So anyway, the stranger takes a seat on the side of the bed and starts chatting away to Paddy. Well, he starts asking him a pile of questions about where he was from, what he worked at, and the likes. As soon as Paddy said he was from Kilgarvan, the man replied, 'Oh yes. Do you know the Healy-Raes there?'

Now here was Paddy, inside in the bed, and this complete stranger sitting on the side of the bed talking away to him and the *Playboy* magazine upside down in between them. He couldn't go taking it off the bed because it would look too obvious. As the man was there talking away, Paddy told me afterwards that all he could think was, 'Well, the devil eff you, Michael Healy-Rae, and what you're after doing to me.'

It got worse, though.

At one point during the conversation, Paddy decided to ask the man a few questions about himself.

'And what do you do yourself?'

'Oh, I'm the Bishop of Cork,' came the reply.

That Bishop of Cork, who is still the Bishop of Cork, does this lovely thing whereby he visits people in hospital at night. He noticed Paddy was new to the ward, so he had decided to say hello. As the small talk continued, what did the bishop only go and do but put his hand on the magazine.

'And what are you reading at all tonight?' he says to Paddy.

Before Paddy even had the chance to think of an answer, the bishop had it turned over, and sure there staring back at him was some woman with her double Ds out for all and sundry to see; nothing left to the imagination except for what was going on inside in her head when the picture was being taken.

The poor bishop took one look at the cover, one look at a shell-shocked Paddy, and threw his head back in a fit of laughter. With that, he blessed Paddy and took off to the next ward. I'd say when he left Paddy, he was thinking, ara, there's another lost cause inside in the bed anyway.

Mr Number Plates

I'm going to tell you something now, and you're not going to believe me, but I swear it's the gospel truth. There's a Castletownbere fisherman called Mick Orpen, a highly respected man in the community, who has the most amazing ability to remember the tiniest details from GAA matches that happened decades earlier. You could say to him, 'Mick, I dunno in the name of God but who played in the All-Ireland Football Final back in 1973?'

Mick would turn around to you, and without hesitating or even blinking, he'd reply, 'Oh well now, that was Galway and Cork.'

Then you could say to him, 'Mick, who won that match at all?' and not only would he tell you the winning team, he'd also give you the final score. He'd tell you the name of every footballer who played that day, and he'd also be able to tell you who each one was marking. He'd give you the names of the footballers who scored, and then he'd start giving you the names of the footballers who got sent off, which would be accompanied by an explanation of each sending off. For good measure, Mick would give you the names of anyone who got pulled up by the referee and carded. He could name every bit of activity that happened during that game. He could even tell you what the weather was like on the day.

You could then say to him, 'Mick, I suppose you wouldn't know who played in the All-Ireland Football Quarter-Final in 1953?' and he'd only go and tell you every detail about that match as well. No bother in the world to him. I almost wouldn't believe it myself only for I witnessed it and know it to be a hundred per cent true. You hear of people having a photographic memory and I'd say Mick has a good strain of that.

Since he was a small child, he has never missed a GAA match. Any game he'd watch, it would be embedded in his brain for ever. The whole game would be captured in his head, the ref, the rows, the takings off, the cards, the injuries, if so-and-so shouldered someone, or if so-and-so was taken off and replaced . . . all in his head. I doubt there is one other person in Ireland who can do that. Mick Orpen's head was like the internet before we ever knew what the internet was. He's still alive too, so if you ever need someone for a GAA table quiz, you know who to call on now.

John Michael Randles, the man whose father I bought the garage from, was another one who had an encyclopaedic head on him. You'll never guess what his speciality was. Number plates. Once John Michael saw your face inside in a car, and once he saw the number plate, it could never again leave his memory. My father did so much mileage throughout his political life, he used to change his car annually. He did this for about twenty-five years, I'd say. Well, if you were to ask John Michael to name every car my father had owned over that quarter of a century, and to name them in the order in which he had owned them, he wouldn't even have to think about it. He could reel off all the details straight away. Not alone would he tell you the number plate, he'd tell you the make and the colour of the car as well. He'd even tell you what he had thought of the car at the time.

''Twasn't up to much, that car,' I remember him telling me about my father's purple Toyota Camry.

It wasn't just the details of the cars belonging to certain people that he would remember. There could be a very quiet person living out in the countryside, one you would only see once in a blue moon, but John Michael would still be able to remember the registration of their car and possibly even their tractor as well. He would only need to see you in the vehicle once and he'd remember it. He was still only a young lad when we all discovered that he had this ability.

Giving Up Smoking

Only recently, I was walking through Kilgarvan village, my mind on a thousand and one things, when I spotted the building where George and Claire Maybury's hardware shop used to be. A lot of businesses survived through the generations but, sadly, Maybury's wasn't one of them. After the shop closed, and later when George passed away, Claire left Kilgarvan, and today the shop sits there as a disused building, the remnants of a bygone era.

In my own village, the hardware businesses like the one run by the Mayburys used to employ a practice that you wouldn't even hear of today. It was called 'the tick'. They had a book, sort of like a credit book, and in this book they would put a tick beside your name. This meant that after you had chosen the hardware you needed, you could then pay for it over time. There wasn't even a set timeframe; you paid it off when you could.

Pat Dillon was a hardware merchant I used to get a regular tick from, and honestly, in those early days, I don't think I could have got going in business at all if it hadn't been for Pat and his ticks. I used to buy my cement and the hardware I needed from Pat and his sons. Once I had a bit of money saved up, Pat would make up my bill, which I would then settle, and sure, off I'd go and buy more stuff and start the tick again. It was like banking before there was banking. I had the ideas, but I didn't have the money, so I needed back-up from people like Pat Dillon, and the bank manager I told you about earlier, Denis Cronin. I was very lucky that I had the right people around me at the right time.

When I bought my petrol station in 1991, I borrowed when interest rates were extremely high, but I would have encountered situations where people needed a tick. When your business is not established though, it was a difficult thing to do. Even to keep the door open and the bills paid, all while trying to improve the place, well, it was awful hard for a while, and would have caused me a good few sleepless nights.

The tick system ended up being phased out and replaced with accounts. To have an account was different to having a tick because, unlike a tick, an account had to be paid at a certain time each month. With the tick system, you wouldn't know when the payments would be made. People like George Maybury and Pat Dillon were great for helping people in that they wouldn't dream of refusing anyone a tick.

My father and Pat were lifelong friends. They used to go to dances together, or at least they'd try to. When they were young, neither of them would have any money so they would pool together their change and try to come up with the price of the dance hall entry fee. Once they had that, they would then try to find the price of a gallon of petrol, so they could travel to the dance hall. There were plenty of places they wanted to go, they just didn't have the money. In later life, when Pat was growing tired and the hips were at him, he would say to me, 'And here I am now, money to go anywhere in the world, and I can't go at all.' It always struck me as quite sad that he financially couldn't do the things he had wanted to when youth was on his side, and now that he did have the means to do them, he physically couldn't. I suppose there's a lesson in this for all of us, when you think of it.

One of Pat's sons, Patie, was a great friend of mine. He always used to call in to see me every night in the garage. I'd be delighted to see him coming because when you're working late, a bit of company was nice. One night, he called in, and we had a big long discussion about God knows what. He was supposed to be up early the following morning to drive a lorry for the council, so when he arrived in home that night after chatting with me, one of his family asked him why he was so late. He said, 'I was over with

Mike and you couldn't get away from him with the height of talking.' I always used to think Patie was an awful man for the talking, but it wasn't until a good while later I found out he used to say that I was the one who was the fright for it. We were as bad as each other.

Late one night, anyway, he called into the garage and, as usual, we talked and laughed the hind legs off a donkey. After a bit, Patie left for home and I went back to work. The following morning, I was back in the garage mending a puncture when I got the land of my life. A local called over and broke the news to me that Patie had passed away in his sleep the night before. When life knocks you with a clout like that, there's no getting over it. Patie was only young, too, which made matters worse because it was so unexpected.

I had given up smoking at the time, but I was so down and out after Patie's death that I went into the shop and bought a cigar. I figured the one cigar wouldn't do me any harm. Sure, the following day, I had done a complete U-turn in my thinking and arrived at the conclusion that smoking cigars was actually a pretty good idea. I'd say at one point, I was smoking around twenty-five cigars a day. I would smoke each one and inhale every last bit right down to the tops of my toes, which, as you know, weren't too great in the first place! Would you believe, I was smoking so much that I suddenly decided I wanted to give them up. So I did. And I haven't smoked one since then.

I can only remember one time when my father used to smoke and that was back when he worked the bulldozer in the dump in Kenmare. Dumps that time were fairly severe-smelling so he always liked to have a cigarette in the corner of his mouth to counteract the odour of his workplace. Back then, there was no such thing as transfer stations. Instead the waste was dumped on the site, and my father would then shove the mounds of rubbish back with a bulldozer before covering it with gravel.

When he finished work for the evening, he would have to take the batteries out of the bulldozer and bring them with him, otherwise they'd be stolen. The batteries were so heavy that another man working there would have to help him lift them from the bulldozer to the car. Usually the man who would help him would be Pat O'Shea. He would have been the boss of the dump at the time and a fierce good friend of my father. Each morning, anyway, when my father would return to the dump, he would always have to bring a stick with him. The first thing he would have to do before putting the batteries back in would be to walk around the bulldozer, belting it with the stick to try and get the massive black rats to leave their various hiding places inside it. Whenever my father would switch off the bulldozer, the rats would run in and snuggle in near the engine for heat. One belt of the stick, though, and cripes that would be enough to send them running. It didn't always do the job, however. When he would sit into the bulldozer, it wouldn't be unusual for one or two more rats to jump out. They could arise from anywhere, including underneath his seat. Ara, he was tough enough for it, my father; he never took any notice of them. Sure, if anything, the rats were probably more afraid of him.

I remember after my father got elected in 1997, he had been so busy with the campaign that he hadn't been to his job at the dump in a good while. The place was in an awful state. Right after the election, every reporter and television crew were looking to get a few words from him, but I had to explain that he wasn't available as he had to go to the dump for a few hours. Sure they all thought he was gone with a couple of bags of rubbish. They didn't realise that one of his jobs was bulldozer driver and he actually had tens of thousands of tonnes of rubbish to deal with.

During my father's time as a county councillor in Kerry, there was an occasion when he stood up at a council meeting and started giving out yards about a dump that was on the side of the road between Killarney and Tralee. He told the County Manager that the rats had become so big, they'd stand up and salute him whenever he'd be driving past on his way to the council meeting. The County Manager said something back to him along the lines of, 'Well, Councillor Healy-Rae, I travel that same road and I don't see any rats and the rats don't see me.'

The following week, my father had the last laugh when *The Kerryman* ran with the brilliant headline: 'Rats Recognise County Councillor but Fail to Recognise the County Manager.'

Will You Advertise Me, Denis?

In our locality years back, we never had a matchmaker like some villages would have had, but people still had their own ways of procuring a bit of romance. I remember a relation of mine went into the post office one day and said to Denis P, 'Denis, would you advertise me?' Straight away, he knew what she meant: a personal ad in the 'friends' section on the back page of *Ireland's Own*. She paid him for the postal order, and sure enough Denis submitted her ad.

As expected, her ad appeared in the next issue of *Ireland's Own* and the responses started trickling in not long after. One letter in particular caught her eye. It was from a farmer up the country, somewhere in the midlands, I think. She obviously liked what she read so she replied to him, and sure enough, a steady stream of letters started going back and forth between herself and himself. The gas thing is, neither knew what the other one looked like, so after months of writing to each other, they decided it was time to meet and put faces to the names.

One weekend anyway, the farmer arrived down to Kerry to meet my relation in person for the first time. He stayed in the local guesthouse, of course. He'd have to wait another while if he was hoping to have her keep his feet warm in the bed. Even though they had just met, they already knew they were compatible from everything that had been said in their letters, so during that same weekend they decided that not only should they get married but that she should sell off her property and move up the country with him as he had better-quality farmland. Lo and behold, she found a buyer for the land and off she went to live in the midlands with her new husband. I'm telling you, don't ever underestimate the power of being advertised in *Ireland's Own*!

Doctor Effing Healy-Rae

Patrick Sean, the character who used to accompany me to London whenever I had to go see a specialist there, was a fine, strong man, but he was completely oblivious to his own strength. I remember when his wife was having a baby, he asked me if I would drive them to the hospital if Margaret went into labour during the night. I was happy to oblige, and I told him I'd leave the door open, so he could let himself in and wake me up if they needed me. There were no mobiles then, so if he needed me, that was the only way he'd get me.

As you might remember from the earlier story, Patrick Sean was not a man for polite subtleties. Never was this more apparent than the night Margaret went into labour. Late one night, I was sound asleep in bed, and I remember I had a pyjama top on me. Next thing I knew, I was being grabbed by the neck of the pyjama top and pulled out of the bed and into the hall. I have to say, I hadn't a clue what was after happening.

All I heard were the words, 'Come on, we must go!'

It was Patrick Sean. I took it that Margaret was in labour, so I threw on some clothes and we headed out the door. I wasn't married at that point and I didn't have any children myself, so the urgency of the whole thing was lost on me. I was sauntering along the road to Cork Hospital, grand as could be with Margaret in the front seat and Patrick Sean in the back. I can't remember what we were talking about but at one point, I turned to Margaret and very casually remarked, 'Sure aren't we alright yet; there's no panic.'

Patrick Sean stuck his head out between the two seats. 'And would you tell me, who made an effing doctor out of you?'

He was right too. We had no more landed in the hospital when the baby was born.

Whatever about me not being an effing doctor, I can tell you from experience that Patrick Sean would make a mighty one. All my life, my toes have been dogged with problems. I've had ingrown toenails, toenails removed, crooked toenails, toenails growing in all sorts of random directions . . . it's never-ending with the lot of them. I had been to see a multitude of doctors, chiropodists and consultants and not one of them could solve the problem for me. Patrick Sean, however, was a great man for working with sheep. He was an expert at it, and he had all the equipment necessary if ever their legs got bad. One day it occurred to me, sure why not let Patrick Sean have a go at my toenails and see if he can put them right? He couldn't be any worse than the people I had been to see, and I was right. He wasn't worse. He was a thousand times better.

When Patrick Sean would call up to the house to carry out the all-important procedure on my toes, he'd arrive with the equipment he'd have for his sheep. The first thing he'd look for was boiling water, so he could sterilise the equipment. He'd then disinfect the tools of the trade, one of which would be an actual shears that he'd use for shearing the sheep. What Patrick Sean would do next was start cutting a V out of the centre of the toenail. The purpose of this would be to encourage the toenail to grow to fill the gap that he had cut. It would stop the toenail from growing in a direction I didn't want it to. If it started growing awkwardly, as it appeared predisposed to doing, it would dig into the flesh in either the left or the right side of the nail, which would then cause the skin to get infected. Sure when that'd happen, I'd end up walking lame for God knows how long. By cutting the V from the centre, it enabled us to control the direction in which the nail grew. It worked brilliantly, but my God, I don't know what we'd have done if anybody ever walked in and saw Patrick Sean going at my toenails with a sheep shears.

Keep Calm and Canvass On

One time, a few years back, when myself and my father were out canvassing, we arrived at the door of a woman we knew well. We knocked a couple of times and rang the bell, but there was no response. We knew she was home, so we knocked again. Still no response. Now, there's no one more determined than a politician looking for a vote, so rather than leave it be, himself sticks his head around the door and lets out the mother of all shouts to get the woman's attention in case she's out the back.

'Mary? Are you there at all?'

'Jackie?' comes the reply from upstairs. 'Is that you?'

'It 'tis!'

'I can't come out to yuh Jackie . . . I'm in the bath.'

'Ara you're grand, a girl! 'Tis just canvassing we are!' answers himself.

'Sure come on up to me,' she shouts back.

'Well stay right where you are so . . . I'll be up to you in a minute.'

Sure enough, off he goes up the stairs, cap on his head, canvass cards under his arm, and straight into the bathroom where herself is sitting inside in the tub, nothing but suds covering the bit of modesty. Without batting an eyelid, my father starts canvassing her, even handing her a 'Healy-Rae for No. 1' canvass card for good measure. The gas thing is, the woman inside in the bath didn't mind one bit because not only had she invited him in, she listened intently to what my father had to say and asked all the questions she wanted. Now, I don't know whether we got her vote in the end, I'd say we did somehow, but either way, the moral of the story is that when there's a politician out canvassing, you're not even safe in your own bath.

Gone to the Dogs

Sometimes when you're canvassing, things can go wrong, and my God, when they go wrong, do they go very wrong. One time I canvassed a lovely old woman, the nicest you could ever wish to have the good fortune of meeting. She was living on her own with a little dog she adored. When you're talking to people like her, it's often the case that you'd forget you're up against the clock. You'd become so engrossed in the chat you'd be having that you would be genuinely disappointed when your canvasser tries to move you on. Well, this woman was one of those people. Veteran campaigner Timothy O'Sullivan, or Timothy O as we call him, was with me at the time. I was enjoying her company and having a great time talking to her when Timothy O tapped my arm and told me it was time to make headway.

We said our goodbyes to the woman and sat into the car ready to hit the road. As I went to back up though, I felt a bit of a bump. I remember thinking to myself, God almighty, what's that? I'd say the thought had no sooner gone through my head when it dawned on me what the bump was. I must have gone completely white, because when I looked at Timothy O, I could tell he was wondering what on Earth was wrong with me. In a panic, I jumped out of the car. Sure as God, I had run over the little dog. I was fit to faint right there on the spot.

At that point, the dog was half-alive and in need of a good vet, so I picked him up carefully and ran back to the door to tell the poor woman what had just happened. However upset the woman was, I was worse. Here was this elderly woman living on her own, with only a dog for company, and now here I was, having just run over the dog after asking her to vote for me.

I brought the dog straight to a vet.

'Whatever you have to do, will you try to keep the dog alive? Will you try to bring the life back into him?'

The vet looked at me. 'Michael, I'm a vet, not God.'

The dog had to be kept in the surgery while the poor vet did his best. When I called back to the woman, I sat down inside in the living room, the two of us devastated. I think at one point, she ended up consoling me. She told me that she had always been worried he'd get driven over because old age had rendered him stone deaf and half-blind. It explained a lot, because to be honest, I couldn't get my head around how the dog came to be near my car in the first place. She had been petting him as I was leaving, but obviously he went and wandered under the car sniffing at the wheels like most dogs do. Unfortunately, because this dog was deaf, he didn't hear the car starting. The vet did his best, but unfortunately the outcome was not what we had hoped for, and the little dog went to his eternal reward.

One thing about canvassing is that if something happens, you can be sure it won't stay private; everything gets out. You'll always have the few smart alecs in every campaign, and Kerry is no different in that regard. There was one man in particular, and everywhere he went, he would always say something like, 'Have you heard about Healy-Rae driving over the small dog belonging to the old woman?' Instead of having sympathy for the elderly woman, he thought it would be hilarious to try and get one up on a rival. It was such a horrible motivation to have. He was an auld . . . well I won't say what, but the polite way of putting it would be to say he was a bit of a Connie four stones.

I called to see the woman a good few times after that, just to check in on how she was doing. We ended up becoming really good friends, as it happens. On one occasion, both myself and Timothy O called to see her, and during our visit, she said the one thing neither of us ever expected to hear.

'Michael,' she said, 'you'll get my number one vote.'

We sat into the car, dumbfounded. Timothy O put his hand up to his head and slowly brought it down over his eyes; it was like as if he was thinking away to himself.

'What are you thinking of?' I asked.

'I'm thinking that woman is so nice and so good to us, Goddammit, even killing her dog didn't put her off you!'

Mike the Vet

I'm very fortunate in that I don't really ever get sick, but when I do, it isn't always the doctor I'd make my appointment with. No. I go to the vet.

You know it takes longer to become a vet than it does to become a doctor? And did you know that vets are smarter than doctors? Think about it. A vet's patient can't speak a word, whereas a doctor's patient can pinpoint exactly where the pain is and explain what's wrong. It's because of this logic that I go to Mike the Vet whenever I'm out of sorts. I give him my symptoms and he informs me of exactly what's wrong. His opinion holds an incredible amount of weight as far as I'm concerned, because he's not just a good judge of animals, he's a mighty judge of people. Let's just say if Mike the Vet mentioned that Mr So-and-So was not looking too good, well honestly you'd start getting awful worried about Mr So-and-So. In fact, you'd almost take it as read that Mr So-and-So was going to have to start 'making his arrangements', if you know what I mean.

There were certainly a few times when I could have done with having Mike the Vet around. Eight times now, I have nearly met my maker, and God knows, that's eight times too many for my comfort. It's so easy for people to have an accident, but then there are times when something stupid happens, and I use the word 'stupid' because they're the kind of accidents that could easily be avoided.

One of the many times I came close to death was when I started choking on some food. It was a Saturday in March 2017. Saturday is my day for clinics, so of course I was rushing as usual. My wife Eileen had readied a sandwich for me before she left, so I threw it on to a plate and was wolfing it down while talking to someone on the phone. Next thing I knew, I couldn't breathe. I tried coughing a couple of times to clear my throat, but there wasn't even the slightest bit of improvement. If anything, I could feel it getting progressively worse.

Thanks be to God, my neighbours, Eileen Finnegan and Margaret Doran, were in the house at the time. I'll never forget it, Margaret was on the phone to the emergency services, and at one point, she asked the operator how far away the ambulance was. Eileen was after doing the Heimlich manoeuvre and it wasn't working. I could hear the operator reply, 'They're a couple of minutes away.'

Margaret took one look at me, and then turned back to speak to the operator again. 'His lips are going blue now,' she said.

I knew that once the lips went blue, it meant oxygen wasn't reaching my blood. I got on my knees, put out my two hands and looked at the tips of my fingers. They were going blue also. I knew what was coming. My mind would be the next to go and then I'd fall unconscious. Once that happened, I'd be of no use to anyone. I knew if I didn't do something, I would be on the ground passed-out, and possibly gone, by the time the ambulance arrived.

I gestured at Eileen to do the Heimlich one more time. As she did it, I rammed my two fingers down my throat so hard that my nails actually tore the roof of my mouth. Between my neighbour doing the Heimlich in the strongest way she could, and the turn of my stomach as I rammed my fingers down my throat, it dislodged enough of the food to let in a bit of air. The minute I felt myself taking a breath, the relief was like nothing I have ever experienced. My head started to come back, and it was at that point that I could hear the blare of the ambulance siren getting closer. I looked at my hands. The shade of blue was now gone from the tips of my fingers, and it was right there and then that it hit me just how close I had come to taking my last breath. I know everyone says this, but that line between life and death? It really is frighteningly thin.

On the one hand, death can so easily happen, yet on the other hand, it's such a difficult thing to achieve. You could survive a horrific car accident, which I did, but then something as simple as eating a sandwich could be the death of you, and in my case, it very nearly was. I learned afterwards that an extremely high number of people die from choking and that more often than not, they are discovered on the floor of a bathroom. What happens is they experience a fit of choking and become so embarrassed by it, they slip off to the bathroom to try and overcome it. Next thing it gets worse, their airway gets blocked and they pass out. Sadly, it's almost always too late by the time their friends realise they haven't returned.

When the paramedics arrived and gave me the once over to make sure my airways were fine, it didn't take me long to compose myself. I had a clinic in Killarney that day, so I changed my clothes and then headed for the road. That night, I faced nearly a thousand people at an event I was judging for charity. People are sometimes shocked to hear that I went to work after that, but I was fine, and sure when you love what you do, it's as easy to keep going as it is to stop. The show always goes on.

A Pub for Each Week of the Year

Years ago, the village of Cahersiveen had fifty-two pubs, and not a word of a lie, all fifty-two of them had no problem staying in business. I'll put it to you another way. You could get yourself barred from a different pub each week in Cahersiveen, and you wouldn't have to go back grovelling to the first one until the following year. In my own village of Kilgarvan around that same time, there were six pubs and twenty-six shops and every one of their owners was able to make a decent living, or at the very least a part-time living, from those businesses. In one house, for instance, there'd be a postman who also ran a farm. His wife would run a small shop that she would stock using their own farm produce such as eggs, vegetables and potatoes. People like that were the backbone of Ireland in the way they managed to make a living from their own resources.

If you wanted to see true entrepreneurial spirit, you only had to look at how people made the most out of an event like the fleadh cheoil. When my father was chairman of Kerry Comhaltas, he arranged for Kilgarvan village to host not just the south Kerry fleadh, but the Kerry and Munster fleadhs. Now, if you've ever been to a Munster fleadh, you'll know it takes an almighty big place to hold one. You wouldn't just set one up in any auld spot that took your fancy, and if you saw the size of Kilgarvan village, well you definitely wouldn't believe that a Munster fleadh had ever been held there. Somehow though, my father managed to make it happen.

When an event like that happened, everyone in the village would get behind it. Each home would immediately become a guesthouse and a teahouse. People opened their doors and rented out their rooms, boiled the spuds and fed the revellers. The pubs, for their part, would put on extra counters. I remember in our bar, we not only had two bars downstairs but a makeshift bar upstairs as well. O'Reilly's pub went as far as turning their kitchen into a bar by installing a counter outside the window. They also had a shed out at the back of the house, and sure they went and made a bar out of that as well. People improvised. People did whatever had to be done to make a few pound. They worked day and night, and not one word of a complaint would you hear from them either.

All that health and safety red tape we have today didn't matter a monkey's back then. One night during the fleadh, there was a double booking in the pub, so rather than turn away one band and have them miss out on a night's business, we put them performing upstairs. The other band, the Dublin City Ramblers, took to the stage downstairs. I remember my father standing outside looking in, and without taking his eyes off the place, he said to my uncle Dan, who was standing beside him at the time, 'By God, there's such a crowd in there, 'twill be all right if they don't knock the place down.'

Every fleadh cheoil was about work, even for the young lads. Every one of us had jobs to do, regardless of what age we were. I think I was about five at the time of the Munster fleadh, so my job was collecting glasses. There was an awful competitiveness between myself and the young lad from O'Reilly's pub across the road. Kevin would have been about the same age as myself, and equally territorial about his corner. When we'd be gathering the empty glasses outside our respective pubs, it wouldn't be unusual for a bit of a skirmish to occur between the two of us whenever revellers would leave their glasses in the street between the two pubs. Kevin would claim they were from his pub, while I'd be there arguing they were from ours.

While Reilly's and our own pub are both still open in Kilgarvan, a good few of the pubs in nearby Cahersiveen have since closed their doors. Today, I'd say Cahersiveen has maybe twelve pubs, if even that. A big drop from the fifty-two it once had. You would think it would be the other way around, that there'd be more now than there were then, but the difference now is that you have all these Lidls and Aldis and whatnot. When I hear that lot talk about the number of jobs they have created, I think they should also be made publish the number of jobs they have displaced. They might be creating forty jobs in a town, but in doing so they might be taking away ninety. When it comes to local independent businesses, people need to use them, because it's when they're gone that they will really be missed. The same goes for the local post office. I can't imagine an Irish village without a post office. It just doesn't seem right.

When I was growing up, Denis P was our postmaster, and Denis P ran the post office with his brother, John C. Denis P, you might remember from earlier, was the man who advertised my relative in *Ireland's Own*. You couldn't talk about GAA in Kerry without mentioning Denis P. He dedicated his life to it and was the club secretary at the time. Hurling was his passion, though, not football. He was shocking intelligent too, but you wouldn't think it from his nickname, Batty. That nickname was no insult, though. He got it from the famous play that was held in Kilgarvan. Denis P's character was called Batty and it stuck with him for the rest of his life. With most people, you would address them by their nickname, but not Denis P. It was just an unwritten rule that you never called him Batty to his face. Even though nobody classified the name as an insult, addressing him by that name would have been seen as disrespectful. Anyway, Batty had three passions in his life: his community, his love of the GAA, and his job as the Kilgarvan postmaster. My God did he give each one the greatest of dedication.

I remember when himself and John C were running the post office, an important part of the business was the telephone exchange. The exchange opened at eight in the morning and would stay open until ten that night. If you were making a phone call, you would have to ring the post office first to get what was called 'a line'. Batty or John C would then have to physically pull out a plug and stick it in an outside line to get you a connection. Next, they would ring the number you wanted, and when there was an answer from the other line, they plugged you in and made the connection. It was a big rigmarole but that was the standard procedure when it came to making a simple telephone call. Sure we all thought it was the height of technology.

Batty was also deeply involved in the GAA. His dedication was on another level altogether. He knew every individual who was involved in the GAA, not just in Ireland, but abroad as well. He never married or had children, so to him the GAA was like his extended family. Once you were interested in hurling or football, Batty would dedicate his spare second to training you and taking you to matches. He would always bring the team to wherever they were playing a match, but the amazing thing is, he didn't own any form of transport, not even a car. He couldn't drive either, but that didn't matter one bit. If the team had to be in some far-flung part of Kerry for a match at midday, then you'd be guaranteed Batty would have you there on time. He would do this thing called 'flagging'. If we were going to Waterville to play a match, the whole team would meet at the post office. Batty would count the heads to make sure we were all there and then he'd go out onto the road and start flagging a car down. Thumbing, for him, was too subtle. The second he'd see a car coming, he would stand in the middle of the road, put his hand out and start waving them down. The driver would literally either have to veer around him or stop.

Once the car had pulled to a halt, Batty would explain that the team were going to a match in Waterville, and he would ask if the driver would mind carrying a few lads as far as they could. Once the driver agreed, Batty would then pack as many as was humanly possible into the car. Five or six young lads would go in the back seat, two or three would be stacked in the front, and if space allowed, another two or three would get into the boot. With that, the driver would bring them as far as they could, which might be to the top of the town in Kenmare, for instance. Meanwhile, Batty would stay on the road in Kilgarvan and continue flagging down cars until himself and the last few lads had secured a lift. Once in the car, he'd then keep an eye out for the other young lads that had gone in the cars before them. As soon as he'd spot a few that had been dropped off, he would get out and start flagging again so they'd have a lift to take them another few miles along the road. Batty was like the captain of the ship. He'd get into the last car and pick up the stragglers as he'd go along. He never lost any of us either; he'd land every single one of us down in Waterville, no bother at all. We'd get to the pitch, tog out, play our game and then return home the same way we got there, with Batty flagging down cars. There was no such thing as hiring a bus or anything fancy like that. You got there how you got there and that was it.

Whenever we'd be playing a match, Batty would have these sayings that he'd always come out with. 'A hoocha, a hoocha' was one. That was one he used on us a good bit. If I was going for a ball, Batty would be on the sideline roaring, 'A hoocha, a hoocha, think of your father, think of your father!' This was his way of encouraging me to be as good as my father, who had won three county championship medals in hurling. Funnily enough, Batty was the one who gave my father his first hurley. Himself used to always tell the story of the day he went to pick it up. As he was leaving the post office with the hurley under his arm, Father Rogers spotted him.

'Healy-Rae, where are you going?' he asked.

'Hurling, Father,' came the reply.

'Come back here to me a minute.'

'What do you want?'

'Tell me again where you are going?'

'I told you! Hurling!'

'Well, you are not!' said Fr Rogers. ''Tis trying to hurl you'll be.'

As you can well imagine, that joke didn't go down too well with himself. He was bullin'!

Unfortunately for me, by the time Batty would have us at the pitch, I would usually be quite sick. I was a very bad car passenger, so when we'd land below in Waterville, my stomach would be in knots. I was fairly small and handy too, so there'd usually be a fella twice my weight sitting on top of me for the whole journey to Waterville. My God, was that road a twisty auld one at the best of times. I would be in bits from it. You'd then have to tog out underneath a bit of furze bush in the pouring rain, head out onto the battlefield, and sure with it being Waterville, you had the likes of young Mick O'Dwyers bating the living daylights out of you on the pitch, all the while with Batty shouting, 'A hoocha, a hoocha, think of your father!'

Goddammit, it was like being a terrorist in guerrilla warfare.

I was always of the opinion that everyone on the other team was twice my size and the reason I used to think that was because they probably were. There was the famous time, however, when Batty organised with the GAA to bring the St Barnabas team over from New York to play us in Kilgarvan. Well, when we went out on to the pitch, it was like being in a field with giants. Even our biggest lad was small compared to these boyos. Sure, they weren't just twice our size, they were twice our weight and twice our strength.

I was playing left corner-back and there was no way in the world I could make so much as a dent in the jersey of the lad I was marking. After a while, I decided there was only one thing to do and that was to give up playing the ball and start playing the man. Every time he went for the ball, I would jump and shoulder him to try and knock him off balance. The only way I could do it was when he was mid-air; I hadn't a hope of knocking him when his legs were on the ground because it would be like trying to knock someone the size of Paul O'Connell. It worked a few times, but with all the work we put in, we still didn't win.

We had fellas on the field that day who were highly skilled; some of them have gone down in GAA history as great players, but I was what you would have called a mighty trier. Usually, I would be on the losing side, but once I was out on the field, I always gave hammer and tongs to whatever position I was playing in. I don't think I ever won a GAA medal; in fact, I'd even be hesitant to say I won a match, because I'm not sure if I ever did, but one thing I did win was a GAA scholarship. Only for it happened to myself, I wouldn't believe it either.

Being awarded a hurling scholarship was the highlight of my fleeting GAA career, mainly because it came as a total shock. I had taken part in the scholarship trials along with my friend Pat Twomey, and while Twomey deserved his scholarship win, because in fairness, he was a skilful hurler, I, on the other hand, am still to this day scratching my head as to why they decided to give me one. I'm convinced there must have only been two applicants for the two places. Winning this scholarship meant we got to spend a month in a Gaeltacht summer school, Coláiste Iosagáin in Ballyvourney, County Cork. We didn't learn too much Irish that summer, but didn't we learn a lot about girls, and in particular, girls from Dublin.

We were very lucky in that we got to stay with the nicest bean an tí in all of Cork, Bean Uí Nora Liathain agus a fear chéile Diarmuid. Bean Uí Liathain and her husband Diarmuid ran

Lissyclearig post office, which was attached to their house; it would have been a fair auld walk from the Irish college, which was on the Killarney side of Ballyvourney, but it was worth it, even if only for the rich homely food that Bean Uí Liathain would always make for us.

Bean Uí Liathain was a lovely woman, but she sure did run a very efficient house. Only the Irish language was allowed, and if you couldn't say it in Irish, you couldn't say it at all. She also used to make the lot of us say the rosary in Irish every night. Herself and Diarmuid were deeply religious. I remember they had a statue of Our Lady outside in the garden, and when I would be up before the others in the morning, it wouldn't be unusual for me to see Bean Uí Liathain and Diarmuid outside on the lawn praying by their grotto.

Another thing that happened, and I'd have to say, I'd make a great detective because I can tell you what year it was without even knowing the exact year it was, there was an event on the television at the time, and I remember informing Bean Uí Liathain that I wouldn't watch it because I wasn't a follower of the people involved in the event. You see, I've always been of the belief that the only people who should be in a position of power are the people elected by the public, and not those who were born into it by chance. The people at the centre of this event were born into it, so I put my foot down and refused to sit and watch it. The televised event in question was the wedding of Prince Charles and Lady Diana, and Bean Uí Liathain wanted us all to watch it because she said it was part of history.

'If Charles had been elected by the people,' I started, 'then I might watch him get married, but for him to have the God-given right to be in a position of power all because of who his parents are? No, that doesn't slide with me at all, Bean Uí Liathain. Not one bit.'

Bean Uí Liathain could see how riled up I was that she didn't even scold me for not having voiced the rant in Irish.

During my month at Coláiste Iosagáin, I made friends with a girl from Dublin. Now, making friends with a girl from Dublin was mighty altogether because between struggling with reading and writing, struggling with trying to learn Irish, and then struggling with the hurling and the football, well, life was starting to look like a bit of a battle. This girl just appeared on my radar one day, however, and talk about opposites attracting. I hope she'll never read this book, because she'll surely be offended that I can't remember her name, but I do remember her being easy on the eye and having a very upper-class accent.

Unfortunately I couldn't get at her in any way, shape or form during the day. There'd be a céilí dance at night, but you'd be under strict observation at all times so the only chance we had of meeting was after Bean Uí Liathain had fallen asleep. I would sneak out the window in the bathroom, jump out on to the flat roof, and then head off walking for Ballyvourney, where we'd agreed to meet. Lissyclearig was on the way to Kilnamartyra, so it was a nice walk from there into Ballyvourney, but wouldn't you know there was another problem. Another struggle.

There weren't many cars on the road but if a car did come along, you were scuppered. The thing about Lissyclearig is that it was a very close-knit community, so if you were seen walking along the edge of the road, the driver of the car would know straight away whether or not you were local, and if they saw that you were a student, you could be sure you'd be reported to the school for being out at night unsupervised.

Even though it was summer-time, there were nights when it would be raining and sure when you're young, you might only head out wearing a light shirt. You wouldn't bother with a coat, especially if you were meeting a good-looking girl from Dublin.

Next thing you'd hear a car coming, and what could you do only jump straight into the ditch. I'd say I spent more time in the ditch than I did on the road some nights. Sometimes, there wouldn't even be a ditch, just bushes, but you'd still have to hide, so all you could do was jump in and hope you didn't land on top of thorns and briars. Once the car had passed and you could get out, you'd be a good ten minutes pulling thorns out of your backside. They'd be stuck in all places.

To make matters worse, you might have only just finished pulling out the last thorn when you'd see or hear another car coming, and sure you'd have to jump back in. 'Twas a highly dangerous occupation at the time, but it was all part of going to Coláiste Iosagáin. I was fairly good at covering my tracks, so my misdemeanours were never discovered, thanks be to God.

When we were leaving I was sad to say goodbye to Bean Uí Liathain and Diarmuid. I'd had such great time for them, and I actually had the pleasure of meeting one of their sons at an event in recent years. Unfortunately, Bean Uí Liathain and Diarmuid themselves have both since passed away. It's sad they never got to live the long life they deserved. It was one of those situations where fate was so cruel. By rights they should never have suffered an ounce of ill health. They were good people, clean-living, never drank or smoked. Despite this, they were both struck by illness, and passed away quite young.

When you think about it, it's all well and good living a life so clean, it would even put a saint to shame, but sure God knows you might as well live it up, enjoy your few cigarettes, your few drinks, your desserts, or whatever your vice may be. Death doesn't discriminate or favour those who live healthy lives. It will take anyone, anytime, so you might as well go with a smile on your face.

Turf in the Bogs

Kilgarvan man Paddy Cronin, God be good to him, he's only dead ten years or so, he was one person who was always very much ahead of his time. He would have those bits 'n' pieces that no one else would have, and you know, you'd wreck your head wondering where on Earth he got them from.

Paddy would buy in machinery as well, the kind that almost seemed futuristic. I remember one time he landed in Kilgarvan with what was known as a sausage machine. Now, a sausage machine is something you would attach to the back of a tractor; it was used for cutting turf into a long sausage-like shape. It wasn't like a hopper, though. A hopper would be a different thing altogether – a machine would dig out scoops of bog, load it in the hopper, mix it up with an auger in a big bin, and then put it out in sods. The sausage machine, on the other hand, would sink a blade down into the ground so it could bring up the turf, but if you hit any bit of a root or anything at all, 'twould break a shear pin. If you have ever spent a day in the bog, then you'll know it's long enough without you having to go fixing shear pins and the likes. Well, Paddy, God love him, had to find this out the hard way.

As a young lad, I worked with Paddy as his assistant, so whenever something broke down, I would help him get it going again. One year, after he had cut his share of turf around Kilgarvan, the place he was booked for was Sneem. We didn't have phones that time but honestly, the bush telegraph was every bit as good. When Paddy and myself arrived into the square in Sneem, there was a big crowd waiting for us. They were all out to examine this new turf machine and to see what it was like. Everyone wanted to see what all the talk was about, and by the looks of things, they all seemed suitably impressed. Had they seen the same machine a short while later, however, they might not have been as fascinated. We got to the bog, and I'm telling you, we weren't five minutes cutting turf when the thing broke down. We spent the whole day getting it going, only for it to break down again each time. It was the biggest torture of all time. Needless to say, the only place the sausage machine was ever a success was in the scrapyard.

The thing about turf, however, is that it wasn't ever just another job; it was far more important than that. It was a valuable lifeline that kept the wolf from the door of many a family when times were hard, and every penny hard-earned. Not only did you have the turf for warmth during the cold winters, and God, was there cold in those winters back then, you could also sell bags of turf and timber and make a few pound. I remember my father telling me that when he was a child, his neighbours Tom and Noel Lynch used to get him to fill their pipes with turf so they could smoke it. People at that time used to smoke turf because they simply didn't have the price of tobacco.

My grandfather on my father's side had twelve children; six with his first wife, and another six with the second. There were two sixes, you could say. Well, my father was the eldest of the second six, so he left school to go working full-time and make money for the family. That was his role as the eldest. One of the many things he would do every spring, even as a child, was cut and bag the turf.

One day, anyway, my father was down in the village with his horse and cart, above on which there was a reek of turf. After selling the turf and getting a few pound for it, he went around the village buying flour, butter and all the other usual bits and pieces he knew his mother would want. While he was gone picking up the messages, he tied his horse and cart to a railing outside Cronin's yard, which was adjacent to Maybury's shop. I don't know if the horse got a bit giddy or what, but at some point, didn't the rope come lose and the horse backed up, sending the shaft of the cart in through the big window of Maybury's shop.

Now this was a disaster, because it wasn't just any window that the cart had crashed through, it was the big window. Back then, every village usually had one shop that had what was known as 'the big window'. Well, the big window in Kilgarvan was in George Maybury's hardware shop, but it was a bit of a landmark in itself. At night George used to place ten green boards against the window after the shop had closed. The following day, if George had removed all boards apart from one, it would mean that someone in the village had died. It was like a silent public announcement that a death of a local had occurred. Of course, whenever anyone saw the one board up, the first thing they would do is go straight into the shop and ask who had passed away.

Now, as I have already mentioned, George Maybury was a Protestant, and this meant two things. It meant he was tough, and it meant he was brutally honest. So, when he came out and saw that the horse and cart had broken his big window, he said to my father, who was only a young boy at the time, 'You have to pay for it, but I will give you time.'

Whenever my father came into the village after that, he would sell a load of turf and then head over to the shop to pay George the next instalment towards the cost of replacing the big window. Eventually it was repaid, but my father always said that one of the most upsetting days of his life was having to head up the Bog Road to go home and tell his mother that he had broken Maybury's window and that he now owed George a big debt. It was thanks to the turf, however, that he was able to make those payments.

These days, with the way some people go on, you'd swear even walking through the bog was harmful. When my father heard that a minister had signed an order stopping people cutting turf, well I'd never seen him as angry about anything before in his life. He was outraged. He couldn't understand how in the name of God someone could sign an order to stop people doing something that had been done for generations before them. It bothered him greatly, and I know exactly what he'd say if he heard that some people were now trying to stop the burning of turf as well. He'd turn the air blue, and he wouldn't be the only one.

A Lesson in Economics

When I was a young lad, there were two things of which I was sure. Number one: school children would pay any amount of money for hard-boiled sweets, which meant I could enjoy a decent profit margin when I sold them in the yard at lunch. Number two: if I wanted to get on in life, the only way to do it would be to work every hour God gave me. And that's exactly what I did.

Any type of work that came before me, I would do it. It didn't matter how challenging it was or, in some cases, how gruesome; if it earned me a day's pay, I did it. For years, I worked by day in the forestry cutting timber, and then at night I would work in a fish factory. I also had cows at the time, so when I was making my way from one job to the next, I'd call into the farm and tend to the livestock. I managed everything on a minimum amount of sleep.

Even as a child, hard work interested me, and what I learned during that time stood to me for the rest of my life. For about three years, I sold holly at Christmas to a contractor from outside the county and he would then sell it abroad. I was like Paudie and Timmy Buckley, going around with my saw cutting the branches. I'd say I didn't leave one holly bush growing in Kilgarvan. You got paid by weight, you see, so you had to cut an almighty amount of holly in order to make a few bob.

The first year I worked for them, we disagreed over the weight, which meant I didn't get paid what I thought I should have. There was no arguing with them but I was too stubborn to let it go, so I decided to bide my time and wait until the following year. When the time rolled around, I cut the holly and bagged it just as I had done the year before, but this time, I stuck a stone in each bag, so they'd be that bit heavier, and I'd get paid that bit extra. I saw it as a way of getting the money back. Sure enough, the plan worked. There was no doing it the following year, though. They obviously found out what I had done, because when they gave me the bags to fill the following year, they were all net bags, which meant they would see straight away if any contained stones. To be honest, though, I didn't give a fiddlers once I was paid the right weight and got what I deserved.

That whole experience was like an early lesson in watching my back and making sure I wasn't wronged. It taught me to stand up for myself in life, and it definitely prepared me for the career I'm in now, I can tell you.

Thank You, Mr Jones

I'm a big believer in fate. Sure, you already know that from an earlier story I told you about Bob Lyne. But I do think events unfold the way in which they're meant to, and even though we may not like it at the time, in the long run, we always come to realise that things happened the way they were meant to. I also believe that if two people are meant to cross paths, fate will give them an auld hand. Now, I know that last part sounds a biteen deep, but the reason I believe it is because my own parents are proof of it.

When my mother arrived into Killarney train station on holiday from America, she was greeted on the platform by a man called Michael Jones. Michael was a great man for directing tourists to different businesses in the locality. That was his job. He would fill hotels and guesthouses, and then in the evenings, he'd send customers to different restaurants if they were looking for a nice meal. Michael would never collect his weekly wage, though. He'd let it mount up for the whole year, and then in the winter, he would collect what he was owed. He was a sharp man too, and my God did he hate waste. He would even fatten the pigs on scraps he'd get from hotels.

When my mother got off the train, she was met by Michael Jones, who asked her if she was looking for a hackney. She said she was, so he told her he had the ideal man for her. He brought her out to where a hackney was parked and who was standing there wearing a snow-white beanie hat with a bright red blob of wool on the top, only my father. She was going visiting her relations, so she gave him the address and he brought her to their house. As she was getting out of the car, his exact words to her were, 'Sure you'll go stone mad here. There's a big dance on in Killarney tomorrow night, will you go with me if I collect you?'

She said she would, and that was how they met. I always say if it weren't for Michael Jones, myself, Danny, John, Denis, Rosemary and Joan might not be here at all.

The Brown Fiver

During the summer months, visitors to the area would often be out cycling, and of course, when you have a lot of cyclists on country roads, odds are one of them will get a puncture or need the chain readjusted. Back when I had the shed at the side of the house, I would always have the doors open wide on a summer's day. That way, if I met someone who was having a problem with their bicycle while I was out cycling myself, I would tell them there was a bicycle shop back the road that carried out repairs. They'd always be delighted to hear this and of course they'd head straight for the garage. I would always make sure I got there before them, however, and sure when they'd arrive, they'd get the shock of their life to see me again.

While I was always adept at finding ways to make money, I often did things that lost me money. I remember back when I was doing a lot of house painting, I used to buy paint from a certain individual who would travel around the place selling various different items. He would always have paint by the five gallon drum, so I used to buy it all up from him. The one thing I used to do at the time was check every drum to make sure it was right. It was a habit I had. The lesson I had learned from the incident with the holly never left me. One day, anyway, didn't the man arrive with a big load of paint, but at the time I couldn't deal with him myself because I was knocked out with a dose of the chicken pox. I was sixteen years old at the time, which is a dangerous age to get chicken pox, and my God was I sick.

As I was too ill to even sit up, I gave my mother the money to pay him and reminded her to be sure to count the drums before he left. Now, I was a regular customer of this man, but clearly he was one of those people who just couldn't resist the chance to con someone, even if it meant doing himself out of money in the long run. When he saw my mother taking care of things that day, he figured she would be unlikely to check each drum like I always did, so he decided to use the opportunity to get rid of some rubbish. Half the drums he left us that day were gone off; they were like solid rubber.

He went in for the kill and caught me out that one time, and sure enough, he never called again. He made a killing that day because he got rid of a lot of crap, but it was so stupid because it was such a short-lived win. It didn't make sense. I had been buying paint from him for two or three years at that point, and I was buying more and more paint each time, but yet he still couldn't resist the temptation to pull a fast one. I think it was the first time I had seen a first-hand example of someone being penny wise and pound foolish.

At the other end of the spectrum, you have people that are terribly straight. I have seen it all throughout my life. I remember one time when a person's car broke down at the side of the road, their wheel was flat, and they had no spare. I went to my garage, got a wheel for them, and then cycled back, holding on to it. After I put the wheel on and got them sorted, they asked me how much they owed. The car I had taken the wheel from, I think I had bought it for maybe forty or fifty pounds, so I told them a fiver would be grand. They wouldn't hear of it. They wanted right or wrong to give me fifteen pounds. Sure of course I refused, and didn't we end up having a battle on the side of the road over them wanting to give me money and me not wanting to take it. We were like the two in that episode of *Father Ted* where Mrs Doyle and her friend start fighting over who would pay for the cup of tea. I'm telling you, if anyone passed us on the road that day, they would honestly have thought we were about to launch into fisticuffs, we were fighting so much. Little would they have known what we were actually fighting over. In the end, I think we met in the middle and they gave me a tenner.

My father was also very straight and honest like that. One day, when he was young, he spotted a brown five-pound note on the ground. He got off his bicycle and picked it up to examine it. There was no one around who appeared to have misplaced money, so he put the five-pound note in his pocket. He brought it home, found a matchbox and tucked the fiver in safely. It was such a novelty that every now and then he'd take it out and look at it. Every fibre in him wanted to keep it but his conscience was killing him. He felt it would be an awful sin to keep something so valuable that belonged to someone else, so he decided to speak to the priest.

'Father . . .' he started. 'Has anyone been in saying they lost money?'

'No,' said the priest. 'Why? Did you find some?'

'I did.'

'How much?'

'I can't be telling you that! But if you hear of anyone that lost money, tell me.'

Not too long after that, the priest was back in touch. A woman beyond in Inch had lost a five-pound note. Well, my father was a proud man, but he cried some amount of tears when he heard that. Times were tough, which was why he wanted to keep the find, but it was also the reason why he couldn't. The person who lost it probably needed it as much as he did. He couldn't in good faith hold on to the fiver, but he consoled himself with the idea that the lady he would be returning it to would likely give him twenty or thirty pence in return as a reward.

The two met, but himself was still reluctant to hand over the goods until he was sure she was the rightful owner.

'Did you lose money?' my father asked her.

'I did,' she said. 'Did you find money?'

'I did. What did you lose?'

'A fiver.'

'What colour was it?' he asked. It was a valid question as fivers that time came in two different colours.

'It was a brown fiver, Jackie.'

He'd heard enough. It was definitely hers. He took out the matchbox, removed the fiver from it and handed it to her.

'Thanks a million, Jackie, thank you so much,' she said to him, delighted with the return. She then shook my father's hand, and added, 'I'll pray for you when I go home.'

He got his thirty pence alright . . . only the 'currency' was prayer. Decades on, whenever he would tell that story, my God he'd be visibly disgusted as he'd recall what his reward was. I always thought the story was a great example of what goes around comes around, though. Wait 'til I tell you why. Months after returning the five-pound note, he had to bring a couple of relations of ours to Cork. Now, I couldn't tell you where in Cork he was, but as he was walking down one of the streets there, a strange-looking ball of paper caught his eye. He picked it up. Seventy-five pounds.

And the priest, you can be damn well sure, didn't hear about it either.

The Rigmarole with the House Phone

When we got a house phone, it wasn't even our own phone, it was an extension of the bar phone, so contacting the Healy-Rae household was an awful complicated thing altogether. If you wanted to get through to the house, you'd have to ring the operator, who would put you through to the bar. Someone in the bar would then have to turn a big handle on the wall, which would make the phone ring in the house. When one of us would answer, the person in the bar would have to put down their phone but leave the handle turned in a certain way so you could take the call. 'Twas some awful convoluted operation.

I remember when Mick the Atlantic first installed a gambling machine in the bar. The jackpot was a massive one, £30. It was a savage amount of money that time, and one night didn't my brother Denis win it. It was honest to God like winning the Euro millions. Another thing that amazes me about times gone is when I think of the jobs that were once commonplace but are non-existent today. There was a man called Karl Hingwong, for instance, whose speciality was televisions. This was back when televisions would break down an awful lot. If it was a straightforward issue, Karl would come out to the house, open up the TV and usually get it back working again. If it was more complicated, however, you'd have to carry the TV into Karl; he would then put your name on a white sticker and stick it on the screen. There were no computers or any kind of system showing who owned what, just stickers. He had televisions stacked right up to the ceiling of his workshop and he'd always be taking bits from one TV and putting them into another. That's how he got TVs back working again, with bits. These days you'd rarely hear of someone repairing a TV or a radio. You'd just go out and buy a new one. It's great we can do that, but at the same time, isn't it sad that we've become such a disposable society?

A Guinness Barrel and a Funeral Procession

If I were to start naming all the great priests we've had in Kilgarvan, I'd surely sound like Mrs Doyle in that episode of *Father Ted* where she's listing off all the names as she's trying to guess the identity of the randomer who arrived at Ted's awards ceremony. In fairness, though, we did have some great priests down throughout the years.

Father Hegarty, for instance, was a mighty man for the visiting. I remember one night, he called to the house, but it was just myself there. My mother was gone off out somewhere, and I was at home alone. I wasn't married at the time either, so there was no Eileen around. I remember it was maybe ten or eleven o'clock at night when Father Hegarty called, so of course I invited the man inside, made us both a cup of tea and sat down by the fire to have a chat with him. At the time, I was working extremely hard and you know, sometimes, when you'd be pushing yourself hard at work, you'd be burning the candle at both ends, and sure you wouldn't realise just how wrecked you'd be until your body suddenly decides, 'Agh, to hell with this malarkey.'

Anyway, we were sitting there talking away, when next thing I look around and there's no sign of Father Hegarty. Well, I couldn't understand it at all. He had been there a minute before. My cup of tea was still beside me, and it full; the television was still on, but the screen was blank. I looked at my watch . . . mother of God, it was ten past four in the morning. I had fallen asleep on the priest while he was chatting, and the poor man obviously had to let himself out. I was never as mortified in my life and had to apologise profusely to him the following day. I can't remember what he said back to me, but sure knowing Father Hegarty, he probably cracked some joke about being used to having people fall asleep on him at Mass.

I remember we then had Father Kelly, an uncle of the MEP Seán Kelly. Father Kelly was a very interesting gentleman; I always had great time for him. I mean this in the most respectful way, but he was an old-school priest. We were chatting one day, and I remember at the time, there were different things coming up on the liberal agenda, so I passed some remark like, 'God, Father Kelly, aren't things getting very complicated in this world? 'Tis moving very fast.'

I'll never forget, he looked at me and he said, 'You know what now, Michael? The way this world is going, the sooner I'm gone out of it the better, because I feel as though I don't have any place here any more.'

I gave out to him for thinking like that and reminded him that what the world actually needed was more people like him; people who would keep the traditional values alive rather than give into a culture where anything goes. He replied with a comment, and now I would hate to misquote the dead, but I think what he said was something along the lines of it being like trying to keep the tide out. He could see the way the country was changing, and it worried him. He had this vision of the culture moving in such a way that he would be left behind, and it was such a sad remark to hear from a man who had lived such a dedicated life.

Another great priest we had in Kilgarvan was an awful sound man by the name of Father Jeremiah Dillon. After he arrived in the village, he set about doing so many good things. The church was in very bad disrepair, so straight away he had the necessary works carried out. Our school likewise was in bad shape, so he had a new one built for us. He improved the community centre, fixed up the graveyard; whatever needed to be done, he was the man to make it happen. When I was a young lad, I used to do a lot of work for him, things like cutting the grass in the graveyard and around the presbytery as well. With all the construction work that was going on around the church, however, sometimes I would have to wait until a Sunday to cut the grass. One day, didn't a very religious woman storm into the church complaining to Father Jeremiah that I was working on sacred grounds on a Sunday. It was blasphemous, she said. Of course, she thought she'd get a good hearing. Instead, Fr Jeremiah said to her, 'For God's sake, woman, did it ever occur to you that Sunday might be the only day he can do it?' Well, she wasn't long hopping off her high horse, I can tell you.

Of all the priests we had, I'll never forget Father O'Connor. Back in the early '70s when we were young, we would always have a funeral whenever a pet would die. Our house was situated on the side of the main road so pet fatalities were unfortunately very common. We wouldn't just get an auld box and dig a hole for the deceased animal, we'd have the full funeral, pallbearers and all. We'd walk up to the grave with the 'coffin' and lower it down into the ground. All very official altogether. One evening, anyway, I decided to go all out with the funeral proceedings for a dog we were burying.

At the time, the drum of gas for the house was sitting up on an empty Guinness barrel, so I found a metal bar and started slowly banging the side of the barrel while the funeral procession was going past. As I was doing this, who do you think was walking along the road only Father O'Connor. Out of the corner of my eye, I saw him stop dead in his tracks, if you'll excuse the pun, look at his watch and start fiddling with the side of it. The poor man honestly thought it was the Angelus bells he was hearing. 'Twasn't the Angelus at all, but a Guinness barrel being used as a funeral bell for a dead dog. He wasn't on Greenwich time, he was on Healy-Rae funeral time.

Speaking of pets, you know the way some people would arrive

home with a stray kitten or a lost dog? Well, my mother once arrived home with a fully grown Alsatian. Back then, the guide dogs for the blind were always Alsatians and there was a centre in Cork that used to train them. They would invest a lot of time and money in training these dogs, so they would be the best of the best, but if, for some reason, the dog was later deemed unsuitable for a blind person, the centre had a system in place whereby a member of the public could adopt it. There was such a demand, though, that you had to join a waiting list if you wanted one. My mother had put her name down and sure enough, a year or so later, she got a phone call telling her there was a lovely Alsatian looking for a new home.

What she brought home was an absolute genius of a dog. He was sweet, but my God was he strong; a right guard dog. We decided to call him Ali because at the time Muhammad Ali was so popular and given that the dog was so strong and so smart, it seemed appropriate to name him after the boxing juggernaut.

I remember one famous night Ali was patrolling around the yard at home when a car pulled up at the bottom of the road. Sure of course Ali was worse than any guard in that he'd have to find out who was in it, so he went down to investigate. Who was inside in the car but my sister and her boyfriend. I won't say which sister, and I won't say which boyfriend. I couldn't be telling ye that! Now, I don't know what Ali saw going on in the car, but he got the impression that my sister was being attacked. Within a couple of seconds, he was up on the bonnet growling in the window at the two. He was all but frothing at the mouth, waiting to tear into the poor lad that was with my sister.

That put an end to their carry-on fairly fast!

The *Farmers Journal*

Back when I was working as a county councillor, I was still working as a machine driver. I also had the shop, so each morning, before I would head off to my job on the digger, I would go in and open up the shop. One morning, as I was about to leave the shop, I glanced at the magazine stand. I looked at the stack of *Farmers Journals*. Then I looked up at the monthly supply of *Playboy*. It suddenly occurred to me that there was more of the former than the latter. I went to work on the digger anyway, and sure I was no sooner there when a journalist rang me.

'God, Michael, there's no news at all whatsoever,' he says. 'Is there anything happening at the moment?'

It was August, there wasn't a blessed thing happening. My father was the TD but the Dáil was on holiday, so there was nothing happening on that side. The council wasn't sitting, and neither was the Seanad. This lad was desperate for a story, so I thought to myself, well, my decent man, if you don't have a story, I'll give you one.

'Actually, d'you know what?' I said to him. 'This morning, as I was leaving my shop, I spotted something very unusual. I've seen it happening with a while, but it has really become more and more evident to me.'

'What's that?' he said.

'Would you believe, my sales of *Playboy* magazine outsell my sales of the *Farmers Journal*?'

The journalist nearly jumped through the phone, 'WHAT? What did you say?'

'Are you deaf?' I said. 'My *Playboys* outsell my *Farmers Journals* by nearly two to one.'

Well, he couldn't get enough of it.

Every newspaper went with the story. I'd say I did so many radio interviews about *Playboy* magazine and the *Farmers Journal*, I should have sent them both an invoice for all the publicity I gave them. It was the best marketing ploy of all for *Playboy* in particular because their sales actually spiked in Kerry after that. There were people who didn't even know the magazine existed until they heard the story of it outselling the *Journal*. I'd honestly say the lads beyond in the *Playboy* offices in America were wondering what in the hell was going on with their sales in Ireland during August and September of that year.

The funny thing is, when people would come into the shop to buy *Playboy* after that, they'd buy the *Farmers Journal* along with it and then tuck the *Playboy* into the centre of it. They didn't want to be seen leaving the shop with an adult magazine. For a while there, the *Farmers Journal* had a very different type of centrefold.

Johnny Hasn't Got
You Covered

I'll never forget the first time there was a condom machine installed near the gents' toilets in the pub. It was a Friday when the man came out to attach the machine to the wall, but it would be Monday before he would have the condoms to put in it. So that was grand anyway, Monday rolled around, and as promised, the man arrived out to stock up the machine. He opened up the machine and what did he find in it, only a pile of money. There was something like £86. The gas thing is, not one person had approached the bar during the weekend to complain that the machine had failed to dispense the condoms after they put their money in. There are things people will complain about, and there are things they won't, but back then if they paid for a condom and didn't get one, well, they weren't too inclined to make their annoyance known.

Pa

Pa O'Brien, God be good to him he's above in heaven, was the King of the Travellers. No question about it. Back when I was working in the Black Valley, there were a few people I would be guaranteed to meet every morning. The first was always Pa, and the second was a man called Jim Grady.

Before I get on to Pa, let me tell you about Jim. First and foremost, everyone called him Grady, never Jim. Grady worked as a jarvey, but he lived at the end of the valley. Now, to get from the end of the valley all the way over to Kate Kearney's where the tourists would be, well 'tis one long journey on a horse. Fortunately for Grady, though, he had a horse that was awful smart.

Every morning, Grady would have the same routine. He'd saddle up the horse, sometimes he might even have more than one with him, then he'd get everything ready, put on their reins, make sure they were fed and watered and their legs were right. Then he'd hop up on the cart, but the minute he'd sit down, you know the first thing he'd do? He'd fall fast asleep. Not a word of a lie, he'd put the head down and nod off. The horse would also put the head down, but she'd take off walking to Kate Kearney's, and she wouldn't stop either until she was outside it, which was always when Grady would wake up. This happened every day, like clockwork.

When I was working in the Black Valley, I'd always see Grady and the horse passing but sure there'd be no point in waving or saying hello as he'd be above on the cart, sound asleep.

I would leave my house at half five in the morning, and I wouldn't see a soul until I got to the square in Kenmare and saw Pa O'Brien setting up his vegetable stall. It reached a stage where we'd be so used to seeing each other every morning that if he had his back turned when I'd be passing, he wouldn't even need to turn around to know it was me. I'd just shout 'Hello, Pa!' and without turning around at all, Pa would shout back, 'How's young Rae?' It's funny, regardless of where I am in the country, if I ring Directory Enquiries, and I always get a kick out of this, but if I ring them looking for a number, they'd give me the number and then next thing they'd say out of the blue, 'Good luck now, Michael.' They'd know it was me. Pa was the same. He'd know my voice without even looking.

It was only a couple of years ago that Pa sadly passed away. I spoke to him not long before he died. I was above in the Dáil when one of his sons rang me. He told me who he was, and explained that he was there with his father, Pa. Now, I knew Pa was very sick, but I didn't realise he was as near to the end as he was until his son said, 'He wants to say hello to you before he dies.'

Sure enough, that familiar voice came on the phone.

'Is that you, Rae?'

'Well it is, Pa,' I said.

'Are you still out early in the morning?' he asked.

'Oh, I am of course, Pa. Are you doing all right?'

'Am I doing all right? Sure, amn't I dying, Rae?' he says straight back to me.

'Ara, you are not, Pa, you're doing fine.'

'When I'm dying, I know I'm dying,' he said. The man was at death's door and he still wasn't going to be argued with.

We said our goodbyes after that, and sure within the next twenty-four hours, poor Pa had left this world and was on his way to the next. His funeral was one of the biggest the Travelling community ever had. They came from all over Ireland, England, Scotland and Wales to say goodbye to Pa O'Brien. A workman to the marrow of his bones, he was one of a kind; revered to the end of his days and beyond. And rightly so.

Lily of the Valley

The most eccentric person in the Black Valley was undoubtedly a woman by the name of Lily van Oost. She was famous for her knitting, so much so that she was once commissioned to knit a jumper for a double decker bus. I think it had something to do with commemorating the millennium; she did it too, no bother at all to her. Known locally as Lily of the Valley, Lily was an absolute character and one I found awful interesting. She was massively into her art, and would find it in the most random of places. This was where her eccentric side would come out.

I'll never forget when she found a dead sheep. Now, I couldn't tell you where she found it, but I can tell you what she did with it. She took its head, put it on a stick, and then landed the stick down into the soil in her front garden. The reason she did this, she told me herself, was because she wanted to see it deteriorate over time. She said the sight of it changing over the days, weeks and months, well, that was true art to her.

Sure look, plonking the head of dead sheep in your front garden was unusual, but it was Lily, so we used to take no notice of things like that. She was eccentric, but I always found her entertaining and sure if we were all the same, it'd be a very boring place altogether.

The Fada Brothers

The Fada brothers, Paddy and John, were two well-known Black Valley bachelors. I did a good bit of work for them, and I'd say somehow I was the one of the first 'outsiders' they let in. They were very much set in their ways, these two. Mother of God were they stubborn, but when it came to business and money, they would buy and sell you, no bother in the world to them. They started with nothing and ended up owning around thirteen-hundred breeding ewes. Considering the times they were living in, it was very unusual to have that many, and sure when the ewes would lamb, that would have brought the herd to over two thousand; an awful amount of stock altogether. For two men living on their own, looking after that number of sheep was no easy feat.

I always got on well with them both, but I would have been on friendlier terms with Paddy than I was with John. Paddy was the boss of the two, so you had to make sure you were in with him or you wouldn't be employed. Paddy was more progressive, whereas John would have been the opposite. I remember one day, I was working on the machine doing some sort of a job for them, when John suddenly took a notion and decided he didn't want the job done. He tried to start an all merciful row with me and while I wasn't giving into it, he kept picking and picking at me, as if he was gunning for a fight.

It reached a point where he picked just a little bit too much off my patience, so I jumped out of the machine ready to give him a fight. God, his bravery wasn't long waning, and didn't he take off in full flight across the yard. I was hoppin' with the anger, though, so I caught hold of the nearest thing to me, a grease gun, and let it fly with the height of temper. The grease gun went speeding through the air, and sure it walloped the back of poor John's head. Down he went, roaring.

Until he rose to his feet again and ran, I was sure I had killed him. I was worried it was going to be the cause of some problems, so I decided the best thing to do would be to get to Paddy first and explain what had happened. Paddy hadn't witnessed the drama as he had been over on another part of the farm overseeing whatever work was being carried out there.

'Jesus, Paddy . . . myself and John are after having a bit of a row . . .'

'How bad a row was it?' he said.

'Well . . . I'm after stretching him abroad in the yard with the grease gun, a belt in the back of the head I gave him. By accident.'

'Well, 'twasn't without good reason you did that.'

The minute he said that, I knew there'd be no more about it. If that happened today, not only would I be fired, there'd be solicitors' letters flying on all sides. The last time I saw Paddy and John, it was during an election and I was out canvassing. We got chatting and I remember Paddy at one point saying to me, 'Michael, we won't be letting you down. We've known you a long time and we'll be sticking with you.'

A few nights later, I was driving along when I saw these blue flashing lights ahead of me. I had to pull in the car because the road had been closed off, so I parked up and walked over to where a garda was standing. The first thing I noticed was the ambulance; I could see someone being treated inside, but I couldn't make out who. A large white blanket stretched out on the road caught my eye. As I looked at it from where I was standing, I realised it had been placed over a body. My eyes immediately went to the wreckage, and I'm not exaggerating when I say I got the land of my life when it dawned on me that I recognised the car. It was Paddy and John's. I went over to a nearby garda to ask if it was them. He didn't know but he asked me if I could identify the man in the ambulance. It was John. Paddy had lost his life.

I went into the ambulance and spoke to John. He told me they had hit a tractor as it pulled out from a gap. I could see from the crash site myself that the impact had even turned the tractor upside down. Paddy was thrown from the car and died on the road. John survived his injuries, but that night was the beginning of the end for him. He and Paddy had been inseparable, and he was never the same afterwards.

The Fada brothers were bachelor farmers, but behind it all, they were businessmen in a way. Not that they'd make their affairs known, mind you. The one thing you'd never do is ask them their business. I remember one day I was out working in their yard when I spotted them leaving the house looking better dressed than normal. They were clean-shaven and looked so smart that only for I knew where they were actually going, I'd have thought they were on their way to a funeral. Where they were going was to an auction. The farm beside them was up for buying and I knew Paddy was gung-ho to get it. I couldn't let on that I knew where they were going, though. That would have annoyed them no end. When they arrived home that evening, Paddy came up talking to me.

'I was at that auld auction today,' he said.

'Oh, very good,' I said back to him. 'How did you get on?'

'Sure I bought the farm of course. But you know, and this will tell you how foolish some people are, a few of my neighbours actually thought they were going to be able to outbid me! Where would they be going with it? Sure didn't they know I wanted it?'

He was wildly amused by the idea that there were people who honestly thought they could outbid him. It was as if he'd never heard the likes of anything so stupid in his life. I remember thinking to myself, well there's a lesson in determination and self-belief if ever there was one.

Not a Hen Left After Healy-Rae

I always began work in the Black Valley at exactly the same time every morning. I'd leave the house at 5.30 a.m., and at 7.30 a.m. on the dot I'd be sitting up on the digger with the radio on. I travelled the road through the Black Valley so often, I was as good as Grady's horse for knowing every foot of it. I knew it so well, however, that my foot was often a little heavy on the accelerator. Now, along this road lived a lovely family called the Caseys. The lady of the house was Chrissy; her husband, Jack, was the postman.

But Chrissy anyway was a great woman for keeping hens. She had a mighty amount of them. The thing is, the hens had a tendency to roam free, and whenever I'd be passing Chrissy's house, they would never hear my van in time to get out of the way. Unfortunately, many's the hen that failed to shift, and as a result, there were mornings when I'd have left a trail of feathered roadkill in my wake as I'd be passing through. If I'd had a hen for every time poor Chrissy would say, 'I don't have a hen left after Healy-Rae', well I'd have been able to have replaced the entire lot of them for her.

I'd say I have carried out machine work for literally every single farmer in the Black Valley, and you know, it was an absolute pleasure to do so because I adored every single one of them. They were the finest of people. I remember I was heading to work there early one morning, but I hadn't so much as seen my bed the night before, as I had been out all night at the Rose of Tralee Festival. Whatever happened me, anyway, I must have closed my eyes for a second too long, because didn't I finish up in such a way that the van was stuck in the ditch at the side of the road. 'Twas like a stubborn horse; there was absolutely no moving it backwards or forwards. No, there was only one way that van was going to leave the ditch and that was with a fine tractor pulling it. I headed off walking to a nearby house that I knew belonged to a local farmer. I had done some work for him in the past and knew him well, but I was in an awful way over the idea of having to wake him up at such a godforsaken hour of the morning. I knocked on the window and called his name, and sure enough, didn't he appear after a minute or so, looking tired and cross. He opened the window.

'Rae, what time is it?'

I looked at my watch. 'Oh, 'tis half eight.' It was half five, but I couldn't tell him that for fear he'd have a grease gun nearby that he might throw at me in temper. It'd be just like what would happen to me after what I did to Johnny Fada.

'Oh my God man, I slept it out,' he said, still rubbing his eyes with the sleep.

'Well, I'm in a bit of trouble, can you bring out the tractor and give me a hand moving my van out of the ditch?'

'I will of course,' he replied. 'Sure I should have been up long ago.'

A couple of minutes later, myself and the farmer were walking across the yard towards his tractor, he there in a bit of a daze wondering how he slept it out, and me there hoping he wouldn't look at his watch.

'Musha, haven't you been working awful hours lately?' I reasoned. 'Sure aren't you killed out, man? Happens to us all.'

'True, true, but Christ Rae, I still should have been up hours ago.'

When we reached the ditch, the farmer hitched the van to the tractor while I sat into the driver's seat to steer the van back on to the road. Just as we got the van out of the ditch and back on the road, didn't he look down at his watch. Next thing came the roar, and I'd almost swear it was heard thirty miles away over in Caherdaniel.

'Ara God blasht you, Healy-Rae!' he fumed, his face the colour of red I hadn't seen in years. "Tis only half past five, you raving lunatic, you!'

No Place Like the Valley

It was a well-known and accepted fact that Johnny Denis was a God-given genius. His right name was Johnny Donoghue, but we used to call him Johnny Denis. Well, Johnny lived in the Black Valley in a place called Cloghernoosh, and you know I'd say there was never a man who took as much pride in living there as Johnny did. I always knew he loved the place but one day it became clear just how much it meant to him.

Years back, the Land Commission offered him the finest of farming land above in Kildare but in return, he would have to give up his land in the Black Valley. The land in the Black Valley wouldn't have been renowned for its quality, so when this group came along and proposed that he swap it for a pile of land that was extremely valuable, what do you think he did? He refused it.

I asked him years later why he didn't accept their offer. 'Michael,' he said to me, 'sure wouldn't it mean having to leave the Black Valley?' That put it all into context for me.

There's something very special about the people in the Black Valley, and I can honestly tell you that every person I knew from there, I didn't just like them, I adored them. Some of the valley's greatest characters have since gone to their eternal reward, Johnny Denis being one, God be good to him, and not only was the Black Valley the worse off for losing them, but all of Kerry was as well.

The Day is Nearly Gone and We've Nothing Done

I honestly don't think there's a house in Kilgarvan that I didn't paint at some stage as a teenager. Myself and another man joined forces to create a mini painting business and we ended up working on every single solitary house in the village. I had a great head for heights and so too did he, not that we were painting skyscrapers or anything, but if you had seen the 'going on' of us above on the ladders, well you'd be inclined to call the doctors if not the guards. We could see no danger; we thought we were invincible.

There was one particular occasion when we had the outsides of three houses to paint, but I had it figured it out in my head that we could easily do it in one day if we started early enough. I was sure of it, so I went ahead and promised the three people that it would be done. After finishing up my shift in the fish factory, I headed over to my painting partner's house to collect him, so we could get a start on our long day of work, but when I got there, there wasn't a sign of him. I started knocking at the door, but there was nothin' doin', so I started throwing stones up at the window and shouting at him to hurry up.

'Will you come on, for God's sake! The day is nearly gone and we've nothing done!'

I kept shouting about the day being nearly gone when next thing didn't his father stick his head out the window. I don't think I ever got as much of an effing and a blinding as I did that day. He turned the air so blue, that what he didn't call me wasn't worth mentioning.

'You're standing outside my effing window shouting about the day being nearly effing gone . . .'

'But it is!' I said to him

'Goddammit, man, 'tis four o'clock in the effing morning!'

I looked at my watch. He was right, but in my head, if we didn't get moving, we wouldn't have stood a chance of getting all the work done in a day. Eventually, I got him up and out, and within the half-hour we were painting the first of the day's houses. We stayed true to our promise, too. By midnight that night, we had all three houses painted!

The one thing I loved as a young lad was a challenge, and the harder, rougher and tougher it was, the better. I loved trying to beat the clock and cramming as much as possible into each day. I enjoyed working, and sure when you're young, you can work all the hours you have to without a bother in the world. I have worked so hard all my life and I know so many others who have been Trojan workers all their lives, which is why nothing infuriates me more than when certain individuals in a position of power try to give the impression that they are among the working people. These are the individuals whose hands look so soft, you know the only hard work they ever did was stir a cup of tea they probably didn't even pour themselves.

I remember one day in the not so distant past, I lost it a small bit when one such individual started banging on about the working man. Nothing out of him but 'The working man this' and 'The working man that.' Now, the same individual, if you put him footing turf in the bog, would probably collapse with exhaustion after handling a few sods. Anyway, in the middle of it all, I said to him, 'Listen here . . . you're talking about the working man, but yet you've never done a day's work in your life. The toughest thing you have ever had to do is come inside here and talk about the working man.'

Well thanks be to Christ, that quietened his rubbish talk for a while.

Learning from Students

Throughout my life, I never worked just one job. I was always tipping away at a number of different things, and I put that down to the influence of people like my father and Master Hickey. The reason I had a strong interest in business and in the value of making a pound was because I had seen them doing it. They stuck at everything.

When I give a talk in school, I try to instil in young children the importance of earning money, valuing it and, above all, saving it. While I offer plenty of advice during these talks, I actually find I'm the one doing the learning. If you hear the questions the young people ask, then you know what the parents are talking about and asking. When I was visiting a national school recently, the class were asked if they had any questions they wanted to put to me. One young girl, she couldn't have been more than nine or ten, put up her hand. I thought maybe she was going to ask me something run of the mill like, 'What's it like being a politician?' or 'What would you be if you weren't in politics?'

My God, she stood up and said, 'Michael . . . why were the farmers' grants being cut by, on average, five per cent?'

Well, she had definitely heard that one at home! When you are talking to students, you are also talking to their parents in an indirect way. I remember one time when we were canvassing, we were below in Waterville and myself and the team were leaving a chip shop after having canvassed the staff there. As we were leaving, I spotted three or four young ones around a table in the corner, so I walked over to them, introduced myself and started chatting.

One of them pipes up. 'We had our election today.'

'How do you mean?' I asked.

'The class voted in our school today. It was a mock election.'

'How did it go?'

Well I got the full run-down. The nearest candidate to them was the then-minister's brother Paul O'Donoghue. He got something like three votes. Then someone else got three or four votes, another candidate got two, but then he tells me that I received nine votes. I remember walking out the door of the chip shop after that, and the lads that were waiting for me were giving out yards asking what delayed me. I told them I had just had a very important conversation.

'With who?' they asked.

'With those young lads there inside in the chip shop.'

'Sure they have no vote!' came the reply. 'They're not old enough.'

I remember smiling but not answering them; I let it go over my head. I knew in my heart and soul right there and then that the results of a simple primary school mock election were in fact a very telling measure of what was going on in the homes of that area. Sure enough, when the votes were counted in the council election, I received the highest-ever number of votes from that electoral area. When I heard the final result that day, I thought back to the conversation in the chip shop. You can keep your polls, and your research reports; for me, it was something as inconspicuous as a primary-school mock vote that confirmed we had the winning of the election in sight.

Maybe Next Time

About a week after my first election, I was in a petrol station with veteran campaigners Jimmy Breen and Teddy McCarthy. As we were walking through the forecourt, we bumped into two sisters we'd known for years. Now, I would have been of the opinion that a vote from both of these women was a fair certainty, but the one thing you need to know about Jimmy and Teddy is that they're as sharp as they come. I don't know if it's a side effect of having spent years canvassing for myself and my father, but they can read people as easy as they'd read they daily newspaper.

Anyway, we stopped and said hello to the two ladies and straight away Jimmy leaned in to shake the hand of one. As he did, he said to her, 'Oh thanks very much for voting for Michael, thank you.' Next thing he turned to the other lady and said, 'Sure maybe you might vote for us the next time.'

Well, she looked at him, and truth be told, even I was doing some lookin' at him. The poor woman was astonished that he knew she hadn't voted for me. The truth of the matter is, Jimmy didn't know she hadn't voted for me, but he knew by the gimp of her when she spotted us that something was off, so he figured it must be something to do with the vote the week earlier.

'Jimmy, I thought the vote was private!' she said.

Sure as soon as she said that to him, she as good as confirmed that she hadn't voted for me. Jimmy looked at her.

'Oh, there's nothing private when it comes to politics,' he smiled.

A Roof Over Your Head

These days we have everything, but wouldn't it be a grand world altogether if everyone treated each other and looked out for each other in the same way neighbours used to back in the days when no one had anything? I think we've started to lose that trait, not intentionally, but in this day and age everyone is so caught up in their own lives and their own problems that sometimes it's the very struggle taking place right in front of them that they don't see.

When I was canvassing back in 1999, one of the houses I called to belonged to a woman who was living on her own. I knew she was home because her bicycle was there but there was no sign of her, so I had a look around in case, God forbid, something had happened. As I walked around to the other side of the house, I noticed things looked very rough. At this point, I could see that the door into the kitchen had been left wide open, so I headed for that. Little did I know at the time, but that door was never closed, not even at night.

I walked up to the open door and what do you think I saw inside in the kitchen? Cows. They hadn't just wandered in either. I realised this when I spotted a layer of cow dung in the room. It had become encrusted in a hard casing too, so God knows how long it had been sitting there. Now remember, this was where the woman was living. She had to eat off the table inside in that kitchen, and yet here were the calves from the yard going in and out of the place of their own free will. It was also perishing cold in there with the door being open all the time.

Eventually I found the woman out working and I got talking to her. We chatted for a bit and she took my card and told me she would vote for me. I hadn't said anything about the condition in which she was living at the time, but it bothered me, so much so that about a month or so after I got elected, she popped back into my head. I went to one of the head people in the housing department at the time, and I told her the story about the woman living with the calves inside in her kitchen. I was only a new county councillor at the time, so I asked her what I could do to help the woman. She explained that if the situation was bad enough, and if the woman signed the relevant forms permitting the council to build her a new house on the land, then the wheels could be put in motion.

The next chance I had, I went back to the woman and told her I could get a new council house built on the land for her. What do you think her first words were when I told her?

'Goddamn you!' she started. 'You came looking for a vote and I voted for you, and here you are now coming back bothering me about a house. Sure I don't want any house, now leave me alone. I'm quite happy as I am.'

There I was thinking she'd be delighted by the offer. Instead she went absolutely mental. Well, that was grand, she had given me her answer . . . so I went back a week later. The same story. I'd say I made three or four different attempts to get her to listen to me. It was the height of battle. Honest to God, there's wars that have been won with less difficulty.

Eventually she heard me out.

'If I sign this will you leave me alone?' she said.

'I will,' I promised.

After I arrived back at Kerry County Council with signed documentation that a new house was being sought, an investigating officer and an engineer were dispatched to inspect her current house, so as to ensure she really needed one. They also had to see if she had a suitable site on which the house could be built. When they went and investigated the conditions the woman was living in, every alarm bell inside in their heads went off. They could see that not only was this an awful serious case, but an urgent one. Right away, Kerry County Council set about putting the wheels in motion and applied to the planning department for planning permission. They were basically applying for planning permission from themselves, you could say. Once it came through, a construction team was sent out to start the build. Even as the house was going up, locals were convinced she wouldn't move into it, she was so set in her ways. Once it was finished and she saw what it was like to have comfort and heat, she was absolutely delighted with herself. She used to always say to me afterwards, 'God, 'tis great to have comfort and to have running water,' neither of which she'd had in her old house.

That to me was politics working at its best. Here was a person living in horrendous conditions but still not actually looking for anything, yet someone took the bull by the horns and got them what they needed anyway. It took a person like that nice official in Kerry County Council to trust my word on the matter and to give the case the attention it needed. That's politics. I have never made any secret of the fact that I have great time for Kerry County Council as a body, but the individuals within the council, in my opinion . . . well, you could search Ireland and I don't think you could find people of the same calibre as those who work on that council.

On another occasion, I came across a case where a man was living in a house with a roof that was leaking so badly that each night when he would get into his bed, he'd have to take a roll of black silage plastic and pull it up over the bed to try to keep himself dry. There was no avoiding the drops because they'd be coming in all sides, so all he could do was sleep under this wet black plastic. The house was a health hazard. I'd say he'd have died from pneumonia if he stayed living there, so I spoke to the relevant people, got the permission that was needed to have the roof fixed and while the work was being carried out, we moved the man into a mobile unit. The sad reality is that in most cases, it's the person who is not looking for help who needs it the most. Some people are very aware of their rights and entitlements, whereas others would just suffer in silence and look for nothing. That's where it takes people who are awake and can recognise when a person is in need of a bit of help and support.

I remember there was a case where the council wanted to erect a mobile unit but the person they wanted to house had no place to put the unit. A mobile unit is like a caravan, just not on wheels. It would have all the basics – a bedroom, a kitchen, a bathroom; it would be small but functional, very compact and easy to heat. An engineer in the housing department approached me and explained that while he could arrange a mobile unit for the people I wanted to house, he had nowhere to install it. He needed a site that had water, electricity and was located in a populated place where there'd be a sewer, a mains, and the likes. He also needed someone who wouldn't be looking for any rent in return for putting the unit on the site. I remember laughing when I heard that and saying to him, 'God, you don't want much!'

I was racking my brain, trying to think of who would have a place that met all the criteria; who would give the bit of ground and not look for anything in return? It occurred to me I knew just the man. I rang the engineer back and told him I had the person he was looking for.

'Have they everything?' he asked, expecting there to be a catch.

'They do,' I said.

'Have you asked for their permission?'

''Tis all sorted,' I told him.

'That's great, Michael. Who is it?'

''Tis only myself.'

I had been thinking of all the people who lived in the locality, trying to figure out who would have the kind of site we needed when next thing it dawned on me that I had the ideal site myself. I arranged for the unit to be installed on the site, and it ended up staying in place for around five or six years afterwards. It housed a number of people who found themselves in need of accommodation. It was only a bit of ground, but for anyone who lived there in that unit, it was a warm safe home. That's what community politics is about. Giving the people the help they need, even if they don't ask you for it.

Inspirations

I've always thought it a privilege to be invited into someone's home. When you're on the canvassing trail, and someone welcomes you in, well, they're inviting you into their lives in a way. I remember when I was canvassing one particular area; it was in an awful secluded spot. Very inaccessible. I went to one of the few houses there, and when we started chatting they invited me inside. It turned out that a young girl living in this house was on the waiting list for a transplant. I sat down and had a grand chat with the girl and her family. They explained to me what the whole process involved and how they would have to leave right away as soon as the call would come. There would be a mad rush to the nearest main airport, then there'd have to be a flight to take the girl to England where the transplant would be performed. I was sitting there listening to this and it occurred to me that it wouldn't work.

Straight away, I took on the case, because, to be honest, it really bothered me that a lifesaving opportunity could potentially be missed in the event of them getting that much-anticipated call. At the time, I was a young, ambitious politician on the health board, so at my first Southern Health Board meeting following my visit to the house, I raised the case and explained the situation. I told them a system would have to be put in place. They agreed, and it was decided that a helicopter should be made available whenever the call would come, weather permitting. To ensure everything would run smoothly when the time would come, the pilot even did a test run, to see if he could land by the house. They had everything in place. All we needed now was the call to action.

Every Christmas Eve, right before going to Mass, I would ring her and ask how she was doing. When she'd answer the phone, straight away she'd say, 'I'm still here and you didn't forget me!'

We would have a great chat and she would give me the update on her situation. I always used to enjoy talking to her at Christmas because it was the dawning of a new year; she was still alive and there was still hope.

There were some false alarms, but despite that, everyone was keeping positive that her time would come. Sadly, it wasn't to be. Her illness took over and before she could get the transplant she needed, she passed away. I'll never forget the next Christmas after that. It was Christmas Eve right before Mass, and I was so lonesome over not being able to speak to her, so instead I called her family to let them know I was thinking of them. I did what I could to help that girl, but I genuinely believe that she helped me a thousand times more. Her fight gave me a greater understanding of the trials and tribulations people go through, the uncertainty they have to put up with, and what they endure with bravery and lack of self-pity.

Ian O'Connell is another person who has taught me so much. He's like a beacon of inspiration to the whole county, if not the country. Ian is a sixteen-year-old teenager from Killarney who had been out riding his bicycle with his friends when he fell and damaged his neck. The injury left him paralysed from the neck down. It has been just over a year since his accident, and he's one of the most positive uplifting people you could ever be blessed to meet. He has even been on *The Late Late Show* giving his views on the cards life dealt him. Ian is dealing with a level of adversity most of us can't even fathom, yet he takes it all in his stride. His motto is, 'If I can't stand up, I'll stand out,' and my God do people like Ian stand out.

Flustered and Foosterin'

After I first bought the garage, I really struggled to pay my way and make a living from it. The one way I made ends meet was by working every God-given hour I could, even late into the night. I used to be out filling petrol, putting tyres on cars, changing oil, anything that had to be done I would do, regardless of whether it was one o'clock in the day or one o'clock in the morning.

One Friday night anyway, my father was to appear on *The Late Late Show* for the first time. He was a county councillor then, but a well-known one, so they invited him on. It was such a big deal to be on *The Late Late Show* and there was no way I was going to miss it, so I put a notice on the window saying: 'SELF-SERVICE AS MY FATHER IS ON *THE LATE LATE SHOW* TONIGHT AND I WANT TO WATCH IT.' Might as well be honest, like.

In the forecourt, I had a small hut, and in this hut, there was a television underneath the counter where I'd make the tea, so I threw it up on the table and turned on the *Late Late*, ready to see himself make his debut. Another fine Kerryman, John B Keane, was on in the same segment. As my father walked out on to the set after being introduced by Gaybo, I noticed something wasn't right about him. 'Twas like he was a bit addled. He had a red head on him as well, as if he was a bit flustered. I parked it in my head and continued watching.

The next time I saw my father, what do you think was the first thing he said to me? 'Did you see the *Late Late*?'

'I did,' I told him.

He lowered his voice a little. 'Jesus Christ almighty, did you hear the story at all?'

'What story?' said I back to him.

'Ah, there was war on the programme,' he started. 'Did you see the women that had been on earlier in the show? The ones with the costumes?' Before my father's interview, the *Late Late* had had a sort of fashion slot where these ladies were modelling swimming togs.

'Do you know what happened with them?' he continued.

'I know nothing about it sure!'

'We were all there getting ready,' he explained, 'and the women were there as well, and the next thing there was some mix-up over their costumes.'

'What was the mix-up?'

'Ara, whatever auld foostering that went on, wasn't there this big panic and suddenly they were looking for scissors, razors, tweezers and sure weren't myself and John B drafted in to help out and get them ready to go out on stage.'

There I was trying to imagine my father and John B Keane with their tweezers and their makeup trying to beautify these young ones. Yeah right, I thought to myself, a very likely story. I was sure he was pulling my leg but in saying that, he seemed very convincing, and in fairness he did look stressed and flustered as he was walking out onto the set. Something in the back of my head made me wonder, was there any fear he was telling me the truth?

Go forward a few years, myself and the man I call the chief of staff, Paudie O'Callaghan of the Failte Hotel in Killarney, were at the Killarney Races. Paudie, because of his connections, had these 'All Access' badges for the racecourse; we could go anywhere we wanted, so we went straight to the bar. Sure who was the first person we saw as we were walking in, only the great writer himself, John B Keane.

'You're young Healy-Rae!' he said to me as I approached him.

'John B, how are you?' I asked. I bought us all a drink. As we continued talking, he wrapped his two hands around the glass, sipping from it every so often. He had become quite feeble by that point, and his health was not too good, I had heard. The next thing he said to me was, 'Well, Michael, I'll never forget one night years ago, myself and your father were on the *Late Late* . . .'

'What about it, John B?' said I.

'Ara Michael, surely your father must have told you the story?'

I looked at John B, and I'd say I had the most innocent head you ever in your life seen on any man.

'John B' I said, 'I have no idea what you're talking about.'

Well sure he got awful interested then. 'C'mere and I'll tell you the story so,' he starts. 'Sure that was the most famous night ever. There was a group of women, something happened before they went out on stage and didn't they all discover they had the wrong costumes on them.'

'And what about it?'

'Ah for God's sake, there was some mix-up and sure the next thing there was a panic because they were due to go out next. Your father was given a scissors, I was given a razor, we were both told to get down to work and sure Jesus we didn't know where to look . . .'

At that stage in his life, John B certainly wasn't going around with a lie in his head, so what my father had told me that time was actually correct. My God, no wonder the poor man had been looking so flustered that night.

How to Win Votes and Influence People

From the time I was knee high, I copped on to the fact that if I applied the sage old advice of keeping kept my mouth shut and my ears open, a good political campaign would teach me far more than the best school ever could. I learned from everybody; all sorts of people from all sorts of backgrounds with all sorts of expertise.

Some of the finest people from whom I would have learned a great deal, and who are now sadly deceased, would include, Bernard Collins, Arthur Lenihan, Maurice Gallivan, Dermot O'Callaghan, Johnny Mahony, Donie O'Sullivan, James Sullivan, and Ned Carey. I remember in the 1997 election, we had a lot of new people getting involved in canvassing for the first time. One morning, a young man arrived into the campaign office, and he was no sooner in the door when this expression came over his face as though he'd just realised he had forgotten something. He quickly put his hand into his left pocket. Sure enough, he had forgotten to bring his phone; I think it was one of those Nokia 6010's that were all the rage at the time. I remember you could play three games on it and it also had a currency converter, a calculator and a clock. God, we thought it was the height of sophistication. But anyway, to come back to the phoneless young fella.

'Maurice,' he said, 'I'll have to go home for my phone, I forgot it.'

Now, I won't repeat everything Maurice said when he heard this, and I won't use the exact same language as he, but all I will say is he wasn't long turning the air in the room a bright blue.

'Now you listen here to me, young lad,' he started. 'We fought elections, we won some and we lost some, but we had no effing phones in our pockets, just brains between our two ears. We canvassed the same way every other fella canvassed, so don't be minding your effing phone.'

It probably wasn't the most diplomatic way of making his point, but the gist of what he was saying to the lad was spot on. I'm not trying to downplay the importance of phones today; back then, it was a different world, but the fact still applies that phones don't win elections. Old Joe Kennedy spent a fortune on hiring people to find out the best ways to win votes. Naturally he expected them to come back with some big answer as to how it could be done. What do you think they came back and said to him after all their study?

'If you want people to vote for you . . . you have to go out and ask them to.'

I'd say I've read hundreds of books on the Kennedys. In fact, I think I'm after running out of Kennedy books; I don't think I have anything left to read about them. For a person that couldn't read until he was just shy of his teenage years, I own a savage number of books in general. I give away a lot of them as well, though. When I come across ones that I don't have any need for any more, I like to pass them on to people who will appreciate them. I do it pure randomly and out of the blue too. The reason I like to do it is because I remember loving nothing more than when my mother would hand me a new book.

A wide variety of topics can be found in the books on my shelves, but the topic of the Kennedys definitely accounts for the most, I'd say. During my time as Mayor of Kerry, I met Ted Kennedy over in Washington, and I'd say the one thing that rattled him a small bit was the level of detail I knew not just about himself, but about all his family members. I just always found them so interesting. I remember my mother always saying about my father, 'Well, nobody could ever accuse him of being boring or dull,' and you know, the exact same could be said about the Kennedys.

Throughout all my reading material on them, the one thing I have always noticed was how sharp old Joe Kennedy was. He was like Daniel Stephen; he was desperate cute. He was also a great man when it came to foresight. One story that always stayed with me was the massive impact of a random encounter Joe once had. When he was going into his office one day, he noticed a spot of dirt on his shoes. Now Joe was obsessive about having clean shoes, so when he saw this bit of dirt on his shoes, he went to the nearest shoeshine stand and sat up on the chair while the lad got to work. While the shoe-shiner was shoe-shining, he started telling Joe about shares he had bought in a certain company. He was convinced they were on the rise, and he encouraged Joe to buy into them too. Joe listened intently to all the man's tips, paid him for his work, and thanked him for the advice. A few minutes later he arrived into his company headquarters and summoned every member of staff into his office. There he delivered the urgent order that he was to be dissolved of every share he owned by close of trade that evening. He wanted cash for the lot.

His staff were sure he had gone mad, convinced old Joe had lost the plot; but they did as they were ordered, and by that evening, every share Joe owned had been sold at top market price. He didn't have one to his name by close of business. A couple of weeks went by, and what do you think happened? The infamous Wall Street Crash of 1929. I remember my own mother telling me that her father had personally known people who had jumped from the windows of their office buildings.

Joe sold his shares based solely on what the man had said to him while shining his shoes. It was a bit like the property bubble in Ireland; the bubble had to burst. Old Joe could see the same thing happening with the shares. They were going up and up and it was obvious their breaking point wasn't too far off. When the shares did plummet, just as he had predicted they would, no one had a bob to spend, but Joe of course was cash rich, so he bought up every share he could. Shares he had previously sold for a fortune he bought back for next to nothing. His net worth went up thousand-fold.

That story resonated with me because it showed me the power of the number one rule I had been taught as a child about keeping my mouth shut and my ears open. When that shoe-shiner started taking about shares, Joe could have interrupted him to talk about his own knowledge of the stock market. He could easily have elected to not speak at all in favour of burying his head in a newspaper. He didn't, though. He sat. He stayed quiet. And he listened. And he realised that if even the shoe-shine men were talking about investing in shares, they must be overvalued. Had he not done so, who knows how the future landscape of the Kennedy dynasty would have changed.

A Kennedy and a Kerryman

If you want to stay alive, travel by plane. It's by far and away one of the safest modes of transport, and this advice is coming from a person who hates planes. It is totally against my will to get on one. I don't have a phobia of flying or anything like that; it's more the hassle of the airports that I don't like. Put it this way, I won't ever be accused of clocking up too many air miles. It's an ironic loathing to have, really, because I'm currently the chairperson of the Oireachtas committee on European Union affairs. Hating travelling is almost a contradiction to the committee position I hold.

When you consider how safe it is to travel by air, the statistics about the Kennedys is actually frightening. I won't put an exact figure on it, but an absolute power of them have died in airplane crashes. As I said before, I never believed in piseogs. I didn't believe that a cliff on the side of a mountain would open up whenever a member of the McCarthy Moore clan died, and I certainly didn't at any point believe that it was some curse that was killing off the Kennedy family. They lived life hard. When they worked, they worked hard; when they played, they played hard. They ran risks that most wouldn't. They were no different from any good Kerryman I know, let me tell you that. With the whole family being that way inclined, though, sure it wasn't a curse, it was the law of averages.

No more than my mother being suspicious of Bishop Casey's relationship with his 'cousin' Annie, I've always been suspicious that there was something going on between Jackie and Bobby after Jack died. I'm fully convinced of it. When she saw Bobby being shot and killed in the same public way as Jack, she was full sure that neither herself nor the children were safe. She even said it at the time, 'They'll kill us all.' Not long after that, she met

Aristotle Onassis, or Arishtotle as we'd call him in Kerry, and he started wooing her with all sorts of carry-on.

You see, Arishtotle always had an eye for Jackie. Now, I say he had 'an eye' for her, but that's ironic in itself, because the man couldn't actually keep his eyes open. He was suffering from an illness brought on by chronic fatigue, and one of the symptoms was that he couldn't keep his eyes open. Not many people know this about him, but he was apparently so embarrassed about his eyes drooping that he'd apply clear tape each morning to try to keep them open. Isn't it mad? All his money, and he still had to resort to Sellotape to keep his eyes open.

The reason I loved reading everything I could find about the likes of Arishtotle and the Kennedys was because I enjoyed delving into their minds, finding out what made them tick and how they dealt with challenges. I always found them to be incredibly interesting people. I also always admired their sense of loyalty to those around them. They were damn proud of where they came from, and that always resonated with me.

I'll never forget the night I first met Ted Kennedy. The man who introduced us was my great friend, Senator Dan Kiely, a great character who was known by all the American politicians. Ted was at one side of the room, and myself and Dan were at the other, and sure as soon as Ted spotted Dan, over he walked. 'Dan Kiely! Who is this young man with you?' he asked, as he went to shake my hand. Ted Kennedy is the only person I have ever met in my life whose hands were the exact same size as my grandmother's. They were like shovels. My father had big hands, but Nana Rae's were bigger, and Ted Kennedy was the same. You'd get lost in the palm of his hand, as they'd say.

Anyway, Ted invited us to meet with him the following day in his office. He had this enormous office because of his standing in the Senate at the time, but when we walked in, he led us into what

I could only describe as the living room quarters. We went in and sat down, and as I looked around and took it all in, I realised the room was filled with memorabilia from his childhood. It was one of those surreal moments. I'm proud to say a Kerry number plate made it on to Ted's impressive memorabilia wall. I know this because I gave it to him. I was Mayor of Kerry at the time, and when you travel somewhere representing your county and country, the county council gives you small gifts to present to the various people you would have to meet, people like the speaker of the house, ambassadors, and the likes. Anyway, the stuff that the council used to give me was awful boring altogether, so I decided to research the different people I'd be meeting during my trip to America and then I went away to a motor factors in Killarney and had personalised number plates made up for each of them. This would have been a massive novelty at the time. I had number plates made for everyone, but I made sure the words 'County Kerry' were printed on them, and thanks be to God I had one done up for Ted on the off-chance that I'd meet him. Well, he was delighted with it, and up on the wall it went. In fact, in 2009 my sister Rosemary ended up going to Senator Kennedy's funeral in Boston to represent the Healy-Rae family.

To have met Ted Kennedy in my capacity as Mayor of Kerry is something I will never forget, but to have been made mayor of my county in the first place is something I regard as one of the greatest privileges of my life. The first time I wore the mayoral chain, the pride was immense because I was wearing the same chain my father had worn on three previous occasions. I treated the role extremely seriously too. During my time as mayor, there were challenges, difficulties and the odd banana skin along the way, but the members of the council knew that my best interest was with the county. I had such an appreciation for having been entrusted with the role that I'd have done anything for the job. I'll put it to you this way, if they were opening a matchbox in Donegal and if it was a Kerry matchbox, well I'd be there for the grand opening. I criss-crossed the country, and I even did the one thing I absolutely hate doing . . . I went abroad every time I was asked.

New York Sidewalks

It was during one of these mayoral trips abroad that I learned an awful unusual skill. It was back in 2002, and would you believe, I learned the skill on a New York sidewalk of all places. I was over there in my capacity as Mayor of Kerry, but as I was walking along the street, I spotted a man sitting on the sidewalk holding a biro with a long piece of string attached to it. He was holding it over one of those wire grates that covered a drain. Every few seconds, he'd carefully pull up the string, before then dropping it back down through the grate again. You know how when you were a kid, you'd tie a piece of string to a stick and pretend to fish? That's what it looked like this man was doing, that he was pretending to fish. I looked over at him and every Kerry fibre in my being was screaming at me to go over and ask him what the hell was with the biro and the string. I didn't want to bother him, though, so I kept on walking and thought no more of it.

The following day, I was walking along the same street and sure who did I see in the same spot again, only the same man doing the same thing as the day before. That was it; the curiosity got the better of me and I went over to him. After apologising for disturbing him, I asked if he would mind me asking him a personal question.

'Not at all,' he said, looking up at me as he stayed sitting on the busy sidewalk, holding the biro and its string over the wire grate like it was the most normal thing in the world. 'What is your question?'

'Could you educate me as to what you are doing with the string and the biro?' I asked.

'I'm making my living,' he answered simply.

'And what is your living?'

He went on to explain how a little lead weight was tied to the end of the string, and on this lead weight was a piece of chewing gum. He would then go to a place where people would be rushing while taking change out of their pockets and purses, places like a subway station or a bus stop, where the likelihood of lose change being dropped was high. He'd find a drain, and then into it he would drop the lead weight with the gum and string attached. If the lead weight fell on a coin, it would stick to the gum and he'd pull it up. He was able to make a living and survive in New York doing that. I think I stood there for about an hour speaking to him. Afterwards I gave him a few dollars as a thank you for educating me. He thought this was hilarious. 'Now here I am making money on the double!' he laughed. 'I'm fishing for money and now I have an Irishman willing to give me money to learn about me fishing for money.'

When you think about it, his quality of life was probably better than most. He wasn't rushing about the place and stressing over trivial things. He made a small living doing what he did each day, and through this, he was able to afford a bed at night and food during the day. That street was filled with countless people that day, and I'd easily say he was the happiest one there.

The Field

I'd say there isn't a one in the country that hasn't seen the film or read the book *The Field*. Does the story of *The Field* surprise me? No. Does it shock me that such a thing would happen? Absolutely not. In fact, the story of *The Field* was actually inspired by an incident that occurred in Kerry many years back. Still to this day, I know of people who would literally die for their land, especially land that has been passed down from generation to generation.

I remember one time, a very nice man was living in a rented house in Kenmare, and one day he approached me wanting to buy a particular site I had. It was a very scenic site, and one that I had been fortunate enough to have had passed on to me from my mother. Even though it'd be about seven miles away from Kenmare, if you were to stand there at night, you'd see all the lights of the town turning on. Day or night, the view there is just beautiful, so I wasn't surprised really when this man put an offer to me. It would have been a fabulous site for a house and sure back at that time, he'd have had no problem getting planning. He wouldn't have a hope of it these days. As part of his proposal, he offered me a considerable amount of money. Now you have to remember, I didn't have a bob to my name. I was borrowing money from the bank left, right and centre. I was working all the hours I could to make the repayments and keep afloat, so when this man came along with his offer, it was like the golden goose had laid the golden egg that would solve all my not-so-golden problems. I thanked him, but I declined. He misunderstood and returned with an increased offer. It was a tasty sum of money, but again I said no. He arrived back a third time with not just an increased offer, but an increased-increased offer. Let me put it to you this way, the money he was offering would buy a farm of land, and when I think back on it now, I was probably foolish that I didn't do just that, take the money and buy a farm of land. At the time, though, I was adamant it wasn't for sale. He asked me one very polite question.

'Why?'

'Well, I'll tell you the truth,' I said. 'You're offering an awful lot of money, and 'tis actually more than what I think the place is worth, but the reason I won't sell it to you is because I don't feel I'm allowed to.'

'I don't understand,' he said to me. 'Do you own the land?'

'Oh by God, I do. 'Tis mine and no one else's.'

'So why can't you sell it?'

'I don't feel I can.'

'Will you explain why?'

'Because it's not really my land.'

And again, he looked at me very confused.

'But you own it?'

I explained to him that I owned it 'for now'. I had inherited the land, so I felt as though I was only a custodian of it; that it was my job to mind it and do whatever I needed to do with it while I was alive and well, but then it was my duty to pass it on to the next generation. I told him that if I were to sell it, it would feel like a disrespectful thing to do given that it had been entrusted to me by the previous generation. Now, if I had my time back, I'd probably do things differently, but in general, I do feel that if you inherit something, it's nice to keep it and pass it on to the next generation. That said, where there's land there's money, and there'll always be issues and problems. The one bit of advice that I would give to people fighting over nothing is that they should be smart enough to realise that it's a simple hole in the ground that's going to hold us all. In the grand scheme of things, the only important asset in anyone's life is their health. Sure everything else is just trivial nonsense.

Putting Problems into Perspective

There's a great line, 'If everyone threw their problems in a pile, you wouldn't be long taking yours back.' I think there's a lot of truth in this. You realise that whatever is going on in your life, someone else is dealing with something way worse. I'm not trying to play down life's day-to-day problems, not at all, but I do think we all let the small stuff get to us more than we should. I remember a case in my clinic that really put things into perspective for me.

A good few years back, an absolutely beautiful young girl in her mid-twenties came in to see me. I'll never forget her first words to me. 'I'm in trouble,' she said. Now, this girl could have been a catwalk model, she was so tall and striking, and she could have been a professor as well, she was so brainy. After she sat down, she explained to me that she was due to undergo a hemicorporectomy. She showed me a diagram of what it meant. When I saw it, I couldn't believe what I was looking at. A hemicorporectomy is the complete amputation of everything from the waist down. The pelvic area, the hips, everything would be removed. She had been diagnosed with an unusual type of cancer which had made its way into the bones in her pelvic area. The only way you could control it somewhat was by removing everything, but the operation that was needed to do this, the hemicorporectomy, was so serious that it had to be conducted in England as it wasn't performed here at all back then. So much was being removed that there was no possibility of a prosthesis either. As she was talking about the journey ahead of her, one of the things I realised was that she was going to have to go through this torturous life-changing operation, but even with that, her life wasn't going to last very long afterwards.

When she stood up to leave, she shook my hand. I had jobs to do for her; just things that would make her journey a bit easier. The same girl, despite all that was going on in her life, had such a great sense of humour. As I walked her to the door, I remember she pointed to the mini-skirt she was wearing and joked that the reason she was wearing it was because she had mighty legs and wanted to people to look at them while she still had them. You know, most of us would be in a foul mood after a bad day at work, but yet here was this girl, facing the end of her life as she knew it, and she was still all smiles and cracking jokes. Her attitude was incredible.

If you had seen her that day, you'd have said there wasn't a thing wrong with her. She wasn't even limping. That taught me a lesson on not judging the proverbial book by its cover; you don't ever know what's going on in another person's life. I stuck by her; did everything in my power to smooth the rocky road ahead. As planned, she went to Britain for the operation, where the surgeons did what they had to do. It didn't stop the cancer, but it did buy her some extra time. Even with that, however, I'd say there was maybe only just over two years from the time she and I first met in my clinic to the time I was attending her funeral.

Unfortunately, with this job, you come across situations that are so sad, you just have to roll with it and do the best you can for the people involved. I'm hardened to it, but saying that, there will always be stories you're never ready for. Before I was fully involved in politics myself, I would hold my father's clinics for him if he got delayed or couldn't make them. Quite often, we would do a lot of clinics together. One night, a lady came into us and was talking in a very roundabout way of something that was troubling her. Whatever term she used – I think it was the phrase 'too affectionate' – I realised that what she was telling us was that her husband was mistreating one of their children. Quick as a flash, I said to the woman, 'You do realise we have to report this?' Right away, she changed her tune and backtracked.

'No, God no, you can't do that,' she said. This man had her in his grip as well. I think the sudden enormity of having the gardaí involved overwhelmed her, but I explained to the woman that it wasn't up to her as to what should happen, nor was it up to me. Only the law could decide.

When a person speaks to me in my clinic, it's as confidential as a confessional, except you don't have the hassle of having to recite three Hail Marys afterwards. If, however, someone comes to me and they tell me that a person is in danger or at risk, in that situation, I am honour-bound to act and inform the authorities. After I listened to what the woman had to say about what was going on, I made the call to the guards and explained the situation. Straight away, they dealt with it. It ended up going to court, and the man was found guilty and punished, though to be honest, the punishment for someone who hurts a child should be far more severe than it is.

When that woman first told us what was going on, myself and my father were very small men after hearing it. As the saying goes, it would have been easy to have made a shirt for the two of us that night. You might think that when a person leaves my clinic, they leave my thoughts as well. That's not true. Couldn't be further from the truth, as it happens. They stay inside my head, and to be honest, sometimes you can't get their face or their story out of your mind and it really bothers you. It might be as simple a thing as a person in need of a medical card. In the grand scheme of things, it's a small issue, but you know that to them it's huge, and probably even causing them sleepless nights.

The sadness and the heartbreak of the stories you hear, it does affect you, but you do have to learn how to handle it, so it doesn't overwhelm you. Very recently, I was explaining to a person who had come to me with a financial problem the importance of parking the problem until they were ready to deal with it. You have to compartmentalise your mind and pull down the shutters when necessary. If you let things get to you, you can't function in such a way where you can adequately deal with matters. We get so wound up in the cycle of stress that sometimes even the smallest things can seem like Armageddon. It's easier said than done, but by putting things into perspective, and appreciating the good in our lives, well, isn't that where the solution lies for all of us?

My Uncle Dan

My father's brother Dan, well if any man on this Earth would have you in stitches laughing, it was Dan. He was the sort of man who was just so naturally entertaining and witty that if people heard Dan Rae was sitting inside in the pub, they'd go in just to have a drink with him. He loved calling in to the family bar for a drink, and he'd always sit in the same spot each time. To this day a commemorative plaque bearing his name sits on the wall above his usual spot.

Dan used to do a multitude of things. He'd milk the cows with my father, and drive the diggers for the council, but one of his main jobs was driving the scholars to the national school. The school bus was actually his mode of transportation in general. The children were mad about him. He was always smiling, always in good humour cracking jokes with them; he was just an absolute character, and while I couldn't swear to it, I'm pretty sure I never heard him complain once in his life. Although I do know that he and my father once fell out briefly over a tug of war. Tug of war was taken very seriously in Kilgarvan and on one occasion Dan and my father found themselves on opposing teams. They took it so seriously that they didn't speak for weeks once the pull was over. I don't even know what they were scrapping about exactly, but I think one of them made out the other did something wrong, or that there was some uneven pull. I couldn't tell you if they eventually shook hands on it, or if they just forgot that they weren't speaking, but either way, the silent treatment didn't last too long.

Dan was also a very good-natured sort of person. At Christmas, he would cut holly and go around the village giving it to people. As he had never married, Dan lived with his mother, Nana Rae, and he didn't just idolise her, he worshipped the ground she walked on. Also living in the house with them was a man called Matt Riordan, a nephew of my grandmother's. I used to love calling there because once you'd go into the house, you'd be laughing until you left. The three of them were hilarious together. When Nana Rae passed away, Dan was inconsolable. I don't think I could put into words just how upset he was at the time. They had been as thick as thieves, the two of them, all their lives. He knew her caper, she knew his. Dan, for instance, was a perfectionist when it came to keeping the house clean. He'd always keep it spotless. Every year, he would set aside one day where he'd go so far as washing every wall, ceiling, and door; not an inch of space in the house would be left unwashed. He'd start boiling water in the morning and he'd mix in his bottle of Mr Proper and start washing the whole house. Whenever he'd see people building these big houses, he'd always say, 'I bet you one thing, they won't get around that house in a day.' People wouldn't understand him, but of course what he meant was that they wouldn't be able to wash the place in a day. I think it must be from Dan that I get my aversion to big houses. People building these monstrosities that are too big for them, no, I don't understand it. Sure, you can only sit in one chair, sleep in one bed, watch one television. Why would you be needing a house with a pile of rooms?

As much as I loved being entertained by Dan, I loved learning from him too. I remember whenever he'd be driving the tractor, he'd always pull into the petrol pumps and pour maybe fifty pence worth of petrol into the tank. Now tractors are diesel machines, but Dan would put this little bit of petrol into the tank because he found that it would stop diesel from freezing. He always said it was good for the fuel system to a have a drop of petrol in with the diesel.

My lasting memory of Dan, though, is his love of gold jewellery. You would always see him wearing a gold necklace and bracelet. I remember when our children were small, myself and Eileen brought them on a summer holiday to Lanzarote for a week. The night before we were due to fly home, the Lucky Lucky Men approached us. These were the lads who walked along the street selling all sorts of stuff, and when they came up to me and showed me their wares, the first thing I spotted was this massive gold chunky chain. Now, there wasn't a person in the world that would wear this thing, it was awful, but I knew the one man that would and that was Dan, so I bought it for him as a gift. The following day, we flew home only to be greeted with the news that Dan was in hospital. After he had taken ill, a doctor had tended to him in the house, but he couldn't diagnose what was wrong, so a passing ambulance was instructed to stop and bring him to the hospital in Tralee. What they hadn't realised was that Dan had a blood clot. When I heard the news that Dan had been hospitalised, I headed straight to Tralee to see him. Over the next few days, I visited him constantly, but I decided to hold off on giving him the chain because I thought it would be a nice surprise for when he'd get home. We were sure he'd be back home again within a few days.

The following Wednesday, Dan took ill again. After he collapsed in the hospital, it was too late to do anything to save him. He was only sixty years of age when he was taken from us. Sure even then, that was no age. Sadly, I never got to give him the gold chain he would have loved so much. All these years later, it's still in the corner of a room in my house, wrapped in the same white handkerchief I had placed it in for him. My father was always convinced that Nana Rae had brought Dan over to 'the other side'. He always said, 'She came over to get him.' He was full sure of it because they had always been so close. There was just two years between their deaths.

Forgetting What's Important

I, for one, fully believe in the afterlife. I think it's nice to believe that we'll get to see our loved ones again; that this isn't the end of the journey, only part of it. Sure, isn't it nicer than the alternative, that you're thrown into a hole when you die? That was the belief held by a very good friend of mine, Luke Kallewaard, and I could never understand it. Luke was a Dutchman who had moved from the Netherlands to Kenmare in the 1960s with his wife, Coby. He opened a second-hand furniture store in Master Hickey's hall in Kilgarvan and it was through that I became good friends with him. He provided a great service to the community because when money was scarce, and when people couldn't afford new furniture, they were able to buy it from him at affordable prices. In another part of the hall, he would sell very affordable clothes. He used to buy his stock over in the Netherlands and bring it all back in containers. He and Master Hickey had a business partnership of sorts. Luke and Coby were both extremely talented artists and I'm fortunate enough to have many of their paintings.

Luke anyway was a Trojan worker, and when he wasn't in the hall, he would carry out building work for people – home extensions and the likes. He would also maintain holiday homes for their owners, so he used to hire me to do any digger work he had. We were like two opposites, Luke and I, but we got on so well because he was such a frank and forthright individual. He used to tell me that I was a fool for believing in heaven and hell. Luke didn't believe in God at all, and he'd go mad whenever he'd see me blessing myself or hear me mentioning Mass. He used to always say to me, 'When you die, you're thrown in a hole and that's it!' and sure of course, I would always say back, 'No, Luke, there's more to it than that. There is a God. There is a heaven and a hell.' He would tell me I was crazy.

Luke was a very intelligent, complex character, but he had one big fear. His brother had died from an aggressive form of Alzheimer's, and Luke was always worried that he too would fall victim to the same fate.

'Michael, if I get that Alzheimer's, you must to come to work some day and bring your gun,' he would say to me. 'Shoot me, dig a hole, throw me into it and forget about me.'

'Well, I can't do that, Luke,' I'd say back to him. 'Sure I'd get years in jail. You'd be dead, and I'd be sitting in some prison. What good would we be to anyone then?'

Life can be beautiful, but there are times when it can be terribly cruel, and what happened to Luke was just that. Cruel. He developed Alzheimer's, the one thing he feared most. It started slowly but gradually, as is the nature of the disease, it got worse. I used to visit him at home and when it reached the stage where he couldn't remember my name any more, it was heart-breaking. As Luke's condition worsened, his doctors recommended that the family bring him back to the Netherlands. He had always spoken perfect English – he had been living in Kerry for forty-odd years – but as the disease strengthened its grip on his mind, he forgot how to speak English and reverted back to his native Dutch. Consequently, it was felt that he would be more content in a care home in the Netherlands where they spoke his language. The last time I saw Luke, he was sitting in his own home in Kerry. It was very sad because I knew that the disease was getting stronger, and I knew this would be the last time we'd ever see each other. In his moments of lucidity, it was like having the old Luke back, but each time the Alzheimer's took hold, he'd be taken from us again. It was heart-wrenching.

It's a horrible disease, Alzheimer's. I think there's still a tendency to associate the condition with being elderly, but the frightening reality is that so many people have developed the disease in the prime of their lives. When Luke passed away, he was only in his early sixties. I was speaking to a lovely man recently whose wife had been diagnosed with Alzheimer's around ten years ago. She's now only in her fifties, and she has the condition full blown.

In my opinion, there is nothing in the world as frighteningly powerful as the human mind. When Alzheimer's takes hold of it, it completely changes a person and affects every aspect of their personality and their life, but then the same can be said for illnesses such as depression, anxiety, and so on and so forth. I have always viewed them as being every bit as serious. Even though mental health awareness is more prominent than ever, I don't think we are really heeding the advice as much as we should. I'd say most of us take better care of our car engines than we do of our own mental health. We sometimes speak to ourselves in ways that we would never dream of speaking to anyone else.

And sometimes, sadly, we get so caught up in our own lives that we fail to really realise when someone is speaking to us from a place of great turmoil.

Time to Talk

I am fully convinced, and will be until the day I die, that I was responsible for a good man taking his own life. If I had been as aware of mental health issues back then as I am now, that man would be alive today; I'm absolutely sure of it.

Around ten o'clock one night, my phone rang. It was a constituent of mine; a lovely man who had found himself in some trouble with Revenue as a result of bad advice he had been given by his bank. What happened was, some banks had told their customers that they could use the address of a relation living abroad in order to get more interest on their accounts, but when Revenue found out about this, they went after the account holders hook, line, and sinker. Say if you'd had €30,000 in one of those accounts, by the time Revenue came after you, they were literally looking for the whole €30,000, if not more.

My constituent had been one of the people billed by Revenue for this practice, so he approached me for help. I examined his case and found that a good deal of the money in this man's account was his pension, so he didn't actually have the liability that Revenue claimed he had. Revenue were charging him tax on the pension sum, which they weren't entitled to do. When I challenged them on that, it brought the sum down from €110,000 to €72,000. Unfortunately, the remaining amount owed meant his life savings would be swallowed. One night, as I was driving, he called me to talk about the latest developments. I explained to him the situation, that I had managed to get the bill reduced, but that he would still have to pay the remaining €72,000. I will never forget what he asked me next, and what's more, I will never forget my reply to him.

'Can we do any more about this money?' he asked.

'Oh, God no,' I said.

I basically told him that this was as far as we could go with it and that the remaining sum would have to be paid. I didn't realise it at the time but that was the worst thing I could have said to him because I was removing all hope from the situation.

Right away he said, 'No, no, no, I won't be paying it Michael, I won't.'

We talked a little longer, and before hanging up, he thanked me.

Two days later, I was up on the digger working when the death notices came on Radio Kerry. I was only half-listening, as you would when you'd be working, but the mention of a familiar name knocked me for six. For a second, I wasn't even sure if I had really heard the name in question, so I phoned a person on my team who was from the same parish as the man. Without letting on too much, I told him the name I'd heard on the death notices and asked him if the man was known to me. Straight away he said back, 'Oh, you do of course, Michael, sure that man was in and out to you a lot in your clinics.'

When people speak to me during my clinics, everything they say stays with me. Not a word of it goes any further, so all I said back to him was, 'God, you're right, I think he was. I think I remember him now all right.'

I phoned another person who would have known the man and asked if he knew what had happened.

'We don't know what came over him,' he said, 'He stood up on the kitchen table the night before and hung himself.'

It was at that moment that it dawned on me what the man had really meant when he said, 'I won't be paying it.' I had just been too thick to read between the lines and understand that what he was really saying to me was that he wouldn't be paying it because he wouldn't be alive.

If I got a call like that today, I would know straight away where the person's mind was at. There are people who ring me up and tell me they are going to commit suicide and I know in my heart and soul that they won't, and then there are people who look me straight in the eye and tell me that everything is fine, and I know it's not. I know they're suicidal. I have seen so many thousands of people over the years in different frames of mind, in good states and in bad, that now I just instinctively know what a person is not saying. Back then, however, I didn't, and through that lack of experience, I failed to realise what the man was really telling me on the phone that night. If I had known where his mind was at, I would have dropped everything, driven to his house, invited myself in and then worn him out talking. I would have carried him through to the dawn of a new day.

When I got elected to the Southern Health Board in 1999, you could pick any committee you wanted to be on. Some of the committees were considered more desirable than others. For instance, if you were interested in being on the road, you could pick a committee where your role would involve travelling around the country and visiting other health boards and hospitals. That was grand if you were interested in racking up the expenses and the likes.

There was only one committee I wanted to be on, and that was the committee that no one else wanted a place on back then: the Psychiatric Services Committee. Today the term 'mental health' is like a buzzword of sorts, but back then it was still more of a taboo subject. It was one that I had a huge interest in, however, so I was determined to get on the Psychiatric Services Committee and do the best job I could. Would you believe it, another young man by the name of Simon Coveney was also starting off on the health board around the same time.

As part of my role, I used to visit the different institutions in Kerry. It was through one of these visits that I became great friends with a lovely patient. She was frequently in and out of different institutions, so I became her go-to politician for issues like her medical card, housing, and so on. Whenever she was in hospital, I would call to see her. She loved smoking, so we'd go out and sit in the fresh air and of course she'd have the fag in her hand and be smoking away to her heart's content. One day, anyway, we were sitting in the garden in the middle of having a great chat, and it was during this chat that she promised me she would never commit suicide. I used to always tell her that if she ever felt bad, she had to let me know straight away, I didn't care if it was three o'clock in the day or three o'clock in the morning. She promised me that she'd never do anything without talking to me.

I'll never forget the day we were sitting out in the garden in our usual spot when another patient passed by. Next thing, she turned around, looked straight at me and said, 'Are you here long?'

'I'm not here long at all,' I said. Sure I had only been there half an hour, but I didn't realise she was asking me if I was a patient.

Next thing she says to me, 'Voluntary . . . or involuntary?'

So I answered honestly, 'Voluntary. I can leave at any time I like.'

Without another word, she walked away, but she wasn't gone a few steps when we heard her burst out laughing. To herself and no one else, she said, 'Jesus, you could meet anyone inside in here.'

She thought I was after being committed.

Taking a pull of her cigarette, my friend looked at me and laughed. 'Healy-Rae, you're an awful bloody man! That woman will be going around telling everybody that you're like the rest of us!'

I looked at her dead serious. 'But sure isn't that the whole point? What is the difference between me and the rest of ye? The difference is there is no difference. No difference whatsoever.'

Whether your illness is above the neck or below it, an illness is an illness. It's something to be treated, not something to be scared or ashamed of.

Unfortunately, my lovely friend didn't see it that way. What do you think she did? She did the one thing she promised she would never do. One day, without phoning me, without sending anyone to get me, she decided that she wanted to leave this world once and for all. And sadly, she did. I thought I was on top of the situation because I had spent so much time listening, talking, reassuring her, and just being there whenever she needed someone. But I think once she had made her mind up, that was it. She didn't want to give anyone the chance to talk her out of it.

I remember another lovely young person used to phone me from a payphone whenever he was in hospital. All I would hear is, 'I'm here, Michael, ring me back'. No matter where I was, or what I was doing, I would stop and ring him back immediately. If he was feeling particularly down, I would wear him out talking. Again, it was another situation where I thought I was really on top of things, but sadly, he too made the decision to end his life and didn't tell me. When you know that you're someone's go-to person and that they didn't phone you when they were in trouble, you will always rack your brain wondering why they made that choice. It's agonising. I can never get it out of my head.

Those friends have never left my mind. I don't just go to someone's funeral and think that's the end of that. A year on I might still be thinking about that person, wondering where their life might have taken them, and what they would be doing if they were still with us. I think of their families too because I know they're still suffering. If people could see the devastation they leave behind after taking their own life, you'd wonder would they make the same decision if they had their time back? I know if I had my time back, I would have done things very differently with the man who phoned me about his financial problems with the bank. To this day, the guilt is bad and regardless of what anyone says to me, it will always be there. Some people wondered why I told that story on the *Tommy Tiernan Show*. I hadn't planned on telling it, but the thing is, whenever I'm asked a question, I will answer it honestly. Even if the answer is against myself, gets me into trouble, or paints me in a bad light, I will still answer truthfully.

There are so many smarmy people out there who like to think they're God's gift and that they never make mistakes. I see enough of them at work! I prefer the straight-talking people; the ones who admit their mistakes instead of passing the blame. Michael Noonan is one of the straight talkers for whom I have great admiration. I will never forget listening to a radio interview he did. It was around the time of his birthday and the interviewer asked him a fairly run-of-the-mill question: 'Have you any regrets?' Michael replied that he did in fact harbour one very big regret. He explained that a decision he had made one time ended up costing a young garda his life. I'd say the poor man doing the interview was fit to a have a heart attack when he heard this because he didn't know what he had just unearthed. Michael went on to explain that when he was Minister for Justice, he had sent a number of gardaí from Templemore to a wood in Leitrim where supermarket boss Don Tidey was being held captive. During the course of the rescue, a young garda ended up being shot dead.

As you'd expect, the interviewer went on to say things like, 'Well, Michael, that was not your fault,' but Michael's attitude was very matter-of-fact. He had made the decision to send them out and therefore he felt he was to blame for one of them not returning. I have deep respect for someone like that.

We all make mistakes sometimes.

We all get it wrong.

And as I Was Saying ...

Sure look, when myself and himself got elected to the council in 1999, it wasn't just a special occasion for ourselves but one for the history books as well, because to my knowledge, no county council had ever before had a father and son elected in at the one time. The two of us were so in sync in one way, but then there'd be the odd subject we'd have to agree to disagree on. Even though we worked well together, and were extremely close, we weren't joined at the hip either, as they'd say.

I remember one time there was a big debate going on. Myself and my father were both there. That same day, I had an awful flu and was very chesty. By the time it was my turn to talk, my voice was nearly gone. I persevered anyway and started making a speech all about rural planning and people building houses on the family farm. I was going as hard as I could and making a very impassioned case, but my voice was so bad that eventually I couldn't keep going any longer, so I threw in the towel and sat down. Now, the mayor of the county who was chairing the meeting hadn't seen me sit down because he was busy writing on the page in front of him.

Realising this, my father spotted an opportunity. The second I sat down, didn't himself jump up, 'And as I was saying . . .' he started, picking up where I had left off with my speech. I'm fully convinced that neither the mayor nor about seventy per cent of the members there that day had even realised we had switched places. Not only did my father finish my speech without using any notes, he also managed to make every point I'd had buried in my head.

Pope John Paul II – a Smart Man

I was very sorry I didn't make it to the funeral of Pope John Paul II. I had wanted to go, and came very close to going, but unfortunately in the end, I had commitments I couldn't reschedule. You know, I always considered him to be one of the two most influential people in the world, the other being JFK. In fairness, though, Pope John Paul, God be good to him, was an absolute genius when it came to dealing with people. Never was this more evident than when he went to Cuba to meet Fidel Castro.

One of the things Pope John Paul wanted to discuss with Fidel was the matter of 25 December. We know it as Christmas Day, but in Cuba it was just another working day and Pope John Paul wanted to change this. He wanted it to be a day people could spend at home with their families. Anyway, the two got on mighty during the trip, and when it was time for Pope John Paul to leave, Fidel escorted him to the plane. Now the Pope was a smart man, he was another one we'd call 'cute', so he waited until the trip was over to catch Fidel on the hop. He couldn't just ask Fidel to make 25 December a holy day because he knew what the answer would be, so instead he decided on a different tactic. As they were saying their goodbyes, didn't the Pope pipe up. 'Can I ask you to do me a favour, Fidel?' he says.

Through the translator, Fidel replied with something along the lines of 'Anything you want, your Holiness.'

Now this was Pope John Paul's window. 'The twenty-fifth of December,' he begins. 'Not a holy day, not anything to do with religion, but will you make it a family day?'

And sure what did Fidel say? 'Absolutely no problem.'

Sliotars, Footballs and Shrines

When it comes to Kerry GAA, there are supporters and then there are people who bleed the county colours. A card-carrying member of the latter group would be a close friend of mine, Niall Botty O'Callaghan. Botty is a brother of Paudie O'Callaghan, the man I was with at the Killarney Races when we bumped into John B Keane. Botty works with the Kerry football team in a voluntary capacity, but the amount of personal sacrifice he makes is something else. His passion in life is Kerry and the Kerry team. He's at every single training session. Every night they're out, he's out. Every match they go to, he's there. He organises their bus, makes sure everyone has their gear bags, that their rooms are booked and that everyone knows where they're staying. He ensures everything is running smoothly. He's like their Mr Fix-It and they're damn lucky to have him.

Then there's Kathleen O'Sullivan, a Cahersiveen woman who holds the official title of Kerry's Greatest GAA Supporter. Inside in her house, she has an actual shrine to the Kerry teams of present, past and way in the past. When it comes to shrines, Kathleen's would put Knock to shame. People come from all over the county, the country and abroad to see it. Her home is even called the Upper Deck. Kathleen has never once missed a match in her life either. She'd follow the Kerry team to hell and back.

Speaking of commitment, I have to tell you about another great Kerry GAA follower who has since gone to his eternal reward. His name was Tom Keane. Tom and his lovely wife, Nuala, were the most hardcore supporters you could find. That's the only way to describe them. You might say, 'Well sure everybody follows the Kerry team', but Tom and Nuala followed every Kerry team. They'd be seen at an U12 game in some far-flung part of North Kerry, and sure enough, the following day you could find them in South Kerry at a league match. Anything to do with Kerry GAA, they'd be there on the sidelines taking it all in.

It goes without saying that Tom and Nuala didn't just adore Páidí Ó Sé, they revered him. Every year, Páidí would hold a weekend sports charity event in Ventry, but the launch of the event would take place in a hotel in Dublin. It would go on for about an hour, and in order to create a bit of excitement, Páidí would always invite the Taoiseach to carry out the launch, along with the Minister for Sport as well as figures from the GAA. Sure of course, every TD from Kerry would be asked as well. One particular year, anyway, I was attending the launch in my capacity as Mayor of Kerry. After Páidí had finished making his speech, I got chatting to Tom and Nuala, who had travelled up from Cahersiveen that evening. Now you have to remember, there were no motorways to Dublin back then. The journey to Dublin was four or five hours on bad roads. Next thing Tom turned to me and said, 'Well, Mike, we'll be knocking a mile out of it!' It was a Kerry way of saying he was going to head home.

'Tom, are you really heading for Cahersiveen now?' I asked him.

'Oh God, I am,' he said back to me. 'Sure I've work in the morning, boy.'

I looked at my watch and if my memory serves me right, it was a quarter past ten. Now, Tom was a great man for rising early in the morning, another reason why I liked him, but when I did the calculations on the time it would take for him to get home, I realised that he would just be arriving in the door of his house at the same time he'd normally be getting up to go to work in his hotel. That will tell you the high esteem in which Tom and Nuala held Páidí. They had travelled a total of nine or ten hours, just to spend no more than one hour at Páidí's launch. If that's not the height of commitment and dedication, well I don't know what is.

You Can Eff off with Yourself

If Páidí Ó Sé had been the leader of some cult, he'd have had thousands upon thousands of followers. He was an exceptionally intelligent man, and that's not me plámásing; anyone who ever had the pleasure of being in Páidí's company would say the same thing about him.

Páidí and myself would have been close friends, but if there was one area in life where we would have crossed swords, it was in politics. Páidí had a big interest in Irish politics, and he was a supporter of Fianna Fáil. In the 1997 election, my father had broken away from being a Fianna Fáil councillor to run as an independent and I was his Director of Elections. When you are Director of Elections, you get no praise when things are going right, but the second things go wrong, you'd need a backbone made of pure steel because you're on the receiving end of every verbal bullet going.

Anyway, polling day rolled around, and at the crack of dawn, didn't my phone ring. It had been going off all throughout the night anyway, but this time, it was the gardaí ringing to tell me we were in a bit of trouble. It turns out my father's election posters were too near to a particular polling station, and this was strictly against the rules. No two ways about it, they'd have to come down. Now, I won't say which polling station it was, but let's just say it was out west of Dingle, which was a good distance, and even though we had a mighty team with us, we didn't have as many as we do today, so in short, I had no one to go out and remove them for me.

'Garda, I'm very sorry,' I said to him, 'but we're in an awful way this morning between everything that's going on and trying to ferry people to and from the polling station. I don't know if I'd have anyone who could go out and take them down for me.'

'Well, you'll have to find someone, Michael,' he says back to me. 'If your father's posters are left where they are, the polling station won't be allowed to open.'

'Is there any chance, Guard, that you could . . . get a shovel, give them each a belt, and knock them down yourself?'

'Ara Goddammit, Healy-Rae! I can't be seen to be out knocking down posters for your father. Fellas would say I was knocking them down because I didn't like Jackie.'

'Well sure, what am I going to do so?'

'I don't know, but the polling station will have to stay closed while the posters stay up.'

By the time the call was over, I was at my wits' end, so I started to think about who I could draft in at that hour of the morning to help. Here I was with this massive issue that could cause awful trouble for us, and only had a few seconds to come up with a solution – my phone was already starting to ring with various other problems. We had only one chance to elect my father and I couldn't risk something like this undoing all our good work. I don't know why, but Páidí Ó Sé entered my head. While the phone was ringing – and remember, this was good and early, about four or five o'clock in the morning – I started to think about what I could say that would convince him to help me. Being a Fianna Fáil man, he would likely tell me where to go. Sure, why should he help my father, an independent running against Fianna Fáilers? Next thing, I had it; I knew what I'd say to him. After a few more rings, didn't Páidí pick up, his voice tired and shocking cross.

'Who's this?'

'Páidí, Michael Healy-Rae here, sorry to bother you.'

'Ara, what's wrong with yuh?'

'I'm very sorry, Páidí, but I have an awful problem. We made a mistake. Our posters are up too near a polling station back west. Would you very kindly go out and take them down for me?'

To put the tin hat on it, I then said, 'And would you mind then going back a bit of a distance and putting them up somewhere there for me instead?'

Well, that woke him up.

'Listen here one minute,' he starts. 'Do you know what you can do? You can eff off with yourself if you think I'm going to go taking down posters for you, and then go putting them back up again. What d'you think I am?'

As quick a flash I answered him, 'Well, do you know what, Páidí? I have been sizing this up myself, and do you know what you can do? You can leave the posters there. Don't take them down at all. But that polling station will not open today if they stay up, and I can guarantee you one thing, the man who will pay a dear price for this will be you and not me.'

'What? What are you talking about?' I'd say he was frothing at the mouth at this stage.

'Well, I don't know how many votes my man will get in that box,' I said, 'but I'm fully convinced your man is going to get more. In fact, I'd be absolutely amazed if my man got more votes than your man out there, but if you want to leave the posters up, leave them up. If the guards won't take them down, and you won't take them down, then there's no man to take them down so instead of me effing off, the polling station can go and eff off. Let it stay closed, Páidí, but thanks very much for taking the call.'

And I hung up.

I'd say within five minutes of that call, Páidí was out of his bed, in his car, and driving out to knock down the posters. Sure enough, the polling station opened as planned, but how many votes do you think my father got there that day? Just the one. The man Páidí was backing, just as I predicted, got a lot more votes. I knew it was going to pan out that way, but I had to bluff a bit when I told him I didn't care if the station stayed closed. Mother of God, I couldn't have our posters being responsible for a polling station not opening. Word would spread like wildfire and 'twould look fierce bad on us if we were seen to have been the cause of people not being able to cast their votes. I also didn't want to go bringing the gardaí on us. Sure, I'd enough to be dealing with that day without the boys in blue coming after me.

I'll tell you who nearly did bring the guards after us, though. Pat Spillane. Pat is famous for his routine of driving up to Dublin, recording whatever needs to be recorded for TV and then heading back home to Kerry, whatever hour he finishes. During an interview a while back, a journalist brought up this habit of his. He asked Pat if he found the journey tiring, especially considering he would be leaving Dublin so late at night, and sure Pat said something like, 'Aw well, you know 'tis fine. You'd head for home, and you'd get on the motorway for Kerry, but you'd see no one all the way until you'd land in Kilgarvan and the lights would be on in Healy-Rae's bar and 'twould be full!' I remember the first time I heard Pat had said this and I thought, oh my God, he'll be the cause of drawing every guard in the country on the parish of Kilgarvan.

But coming back to Páidí, I remember another election one time, and this will really show you how smart Páidí was. Myself, my father and couple of others were inside in Ó Sé's pub one night having a drink after a long day of canvassing. Next thing, Páidí turns to my father, and out of the blue he says, 'Jackie, I must take you up the village to do a bit of canvassing.'

Now, this was as random a statement as you could ever expect to hear come out of the mouth of a Fianna Fáil man. I looked at my father, my father looked at me.

The couple of men who were with us were equally baffled, so I broke the ice and said, 'Right, well sure let the two of ye go away so and do as many houses as ye can.' Off they went out the door, and I'm not joking you when I say that for the length of time they were gone, I was scratching my head wondering what in the name of God Páidí was at. What really got me suspicious, though, was their return to the bar just forty minutes later.

During that time, I later found out, Páidí had strategically brought my father to a number of specific houses and bars in the area. When they went into each pub, he stood in the middle of the crowd and announced, 'Lads, I'm here with Jackie Healy-Rae, and I'm asking ye to please give your number one vote to him in the forthcoming general election. He's a good man, a man of the people, and I'm asking ye now to vote for him.'

When we were in the car that night heading home, my father said to me, 'By God, what was Páidí Ó Sé playing at earlier?'

'I'm figuring it out,' I said to him, 'and I think I'm nearly there.'

John O'Donoghue was a government minister at the time, and of course the following morning, he would have no sooner had the spoon in his cornflakes when it would have been reported to him that Páidí Ó Sé had been out canvassing the night before with Jackie Healy-Rae. I'm telling you, every alarm bell that could have possibly gone off in John O'Donoghue's head went off in stereo that morning. You'd swear Páidí had been out canvassing with my father day and night for weeks on end. They weren't even gone forty minutes, but for the minister to hear that such a well-known, well-liked and well-respected Fianna Fáiler was suddenly out endorsing an independent . . . well it was enough to send the stress levels soaring.

Páidí of course just wanted to put down a marker with Fianna Fáil not to be taking him for granted. His 'canvassing' definitely concentrated minds in the party.

Behind it all, Páidí and myself had a strong friendship. We'd ring each other regularly for advice or a general chat. We used to have these lengthy phone conversations while we'd both be driving along the road late at night. We always had the best of craic and I loved calling to his pub to see him. Before I was a TD, myself and a number of friends from Kenmare, Templenoe, and Blackwater had this tradition where we'd go to Dingle for a weekend during the winter. It would be organised by Kieran O'Sullivan and Anne Quinn, very good friends of mine for years. We'd go on a Friday night and stay in Benners Hotel. On Saturday evening, we'd head for Páidí Ó Sé's pub and there we'd be for the night telling stories by the open fire. There was no man better to hold court in a pub than Páidí. I saw him do it on All-Ireland days when he was retired as a player and then as a retired manager. We'd meet him inside in a pub before the game and he'd give his opinion on how he thought the match would pan out. He was always spot on.

I remember on one particular All-Ireland day, he had written in his *Irish Independent* column that morning that Kerry looked set to lose the match. I was with him in a pub in Dublin while the match was on, and to hear him give his version of events and what was going to happen, I'm telling you Páidí didn't think for one second that they were going to lose. He knew if he had predicted a win, sure no one would want to read it. By saying they looked set to lose, sales of the paper increased because everyone wanted to read his reasoning for making such a bold statement. Anyone travelling to the match was buying it and no doubt asking, 'Has Páidí gone out of his mind saying that about Kerry?', but Páidí was doing what Páidí was good at. Creating excitement and buzz. No one could have ever accused Páidí of being dull. Sure, he'd create excitement inside in a funeral home.

He was everyone's friend, Páidí. Thousands upon thousands turned out at his funeral in Dingle, and I'd say every single one of them could have told a different story about him. I still see his

Life, Lore and One Long Chat

Let it never be said that a Healy-Rae can't keep a conversation going. I remember when interviewer Maurice O'Keefe of the Irish Life & Lore website wanted to speak to my father one time. Now, my father, God be good to him, would meet anyone, so when Maurice asked if they could meet to go through his life story for the website, my father said, 'Sure, no bother, Maurice, I'll meet you for a few minutes.'

Of course, Maurice would reply, 'Well, Jackie, I'd really need a few hours with you to get everything.' Sure, once himself heard this, Maurice hadn't a hope of getting what he wanted.

Eventually, he gave up asking my father and decided to ask me instead. 'Will you try and organise it?' he'd say. 'If it's going to happen, you're the one who will make it happen.'

'No bother in the world,' I promised.

I always knew the best time to go bringing up something – I'd know by his form and his humour – so one day I put it to him that he should have the chat with Maurice. Eventually he agreed. We arranged to meet the archivist in a room in a hotel where the chat with my father could be recorded. Maurice had a power of questions, but in the end he only had to ask one.

'Jackie,' he starts. 'What's your earliest memory?'

Well, my father started talking, and do you think he could be stopped? I left after two hours, and he still hadn't paused for breath. Four hours later, he was still in that room talking. He had literally started at the very beginning of his life and talked right up to where they were in the room that day.

Out on a Limb

A job in politics brings with it many responsibilities, and often those responsibilities can range from the usual to the unusual. On occasion, however, you will get a request that's so random, you'd almost have to pause for a second and question if you're being pranked by some radio station. One day some years back, I received a phone call from the matron of a hospital ward where one of my constituents was recovering after having undergone an operation. The purpose of the surgery, very sadly, was to amputate his leg. Prior to the operation however, the patient was asked if he wanted his limb to be cremated or buried. He requested a burial, which was all well and good except for the fact that there was no one available to transport the amputated leg to the family plot and bury it.

'Ask Michael Healy-Rae,' the patient instructed. 'He won't refuse me at all.'

Sure of course with that, the matron duly phoned me with the request. When she first started explaining the situation, I genuinely thought it was a hoax call but the further the conversation progressed, the more I realised the woman was being deadly serious. Naturally, I didn't need to think twice about helping the man, so off I went to the hospital morgue to collect the leg and drive it to its final resting place. I also brought with me a few friends who could help with the dig afterwards.

The patient had asked that a priest be summoned to say a few prayers while the leg was being buried, which of course was only proper order, but unfortunately it was all very short notice so finding an available priest wasn't as easy as we'd hoped. Between the time spent trying to locate a priest, and then wandering around the graveyard with flashlights trying to find the family plot, it was late at night when we picked up the shovels and actually started digging. With no priest to say the prayers, I had decided on the next best thing. I phoned the most religious member of my family and asked them if they would fill in and do the honours.

We all duly did the task and buried the leg in the plot. Let there be no jokes about having one foot in the grave, I won't hear of it. The proper prayers were said for the quick recovery of the person who had lost the limb, and of course for the parents interred in the grave we were after opening. We even had some holy water on hand so that everything could be done accordingly.

The moral of the story is that when you're a politician, you never know what favour someone will ask of you when they ring your phone, but after having buried a leg for someone in the middle of the night, well I doubt there's any favour you could request from me now that would have me bat an eyelid.

Charlie

There was a big radio debate going on one night and I can't swear as to who was doing the interview, but I think it might have been Vincent Browne. The production team phoned me up and asked if I would participate, so I agreed to go on air as long as they didn't tell me in advance what the interview topic was. I hate knowing what I'm going to be asked; I prefer to be put on the spot. Whenever I would agree to go on shows like *Questions and Answers*, I always preferred to go in blind, as they say. If I knew in advance what John Bowman was going to be asking me about, sure I'd do my own head in thinking about it.

Anyway, I joined the radio debate, and the same question that had been put to each of the panel members was put to me: 'Who is the most influential person of all in Irish politics?'

I named an American woman, based in Florida I think she is, or at least she was some years back. Not one of them knew who she was. Sure of course the panel were looking at each other and no doubt thinking, is this lad raving? Who is she? I said to them, 'Well, ye should know who she is because she's the most influential person not just in Irish politics, but in the history of modern-day Irish politics.'

Well, that flummoxed them altogether. They couldn't think who I was talking about. The woman I was referring to was a twenty-two-year-old call girl who, in July of 1992, received a message on her pager from her agency instructing her to go to a room on the seventeenth floor of the Grand Hyatt Hotel in Orlando. She went to the hotel as directed, and and sure we all know whose hotel room she walked into! If that woman hadn't answered the call that night, Charlie Haughey would have been President of Ireland, Michael Lowry would have been leader of

Fine Gael and Taoiseach, people who were ministers wouldn't have become ministers, and many who weren't ministers would have become ones. When the woman answered her pager that night and accepted the booking, she triggered such serious consequences that the ripple effects would be felt for years to come through the tribunals and whatnot. When you are looking at politics, it's often something outside politics that can completely change the landscape in ways you can't imagine.

To be honest, I think history will be kind to Charlie Haughey. It's very easy to look at him in isolation and be critical of him, and for many years it was the popular thing to do, but when people carry on with that kind of condemnation, they become so focused on the flaws that they forget to consider all the good he did. They don't bring any balance to their views of him.

Personally, I had great time for Haughey. We would have been good friends, and my father likewise always enjoyed his company. I remember one day I was up on a digger in Gleesk Pier, South Kerry when Haughey came into my head. Gleesk is a beautiful spot, and Haughey was known to love taking a walk there whenever he was holidaying in nearby Sneem. It's an isolated spot but he adored it. I had heard he was in hospital, so I switched off the digger and rang to see how he was. They put me on to him, and as we were chatting about all sorts, I told him where I was and how he had come into my head. Sure once he heard I was in Gleesk, he was all ears. I'll never forget what he asked me next. 'Tell me what you can see.' I described my view to him; the sight of the seagulls standing on the jagged rocks that sit just a few yards beyond the pier, the sight in the distance of the three very small islands known as the bull, cow, and calf, one of which had been home to a lighthouse one time. I described the noise of the flowing streams heading down towards the sea as the sun beamed down upon it . . . it was such a lovely day and I did my best to paint a vivid picture of what I could see. I knew how much Gleesk meant to Haughey. I left nothing out and he hung on to every word. I could almost picture him in the hospital bed with his eyes closed imagining the scene as I was describing it to him. I'd say he would have given anything to have been down by the pier at that moment, enjoying the fresh air.

When I hear people being critical of Haughey's character and career, I think they're wrong. He was very intelligent, and he had a great understanding of rural issues. He also did a lot of good work for people; there are schemes he brought about that are still in use to this day. For instance, he brought in free travel at a time when it was very imaginative to do so. He was very divisive, but I think, in time, he will be viewed as a person who got things done.

When some of his own were turning their backs on him and plotting against him, I held firm to my opinion that he was fundamentally a good man. I remember one night he was chairing a meeting of the National Executive of Fianna Fáil and a number of party members were standing behind him. This would have been around the same time that Seán Doherty had come out on the *Nighthawks* programme and talked about the phone tapping. I remember everyone in the room that night was dropping Haughey and looking at Albert Reynolds as being the new man in charge. Not one person at the meeting spoke in Haughey's favour that night except me. I stood up and I spoke about what he had done through his health initiatives, the transport initiatives, and so on. I remember I then added, 'Right now, the biggest danger you have are the people who are standing behind you with their knives drawn.' It was ironic that I had phrased it that way because on that particular occasion, standing behind him was Albert Reynolds. It was also convenient, because it was precisely him I had been referring to. And he knew it too.

Haughey told me afterwards how much he appreciated me standing up and speaking out in his defence. There were plenty in the room that night who had been all about him throughout his career, but when the proverbial hit the fan, they quickly dropped him and ran faster than the rats hightailing it from my father's digger in the dump. I wasn't going to do that because it's not in my nature to turn my back on someone I once stood by. Bernard Collins, my lifelong adviser and right-hand man, drummed it into me very early on that the people who are loyal to you are very important, but so too are the people who hate you. To have supporters, you have to create division, and to create division, you have to be a certain type of character. The biggest challenge in life, however, is knowing who you can trust and who you can't. Sometimes it's the very people in whom you place all your trust who then turn around and cut your throat. That's what life has taught me, and that's why loyalty has always been so important in my book.

Dark Times

The road from Dublin to Kerry is a long one. It's one I would often be travelling a good bit at night, and sure, you know what it's like being on the motorway at night, you'd find yourself doing a good bit of thinking. There are times when I would be driving along, and I'd start thinking about the people I have lost. I would find myself asking the question, my God, are they really all gone?

In the space of twelve months, I lost four of the most precious people in my life: my father, my mother, and my friends Bernard Collins and Arthur Lenihan. To put it into context, go on your phone and look at your top five most frequently dialled numbers. Now imagine the first four suddenly being taken away from you. That's what it was like for me. On top of it all, an election was going on at that time. It would rattle the best of people.

I have always said, the one thing we are sure of in life is that nothing stays the same. Every day, something changes. Sometimes that something is minor, sometimes it's major, but whatever its size, the action will always have a reaction. When one person becomes ill or passes away, it has a knock-on effect in so many other ways. Life for a lot of people can change dramatically when one person leaves this Earth.

My father was the first to leave. He passed away in Kerry General Hospital on Friday 5 December 2014. It always bothered me that he didn't get more time to do things that I know he'd have loved to have done. He'd have been in his element walking around Kilgarvan, popping into the bar and being the boss of the place, maybe heading over to my shop and throwing his weight around there for a bit, before going up to the farm to do some jobs and see his pony Peig. When he'd feed Peig, he'd catch a hold of her head and pull her into his chest and rub her nose. Whenever he'd come back from feeding her, there'd be all this hair and drool all over his suit. I used to give out to him for it while trying to wipe it off. Every single time I did, he'd laugh it off, 'Ara sure that's only auld Peig's. 'Twill be all right.'

After he passed away, I spoke to the nurses. They had known a few days earlier that he was dying. Did I know it? I actually don't think I'll ever be able to answer that because on the one hand, I kept thinking he was going to improve, but on the other hand, I knew his body was tired and worn out.

About an hour after my father passed away, I heard that a friend of ours, John Pigott, had died in Glenbeigh, Killorglin. There was around two hours where there was nothing we could do only just sit around, so after a discussion, we decided I would go to the funeral along with my nephew Johnny and my son Kevin. We sat into the car and when I turned the key, the radio came on. Who was on it only Bertie Ahern talking about my father. The news of his passing had obviously reached Dublin.

As the three of us were listening to the radio, the phone rang, and this very nice man called Martin came on. Now when the phone rings in my car, the radio automatically shuts off because the system puts the caller on loudspeaker. Sure the three of us had wanted to hear what Bertie was saying about my father, but when Martin called, we couldn't hear a thing because the call cut off the radio. Anyway, Martin had just heard the news and very kindly wanted to extend his sympathies to me. Just as we thought he was about to say goodbye, what does poor Martin go and say? 'I must put you on to Mary for a minute, Michael.'

Now at this stage, my nephew Johnny was getting fierce impatient and anxious about the fact that we were missing Bertie's interview about my father. When he heard that this Mary was now coming on the phone, it all got too much for him and without thinking, and in pure frustration, he said, 'Ara, who in the name of God is Mary?'

Just as the words had left his mouth, Mary was on the phone giving her sympathies *as Gaeilge*. Next thing, the biggest look of horror appeared on Johnny's face as he realised he recognised the voice. He put his hand up to his forehead and started mouthing the words, 'Oh, mother of God,' as it dawned on him that the 'Mary' in question was none other than our wonderful former president, Mary McAleese. Mary's own father had been good friends with my father and as a result of that friendship, she too became close friends with him. Poor Mary only came on to pay her condolences and all she was greeted with on the other end of the line was, 'Ara Jesus, who in the name of God is Mary?'

Thousands of people attended my father's funeral, and I have to say, given his reputation for being a master Director of Elections, he would have been proud of the way his send-off had been organised. A great group of people took care of proceedings and every last detail was tended to with military precision. I'd say anyone who was there as the coffin was being carried through the village from the church to the graveyard will tell you they witnessed one of the saddest and most unusual sights. As the pallbearers were carrying the coffin, they paused outside the pub and faced the coffin in as a salute. A local man, Dick Hart, had brought along my father's beloved pony Peig, so she would be there as the coffin was passing. When the pallbearers paused, however, didn't Peig take it upon herself to walk over to the coffin and start sniffing and nuzzling it. After about a minute or so she walked back. Reporters of course wrote that Peig came up and kissed the coffin. What happened was, my father used to always wear the same Brut aftershave, and sure of course, Peig had obviously picked up on the scent, which was why she started sniffing the coffin. She knew he was inside, but she backed off because she couldn't understand why he wasn't holding on to her head like he always used to. It was awful heart-breaking to see her nuzzling his coffin because anyone who knew my father knew he absolutely adored Peig, and she him.

This book isn't about politics, but you can't talk about loyalty without mentioning politics, because in that particular sphere, loyalty is what it's all about. I count myself extremely lucky in that regard to have been blessed with the most loyal of friends, neighbours and constituents. There are people who have done so much for me; they stuck by me through thick and thin, and until the lid is closed on my own box I'll never forget them. Two of those people were undoubtedly Bernard Collins and Arthur Lenihan.

I remember I was speaking to Arthur on Monday 30 March 2015. My son had a hospital appointment the following Wednesday, but I had to be in Dublin that same day and my wife Eileen was also working, so it meant there wasn't anyone there to drive the young lad to the appointment. I phoned Arthur. The one thing about Arthur is that he was always extremely reliable. He used to go everywhere with me, and I'd say there was rarely a day when we wouldn't see each other.

'Arthur? The young lad needs to go to the hospital on Wednesday. I thought I'd be able to bring him, but sure I'll be in Dublin. Would you by any chance be free to give him a lift in?'

'I will of course,' he said back to me. 'The only way I won't be able to do it is if I'm dead. If I'm dead, sure I won't be able to do it at all. Once I'm alive, I'll drive him.'

'Well, Arthur,' I laughed. 'There'll be no fear of you being dead by Wednesday.' Those were my exact words back to him.

That night I was holding clinics in South Kerry and as I was leaving a place called the Inny Tavern, I got a phone call from Arthur's daughter. She broke the news to me that her dad had collapsed and died. You could have knocked me with the shock. The following Wednesday, the day he was to meet my son, we were getting to ready to bury him. I remember thinking back to that conversation and the joke he had made about how only death would stop him from driving my son to the hospital. I don't know if you'd call it an omen or just a coincidence, but either way it was very strange, that last conversation we had.

It still hits me that he's gone. Any time I spot something that reminds me of him, it gets me thinking about the good times we had, the chats we shared, and the battles we fought, be they of a political nature or any other matter. Arthur travelled everywhere with me and was so instrumental in all parts of my life. So too was Bernard Collins.

Bernard gave many years advising and guiding me. He took me under his wing and educated me so much. He taught me a lot about what was important in life and what wasn't, and throughout it all, we became firm friends. I'm genuinely convinced his IQ level ranked at genius. He was exceptionally intelligent and could have been anything he wanted in life. He could have been a professor, a mathematician, the man could have been a rocket scientist if he felt like it, not that there'd have been much demand for one in Kerry, mind you.

He once gave me a key piece of advice that always stuck with me. He used to say, 'Take ten people. Out of the ten people, three have to like you. If three don't like you, you're in trouble. Three have to hate you. If they don't hate you, you're in trouble. The rest don't have to have to have any opinion of you. You have to polarise opinion.'

That advice resonated with me most after I did an interview on *Ireland AM*. As I was walking off set, I happened to hear Aidan Cooney, I think it was, talking about me on air. 'I don't know about Michael Healy-Rae . . . I think a lot of people are right, he's a bit like Marmite. You either like him or you really hate him, but I do know one thing, if I was in his constituency, and if I had a problem, I would go to no one else but him.' Bernard was right. It's about polarising opinion. Anything Bernard ever sized up, he got right. Politically, the man could see into the future.

As he grew sicker and sicker, he knew he was reaching the end. The rest of us were probably holding on to a little denial, but he knew. It was a devastating realisation to have to come to, because Bernard had so much left to give in life; he had so much to do and so much still to offer. There are farmers today who have benefited financially from his brain. He helped with the development of wind farms, and he was instrumental in orchestrating on behalf of the local community what we'd call a community fund. At one point, I was chairman of the Strategic Environmental Committee for the county and I worked very closely with Bernard in formulating policies and plans to deal with our waste in Kerry. In other words, we developed proper transfer and recycling facilities for the dumps – prior to that, we would have just put the rubbish in a hole in the ground and covered it with gravel.

There was a major landfill facility in Bernard's community, and we worked together to ensure that massive improvements were made in how it was managed and run. The road leading into it went from being the type that no one wanted to live on to being a very desirable location. The road itself was good, the lorries were sufficiently covered, and we also hired a professional falconer to put birds of prey into the air, so they would hunt away the crows and stop them swooping down and picking up bits of rubbish that were being deposited in cells. The community fund was then used to help elderly people install alarms, paint their houses and tar their roads, help them improve the water supply and septic tanks, and so on. I always used to say that if you had a choice between having Bernard Collins or a government minister living in your parish, you'd be way better off having Bernard because Bernard would do something for you.

Would you believe, Bernard passed away the same week as my mother. My mother passed away on Monday 28 September 2015, then Bernard left us the following Monday 5 October. There were nights when I would leave my mother's bedside, and go to sit by Bernard's bedside. It was the most difficult time. In the middle of it all, we were in the throes of an election. Your head would be bad enough during an election but to have all that going on in your personal life was hell altogether.

Bernard was the brains, Arthur was the constant companion by my side, and my mother and father were always there for advice, late night calls, early morning chats.

And suddenly, just like that, they were all gone.

I'll Keep a Seat for You Next Year

Even though it is devastating, when you look at death as a subject, there are few things more interesting. When it comes down to the fact of it, death is the one thing we all have in common. No matter what you do in the world, you're not getting away with it. That's why I'm obsessive about using every hour of every day. Sure, why would you want to be lying down in bed asleep when you know you're going to be giving so much of your time lying down after death has come calling for you?

Each year I have the privilege of having Christmas dinner at The Oaks Hotel with the Active Retired, or as my mother used to call them, the young at heart. It takes place the week before Christmas and there is always a seat kept for me. I sit beside the finest of gentlemen, Michael O'Connor from Muckross. He's a hundred and four years of age. In his prime, he is. He only stopped driving four or five months ago. Michael used to get up early in the morning and drive into town to pick up his home help because she had no car to get to his house. It was against his will he stopped driving, and the only reason he did was because he had failed the eyesight test. Eighty-six years he had been on the road, and not once did he ever have an accident.

When the Christmas dinner would end each year, Michael would always say to me, 'I'll keep your seat for you next year.' It used to be different though. When I first started going to the Active Retired Christmas Dinner, I would be with my mother. We started this routine of me sitting in the middle, Michael on one side and my mother on the other. The three of us would have the mightiest time laughing and chatting away about all sorts. The first time I was there without her ... God, it was heart-breaking.

She had passed away on 28 September that year, so the grief, as you can imagine, was still raw. The dinner had been my first main outing since the funeral. In the run-up to the event, I was in an awful conundrum over whether or not to go. On the one hand I felt I should, but on the other hand, well, 'tis like a wedding, you can't go unless you're asked. Valerie and Eamon Courtney, who own The Oaks Hotel and who very generously host the dinner for Active Retired and the local community, at their own expense, would have known the position I was in and a couple of days beforehand they contacted me and said they would like me to be there. That took the pressure off in a way, but it still felt awful strange walking in there without my mother beside me. She should have been with me. The second Michael saw me coming into the room that day, straight away he beckoned me over. 'I have your seat here for you,' he said.

Every year I make a speech at the event, but on that particular day, it was so difficult to get up and speak. There were hundreds of people in the room and every one of them had been a friend of my mother. The whole day was an emotional one, but that speech . . . my God, that speech was tough. Everybody will tell you that I don't do emotions very well. I'm just not wired that way. When I have a problem, I tend to keep it to myself. I do the opposite of what I'd be telling others to do. I'd honestly be the last person in the world to take the advice I'd be giving everyone else.

The advice I do try to take on board, however was given to me by Michael. You'd learn an awful lot from a man who has spent a hundred and four years on Earth, let me tell you. I remember I asked him for the secret to a long life. He gave it to me, no bother. He said if I wanted to live for a long time, what I had to do was live life in moderation. There's nothing wrong with drinking, nothing wrong with anything, as long as it's in moderation. Don't eat too much, don't eat too little. Have a drink each night if you want, but don't go overboard and start downing a bottle. If you're craving a bit of chocolate, have a small piece, but then leave it at that. Same goes for cigarettes, although I always say if I live long enough, it's highly likely I'll take up smoking again. To be honest, if I don't get this book done in time, I'll definitely be hitting the cigars again.

I do think Michael is right, though. Moderation. That's the real secret.

Just the One

Years ago there was a man who used to phone me early every Sunday morning, and he'd be talking about how things would be getting busy with the calving season coming up. He was in an awful way over it. This went on every Sunday morning for weeks. One morning, anyway, he happened to say, 'Well, thanks be to God, it's over me now.'

'What's over you?' I asked.

'She calved last night,' he says back to me.

And then he mentioned 'she' again a couple of times.

Sure, the penny dropped.

'How many cows have you?' I asked him.

'Ara, just the one,' he says.

Just the one! With the way he had been talking, sure, I thought there was going to be at least fifty cows calving.

Nine Lives

My mother always used to say to me, 'Michael, you're like the cat with nine lives, you really need to slow down.'

Well, if a cat has nine lives, I don't know how many a Kerryman has. I've used up eight of mine already. As you know from the very start of the book, my first near-death experience was before I was born, when my mother, when she was pregnant with me, got a massive electric shock from the fridge and was thrown to the floor. Now, I don't classify myself as a superstitious person, but even I would have to admit, it's not a great auld start to life when you're nearly taken out of the world before you've even had the chance to make your grand entrance into it.

The second of my nine lives was used up during a camping trip in Mayo. My mother brought myself and my sister Rosemary to the grounds of Lord Altamont's house, which was like a resort where you could pitch a tent and camp. Today it's better known as Westport House. I was eight at the time. Rosemary was exactly four years older. I say 'exactly' because I stole her birthday. She was born on 9 January, and then I came along four years later . . . on 9 January. Anyway, we weren't long at the resort when curiosity got the better of me and I decided to head off on my own to do a bit of adventuring. I had walked a fair bit when I came across a tyre swing hanging from a large tree. It was a fair height up from the ground. In fact, to get on the swing, you had to first climb up onto a bank. I climbed up and hopped into the tyre, and the next thing I remember, I was lying in a hospital bed, not having a clue from Adam what had happened to me. It turns out I had fallen from the swing. It wasn't so much the fall that did the damage but rather the one single rock on the ground underneath the swing that also happened to have a sharp edge on it. My head, of course, had to land on top of this one rock. I burst open my mouth, my nose, my cheek . . . I'd say there wasn't one part of my face that hadn't been split open. By pure luck, two very kind gentlemen came upon me. They had spotted me lying beneath the swing in a pool of blood and ran over to help. There was no one nearby so they hadn't a clue who I belonged to, and sure I was no use to them either because I was knocked out for the count. Eventually, they found my mother on the camping site and an ambulance was called. Needless to say, our grand plans to camp out on the grounds of Lord Altamont's mansion were swapped for a week in Castlebar Hospital.

Life number three was used up when I was working in the forestry and a particularly heavy tree fell on top of me. Thankfully, this happened during the height of winter so the ground I was standing on was fairly soft. When the tree fell on me, it almost drove me into the ground, but the soft soil meant there was a bit of 'give', so it stopped the tree breaking my back. That said, the tree still had to be cut off me, but I'm convinced that had I been standing on hard ground, the belt I got would have killed me instantly. Suffice to say, the sore back I had for a few days after that was a small price to pay.

I've already told you about the car accident that left me on crutches for four years; well, I reckon that was definitely life number four used up. Life number five went during an incident that I have never spoken about publicly before. It was a car accident that occurred in a field of ours known as the Baker's field. When I told them all at home about it, I took responsibility for it and said I had been driving, but the truth of the matter is that it was my son Kevin who had been behind the wheel. We had just finished up an election at the time, and because I had been so busy with the campaign, myself and Kevin, who was about eleven years of age at the time, hadn't really had the chance to enjoy much time together. So one day we decided to carry out a bit of fencing work in the Baker's field. I had a small Berlingo van, the sort I'd call an election van, and as we were on our own private farmland, Kevin hopped into the driver's seat and drove it over to the field. It wasn't even thirty seconds of a walk away, so we hadn't bothered to put on our seatbelts. The only reason we were bringing the van was because we had poles and fencing equipment to bring over with us.

As the field was near a river, the soil there was too wet for us to turn the van around, so instead Kevin went to back it up. As he was backing up, didn't he take the turn too fast and we spun off the edge of a bank. Straight away, the van started to flip over. To make matters worse, the field was on a slope, so it wasn't going to stop after just the one flip. If you can imagine a van cartwheeling down a small hill, that's what this was like. I quickly wedged my legs under the passenger seat to prevent myself from being thrown all sides. Kevin, however, was small and as the van turned over for the first time, sure he was in full flight. Instantly, I reached out and grabbed him. I'm not joking when I say the young lad was in mid-air when I caught him. With as much strength as I could muster, I pulled him into my chest and held him tight while the van continued to flip over another five or six times down the slope.

Once the van had come to a stop, I stayed sitting there for about a minute, still with a firm grip of Kevin. To say the two of us were shook would be an understatement. The van we were in was the sort that always had a pile of stuff on the dashboard; nothing of any importance, just random papers and the likes that you'd throw on the dash and sure it'd be there so long, it would almost have a film of dust over it. Well, as the van was flipping over, everything on that dashboard went right out the driver's side window, which had broken. There wasn't a blessed thing left, and I'm convinced that if I hadn't caught a hold of Kevin when I did, he'd have gone out the window also, because God knows he was small enough.

After we got out, Kevin took one look at the wreck and became awful upset. The van was a write-off. 'For God's sake, Kevin,' I said, 'do you realise that this is the best day of our lives?'

'Are you mad?' he said back to me. 'What are you talking about?'

'Do you not realise that if I hadn't caught you, you would have gone out the driver's window and been crushed as the van flipped over? I'd be getting out of the van now and you'd be lying there dead on the ground. Instead here we are now, the two of us alive and well. The van is for the scrap heap but sure what about it? It's only an auld van! And even if it was a brand new one, I still wouldn't give a tuppenny damn about it as long as you were okay.'

All of a sudden, he realised what I meant, and it put a new perspective on things.

Like everything on the Berlingo dashboard, life number six went out the window in December 2011 when I collapsed inside in the Dáil. Before we were due to head into the chamber, I was having lunch in the canteen and I remember feeling out of sorts. Granted, I was upset that same day as there was a controversial issue in the Dáil, and I was inundated with calls from constituents who were at risk of suffering the consequences of the Government's handiwork. As I was walking into the chamber, one of the ushers put his hand on my shoulder and asked if I felt okay. It took me by surprise because even though I didn't feel too hectic, I hadn't thought too much of it. I actually thought he was the mad one, and I even remember thinking afterwards, God, what's wrong with him? Sure aren't I grand?

A few minutes after that, I stood up in the Dáil to say my piece and as I was making a strong impassioned argument, the unwell feeling I had been experiencing suddenly started to overwhelm me. I couldn't breathe, and my heart felt like it was trying to jump out of my skin. The next thing I knew, I was on the floor of the Ceann Comhairle's chamber with my cap on the ground and my shirt and tie off me. On their knees beside me were office personnel who were trained in CPR, the Ceann Comhairle, and the then Minister for Health James Reilly. It's one thing to wake up on the floor of the Ceann Comhairle's chamber, but to see the Minister for Health, who was also a trained doctor, looking at you with a worried expression, well, I knew things couldn't be too great. Following a battery of hospital tests, it was discovered that I had an irregular heartbeat. It's all under control now, thank God. Funnily enough though, a similar thing happened to my father. He was on a train when he took ill. He had palpitations and like myself, he felt as though he couldn't breathe. He was in a bad way so the train ground to a halt, and Dick Spring, who was in the same carriage as him at the time, ended up calling the ambulance. I always liked Dick Spring, but I've had great time for him since then.

That was life number six, you could say. Life number seven was definitely used up when I started choking on food and my lips and fingers started to turn blue. I've already told you about that sure.

Life number eight then was my run-in with the cow. I always call this incident 'the kick in the goolies'. I shouldn't really be making light of it, but if you can't find the humour in something, even if that something nearly killed you, well sure look you're rightly scuppered then. What happened to me could have happened to any farmer out there. It's fine to be talking about farm safety, but the fact of the matter is that in an ideal situation, a farmer would never carry out certain jobs on the farm when they're on their own. That was the first mistake I made. The second mistake I made was not being on my guard around one of the cows. To be honest, I didn't think I needed to. I was used to the cow and her caper, and I thought she was used to me.

As I was doing the farm work one evening, I realised one of my cows had just calved, so I brought the cow and her calf into another pen where there was straw bedding. As I was in the pen, she suddenly turned on me. There was no rhyme or reason to it. In fact, she had always been a very quiet, placid animal. I can only assume the poor thing was on the defensive as she had just calved, and of course, with me being in close proximity, she took it out on me.

And dear God, did she take it out on me.

I got such a bad doing from her that if it hadn't been for my son Kevin and our neighbour John Joe Reilly, I'm convinced she would have killed me. Convinced of it. A lot of people won't understand the strength of a cow, especially if they didn't grow up on a farm, but to give you an idea as to what they're capable of, my one gave me such a blow to the windpipe with her head, she actually broke my ribs. As I was falling on the ground with the force of the belt, I struck my head off the bolt on the gate and in doing so, split it open.

It was reported in the media that the cow kicked me that day. She didn't. Cows don't kick you unless you're behind them. What cows do when they attack is stamp their hoof down on you and then pull it backwards. Once I was on the ground, she stamped her hoof right in the goolies department and then dragged it backwards. That in itself would be enough to paralyse any man with the pain, let me tell you. Next, she stamped her hoof on my chest and did the same thing again, dragging it backwards down my stomach and groin. The last place her hoof went was right between my two eyes, and again she stamped it down and dragged it back. That was the sucker punch that knocked me out altogether. Right before I fell unconscious, I remember thinking, oh God, this is bad. When Kevin and John Joe ran in and lifted me out over the barrier, they were sure I was dead. As they landed me on the silage outside, I must have groaned because John Joe roared, 'God, he's alive all the time!'

No more than the choking incident, I wouldn't be here today if it hadn't been for the good people around me. My recovery time was decent enough; I was back on my feet a day or so later, and then back on the road the day after that. I don't think I missed a day in the Dáil over it. My injuries were painful, and I suffered with them for a bit, but I was awful fortunate in that I had a great team of doctors and nurses who looked after me well.

Well that's eight of my nine lives gone. Despite everything, I would actually consider myself to be a fairly lucky person. Good God, can you imagine the carnage if I was unlucky? My close friend and neighbour, Donal Twomey, always warns me about the law of averages. We'd be speaking on the hands-free late at night when we'd both be on the road in God knows what part of the country and he would always say to me, 'Whatever you do, mind yourself.' The law of averages would dictate that if you spend most of your time on the road it's likely you will be involved in a road accident, so he's constantly reminding me of the law of averages and the fact that I'm running short on lives. Well, I've had eight narrow escapes now, and maybe for someone who has been on this Earth for fifty-one years, eight really isn't too bad, but all I can say is if I do use up the last of my nine lives any time soon, well I hope I defy the odds and carry on into my tenth one.

The Young Lads

The next generation of Healy-Raes . . . myself and Eileen have five of them. I always refer to them as the young lads, but I actually have two girls and three lads. There's Ian, Juliette, Rosie, Jackie Jnr, and Kevin. It's been interesting to see them growing up. They're all hard workers; all doing their own thing in life, and every single one of them have made myself and Eileen proud.

Juliette would be the quiet one. She was named after my mother, and interestingly, she's very like my mother in terms of character also. They have that same quiet reserved, nature. Like my mother, Juliette is also very brainy. I always joke that if Google wanted to know something, it would only have to ask Juliette. She's one of the most organised and dedicated workers I know, and I was very fortunate in that she always had a strong interest in the shop. When she was a child, she loved serving the customers but she was so small in height that she would have to stand on a crate in order to reach the cash register. I always enjoyed walking into the shop and seeing Juliette there in her element.

She has the Healy-Rae trait of being a morning person. Even though she lives in Killarney, she will always have our shop in Kilgarvan open before six every morning. She takes care of the baking and organises everything in the shop, along with Eileen. They're a great combination, and I have to say, it fills me with great pride to see a shop I started years ago being run successfully today by my wife and daughter.

Rosie is the one I was telling you about earlier, the one who made bits of every ditch on the farm while she was learning how to drive. She's very bubbly, very loyal, and massively interested in animals. 'Tis like a joke with us that when my poor mother died, she did the right thing leaving her dog to Rosie. The dog is tiny, you'd hold her in your hand, but it was a good job that Rosie got her because she'd be dead a hundred times over if any of the others had to mind her. I've always said Rosie reminds me an awful lot of my uncle Dan. She's such a happy-go-lucky person, and always smiling. Exactly like the way Uncle Dan used to be. Rosie is one of those people that could make you laugh without having to even say a word. She's very positive by nature; she wouldn't be one for worrying.

My eldest lad Ian takes care of the machinery side of things. He's very organised and keeps the whole operation running like clockwork. Even during the recession, he worked so diligently to ensure the business survived. His interest in diggers started when he was a child. I would always take him with me on a Sunday when I'd be moving the machines. He loved being around them. Sometimes, Ian would even come with me when I'd have to go out working the digger at night. He would be sitting on the floor of the machine, taking it all in. I used to put an auld coat on his back to stop his head from hitting off the cab with all the bouncing and moving the machine would be doing. I would make a little nest for him and he'd be quite happy and content just sitting there. All three lads would have joined me in the digger as children, and through that, they all developed a great love for machinery. It was that kind of experience that really gave Ian a great understanding of the job. It's lovely to see something I started with borrowed money now being run, and run very well, by my son today.

Jackie Jnr then works with me in politics. He's like my shadow. He's awful interested in all things political, which is mighty to see. Growing up, he would have been very close to my mother. I remember he used to spend a lot of time with her and would accompany her to the Active Retired meetings and the likes. I'd say every house with young lads has a story or two about narrow escapes they had when growing up. Well our house is no different.

When Jackie was a young fella, about seven or so, he suffered awful bad travel sickness. One day however, I had to go to Sneem to look at a job for a digger and he wanted right or wrong to come with me. I didn't want him falling ill so I picked up some travel sickness tablets and gave him one before we went. The tablets worked mighty. Unfortunately they looked like smarties. A couple of days later, Eileen rang me, awful worried about Jackie. He was drowsy and not himself. What did she discover only that he had found the box of travel sickness tablets, thought they were sweets and downed the whole lot of them. We rang the poison unit, which is open 24/7, and they instructed us to bring him to the hospital right away, so they could pump out his stomach. The hardest job we had on the way to the hospital was trying to keep him awake. They warned us not to let him drift off to sleep. The procedure itself was one I'll never forget. Mother of God, it was a frightening experience to witness. They had a tube down his throat through which they were pumping black charcoal while sucking out the tablets at the same time. It was awful hard to watch because Jackie was roaring for dear life. It got so bad that Eileen couldn't stick it and had to leave. Fortunately, once it was over, he was right as rain.

Today, Jackie is one of my team and works side-by-side with my secretary Martina Drew and assistant Fiona O'Leary. The three of them work really well, and together they make an amazing team. When people ring the office, it's them they speak to and I honestly couldn't ask for a more intelligent and committed team. Should Jackie decide to carve out a career in politics himself, well I would hope he'd be lucky and do well. He's a people person and a hard worker; a great lad for getting things done so you never know what might await him down the road.

The youngest is Kevin. Mother of God, he nearly got me into awful trouble one day. Myself and Gráinne Seoige were filming a segment for a talent show, but the show was being filmed in the old Cork Jail. The place was absolutely freezing; you'd catch your death there it was so cold. When we broke for lunch, Gráinne and I were walking up the stairs, talking about how cold it had been, when she said to me, 'You know, there's only one thing that will warm us up now, and that's a hot bath.'

After we got our food, Gráinne headed off to her hotel room and I to mine. As I was running the bath, Kevin phoned me. He couldn't have been more than eight at the time I'd say. We were chatting anyway when he asked me what I was doing, so I explained to him that myself and Gráinne were freezing so we decided that the only way we could warm up would be to have a bath. He asked a few more questions but said no more about it. Later that night, I was chatting to Eileen.

'You know Kevin was awful confused when he got off the phone from you earlier?' she laughed.

'Why is that?' I replied.

'Well after he put down the phone, he walked in and said, Mum, do you know what Dad is doing? To get warm, he has to take a bath. And Gráinne Seoige is going taking a bath with him! Can you believe that? They have to take a bath together to get warm!'

Well he was full sure myself and Gráinne Seoige were going hopping into a bath together. And what's more, he had no problem telling Eileen either!

When he was a teenager, Kevin announced he wanted to go to Rockwell College in Tipperary. Jackie Jnr decided he was joining him. With the two of them boarding, God it nearly left me broke but it was a mighty experience for them to live away from home at that age. It helped to instil within them a great sense of independence and it has stood to them to this day. Kevin also went on to attend Pallaskenry Agricultural College. It was nice to see him follow in my footsteps that way. Would you believe, some of the teachers that had taught me when I was there also taught Kevin when he attended? Overall, Kevin would be very outgoing, very sociable. He's also a DJ so he's mad into his music as well. I don't know what kind of music they're listening to these days, but I don't think he's following in my footsteps when it comes to the 1980s music.

We're proud of the children, myself and Eileen. They're hard workers and they each have a good head on their shoulders. When you see the upcoming generation doing well and and keeping their noses to the grindstone, it's reassuring in a way. It's nice to see.

A Drink Too Many

I have long been a good strong spokesman for the vintners. We were always on the same wavelength because in the past, the things that I had wanted were the same things they had wanted, and vice versa. When it came to the debate about whether or not to open pubs on Good Friday, however, I had to disagree with them – in a friendly way. This is just a personal opinion, but I would have been happier for the pubs of Ireland to have stayed closed on Good Friday, but sure look, this is why we live in a democracy. In the end, the majority won out and I respect that.

Close publican friends of mine, some of whom would have even canvassed with me, could not get their heads around why I would want the pubs to remain closed, especially when my own family owned one.

'Michael, you must get with the modern times,' they'd say to me. 'We're losing money with tourists who are here for the Easter and can't go into a pub on Good Friday for a drink.'

To be honest, though, not even Pope John Paul himself, God rest him, could convince me it's a good idea to open the pubs on Good Friday.

No one lost their minds when pubs used to have to close every Sunday between the holy hours of 2 p.m. and 4 p.m. There was even a law one time which stated that if your home was a certain distance from the bar, you could stay inside, but if you were from nearby, then the law for you was different. I remember my father telling me a famous story about when the gardaí raided a pub during the banned hours, and they caught a man on the premises. Sure, they were gung-ho in taking him to court, but the man claimed he was within the permitted distance and therefore allowed to be in the pub. So, what do you think the judge said? He said, 'Guards, you must measure the distance.' At the time, they measured distance with a chain. That's how it was done years ago because once the chain was straight, there was no give in it; you knew the measurement was dead accurate.

When the guards asked the judge for the start and finish points for measuring, the judge, who wanted to give the man every bit of help he could, said, 'From the door of the bar to the leg of the bed.' They measured the distance and sure enough found that the man had been beyond the allowed distance, so was in fact entitled to be in the pub. He couldn't be fined or prosecuted, thanks be to God.

Even though I worked behind a bar as a teenager, would you believe I never used to drink. I can't even remember being tempted. I'd say I was in my late teens easily when I first 'took a sup', as they'd say. I was nineteen when myself and Mikey Reilly decided in our infinite wisdom to head into Killarney and see if we could manage to have a drink in every establishment there. If it had a bar, we would have a drink in it. It would be a sort of test to see if we could manage it. The thing is, Killarney has an awful lot of establishments, so for us to aim to have a drink in every one of them was a highly ambitious notion altogether. The first place we went into was the Castle Heights Hotel. Our next conundrum was deciding what we should drink. If we were to carry out this test, we'd need to pace ourselves. Unseasoned drinkers that we were, we decided to start with a glass of brandy. Knowing now what I didn't know back then, that was not a good idea. Every place we went into after that, we downed a brandy. We made it as far as a pub on Killarney's High Street, which, when I look back now, was a great achievement.

Not so great an achievement was our journey home the following morning. God, our heads felt like they had rusty auld chainsaws inside in them. That morning, we got a lift back to

Kilgarvan with a breadman called Jerry who drove for Keating's bread. Now, Jerry was an awful fast driver because he was under pressure to make the deliveries. You'd need a strong stomach the best day ever to be able to endure Jerry's speed on those bendy roads. He would also have Radio One turned up to the last and sure he'd be there trying to shout over the radio when he'd be talking to you. Between the combination of Jerry speeding around bends, the blaring radio and the smell of the hot bread, we were green by the time we fell out of his van in Kilgarvan. We were sure we were going to die. I'm not exaggerating when I say I haven't so much as tasted a drop of brandy since. That night in Killarney was the only time I drank it, and my God, I drank enough of it then that I would never need to drink it again.

A Hundred Per Cent Irish

'Being a Kerryman, in my opinion, is the greatest gift that God can bestow on any man. When you belong to Kerry you know you have a head start on the other fellow. In belonging to Kerry, you belong to the elements, to the spheres spinning in the heavens. You belong to history and language and romance and ancient song. It's almost unbearable being a Kerryman and it's an awesome responsibility.'

I have to say, John B was on to something when he wrote that gem. I've always said there's a streak of madness in all of us; even the most boring people would have something that sets a spark off inside them. I suppose mine can be attributed to the fridge that nearly electrocuted my mother. Or maybe it's the strain of Cork in me. I'm not too sure. Even though I was born in Cork Hospital, I'd never have considered myself a Cork man. Not a hope of it. I'd say if you were to cut me open at all, 'twouldn't be blood you'd find in my veins, but Kerrygold.

Well, the green and gold flag was all but flying at half-mast over my house one Friday night in 2017 when I was informed on *The Late Late Show* that an ancestry.ie test had revealed my DNA was more associated with Cork than it was with Kerry. To put the tin hat on it, Eamon Dunphy had taken part in the same test that night and was found to have had more Kerry DNA in him than I did in me. I haven't been able to live it down to this day. There's still people who ask me about it. On the upside, they found me to be one of the very rare few who could lay claim to being a hundred per cent Irish.

I was genuinely surprised by the results, so after the show I approached the man who had carried out the test, Mike was his name, and I asked him on the quiet just how accurate it was.

'Oh God, we staked our reputation on this,' he told me. 'And look at it this way. If we said anything incorrect about you live on television, the reputation of the company would be destroyed. Ruined!'

Mike went on to tell me that they had located another person on their system with the same DNA as myself. He gave me the man's name and asked if it meant anything to me.

'He's over in New Jersey,' he said, 'and he's the only person in our database that has the same DNA as you and can claim to be a hundred per cent Irish.'

I started laughing. 'Well, the funny thing is,' I said, 'the name does mean something to me because he's my first cousin!'

To me that proved that the test was accurate. Mike couldn't have known the fella in New Jersey was my cousin because not only were our surnames different, I would never have had any reason to have spoken about him publicly. There was no way Mike could have connected us except through those test results. Now, I don't think I'll be togging out in the Cork jersey any time soon, but I will always cherish the proud honour of being able to say I'm a hundred per cent truly Irish.

A bit like the rashers.

Old Times Come Again

It was always said that a good funeral in Kilgarvan was better than a bad wedding anywhere else. If you had great characters lamenting about the deceased person in the coffin, well sure you were guaranteed a mighty night altogether. I remember wakes were all the go when I was younger. Funeral homes took over for a bit, but the trend for wakes appears to be on the way back again. I remember when the funeral home in Kilgarvan was built. We all thought it was very unusual. I think the last big old-fashioned wake I can remember was for a local man. It was a massive wake because both he and his father were awful popular.

I remember the man being laid out on the old timber seat. At five that afternoon there were people queuing up to pay their condolences, and at five the following morning, there were still as many mourners inside in the house. People were the whole night telling stories and yarns and lamenting about times gone by. The man was a great character, so the stories of his farming life, his family life, and so on, were in plentiful supply that night. Sure you couldn't buy those types of memories.

In the same way we're reverting back to wakes, I can see us become a nation of Mass-goers again. Some people would laugh at that statement, but I'm telling you, I can see it happening. If you think about it, everything goes in cycles. There was a time when people were building houses out of stone and nothing else. Then along came modernisation, and sure everyone went mad for plastering; that was the done thing. Today, it has become fashionable to knock off the plaster and expose the stonework again. The unfashionable has become the fashionable. I would just love to see us go one step further and try to give a new lease of life to the ruins of the derelict old cottages that are all over the countryside. They're so commonplace that most people don't even take any notice of them any more. It would really be something else to see these beauties of the past being restored, and new life brought back into them. I remember when my cousin, Paudie Buckley, passed away, it just wasn't feasible for his brother, Timmy, to live on his own, so he moved into a nursing home. I'm telling you it was a sad day when the door of Paudie and Timmy's house closed for the last time. Like so many other houses in the countryside, it had witnessed so many memories being made and stories told and I hope, in the future, houses like this will get a new lease of life.

By injecting life back into the old houses, we would be reinvigorating the community too. Where I live, I one hundred per cent rely on the people of the village and on my next-door neighbours. If it weren't for the woman on one side of my house, I'd be dead from choking. My neighbour on the other side is Cathal Sullivan, who used to carry me to the digger on his back when the injuries I sustained from the car crash meant I couldn't walk for a while. The house next door to Cathal's belongs to Donal and Cathy Twomey, lifelong friends of mine.

Another lifelong friend of mine is a remarkable man called Seán Jones. Seán and I have been friends since our school days and we have stuck together through thick and thin. Seán was the manager of the fish factory where I worked as a young lad, but he was also into property and storage rental. He had started out with nothing other than a good brain, a strong work ethic and a backbone made of steel and my God did he put them to good use. I remember when he started the storage business, the only people doing it at the time were based in Dublin and Limerick. Seán however saw an opportunity for such a service in Kenmare, so he got it off the ground and turned it into a hugely successful business.

Even as a young fella, you knew Seán would do well in life. He was just a natural hard worker. His parents likewise were the finest people you could meet. I remember one time, there was a house I wanted to buy; it was a great deal, but I couldn't afford it, so I told Seán about it and suggested he buy it for himself. I always believe that if there's something you can't have, well isn't it better that one of your friends have it instead? In the end, Seán's brother bought it. He had that house rented out for years. I used to help out by collecting the rent for him and carrying out any repairs that needed doing. One night anyway, I was standing in the hut of my garage waiting to serve petrol, when who should arrive in only Seán's mother.

Now, Seán's mother, God be good to her, was a lovely woman but a formidable one. You wouldn't argue with her. 'We're going selling the house,' she informed me, 'and you must buy it.' At the time, the idea of buying a house was the furthest thing from my mind. Sure I couldn't have bought so much as a pair of boots with the money I had to my name.

'Oh no, 'tis grand, Mrs Jones,' I replied, 'I don't want it.'

'Now Michael,' she started, in the sternest tone imaginable, 'don't be silly. There's no ifs or buts about it, you're buying the house and that's the end of it.'

She put out her hand and we shook on it. There was no mention of money, it was a case of 'you're buying the house, and that's that.' And off she went in the car, leaving me standing there with my mouth open, thinking, oh mother of God, how will I tell Eileen that I'm after buying a house? There was no backing out either; sure we had shaken hands on it, and as far as I was concerned, a handshake or a voiced promise was as good as a contract. In the end, I went and bought the house. Years later, long after Mrs Jones had gone to her eternal reward, I got a letter in the post. I read it and picked up the phone to call Seán. The letter was from the bank telling me that I had made the last mortgage repayment on what I called the Jones house. Had it not been for Seán's mother, I wouldn't have bought that house, and I have always believed that it's only right to have your manners and thank those who gave you good advice or helped you out in life. I couldn't thank Seán's mother, so I did the next best thing and thanked him instead.

There are so many people that have stuck by me all throughout my life, and dear God, I know it's only when this book is out on the shelves that I'll realise I forgot to mention an absolute pile of them. It has caused me great deal of concern to know that I have more than likely left out names that were worthy of a mention. Not since I went hell for leather on the brandy in Killarney back in my early twenties have I had such a case of the fear, I can tell you! You might wonder what the big deal is, but to me, it really is a big deal because I value every single friendship.

You could have all the money in the world, but what use is it unless you have sincere, good-natured people in your life? 'Tis like when I had to ring one of my neighbours recently. There was a cow of mine in trouble and I couldn't get home to tend to her. I phoned my neighbour and explained my predicament. Straight away, he dropped what he was doing and went to see how my cow was doing. You can't fake that kind of neighbourly loyalty. That's part of the fabric of where you're from. I know that I can call on my neighbours and they know they can call on me.

I remember one day when Donal Twomey, who lives right next door to me, was laying down tarmacadam around my house. There was another man helping Donal, but he wasn't a local. Once they were finished, the two went back to Donal's house which is a no more than a stone's throw away from mine. I'd say they weren't five minutes gone, when I got a phone call from Donal. 'Come quick and bring the gun,' was all he said before he hung up. I did exactly as I was asked. I got the gun, put some cartridges into my pocket, and ran down my yard over to Donal's house. I held the gun in the upright position, ready to load and fire when I'd see exactly what was happening. As I got closer to the house, I could hear this awful screeching going on. What was it only a mink attacking their cat.

Now, I love animals, I do, but this mink was out of control and needed to be disposed of. When I realised what was happening, I quickly dropped to one knee, loaded the gun, took aim and promptly sent the mink into the next world. Donal nodded at me. 'That's alright now,' he said. Without saying a word, I put the two spent cartridges into my pocket and headed back to my house. The man that had been helping Donal with the tarmacadam had witnessed the whole thing, except what he saw was Donal making one phone call and saying nothing more than 'bring the gun'. I wouldn't even have been sixty seconds when I had landed in beside them, dropped to one knee and fired the necessary shots. After I left, the man turned to Donal's wife, Cathy. 'By God Cathy, with a neighbour like that, you'd always want to watch yourself.' Donal and Cathy got mileage out of that for years!

In Kilgarvan, the people of the village look out for each other and stick together, and it's been like that since back in my grandfather's day when the locals collectively ensured the village remained completely silent so as not to wake the patient after his brain surgery in the pub. I've always said it, when a family is going through a hard time, that's when you will really see the supportive spirit of an Irish village.

I've been fortunate all through my life to have been surrounded by great people. From my wife, Eileen, and our children, to my extended family, friends, neighbours, team members, and supporters. God, I've been very lucky with the company I've been keeping all these years.

In politics, I have had mighty people guide me. You already know about the late Bernard Collins, and Arthur Lenihan. Then there are so many people that canvass with me. Mighty people like Tom Shea and his wife Sheila from Waterville. Tom is one of life's gentlemen. I always joke that if you want to improve something, you should ask Tom if he wants a loan of it. If you're lucky, he'll say yes, because when he'll give it back to you, you'll be guaranteed to find it in ten times better condition than when you had it the first day ever. He's such a diligent man, Tom, and you can't but learn so much from a person like that.

I have always deliberately surrounded myself with people who are much smarter than I am. Sure, you can't learn anything if you're the smartest person in the room. Risteard Ó'Lionáird is definitely one of these people. He is a calming influence on me at all times which is very important in politics. Another great couple are Kevin and Judy Tarrant who have been of huge assistance in every election campaign we have taken part in over the years. I was very fortunate in the sense that the individuals in question were people who also happened to be neighbours and friends; good solid sound people who chose to stick with me, guide me and advise me. Ever since I was a young lad, I have always learned an immense amount from the people around me and how they do things.

For instance, there's a brilliant man from Ballinskelligs, Nicholas Browne is his name; I've been friends with him since I was a teenager. Well Nicholas works in plant hire and construction and his whole life has been dedicated to hard work. We started our working lives together and we both continued on in the same business. We have so much in common because every problem I've had, Nicholas has also had. What you need to know about Nicholas however is that he's one smart man, so much so that when he was building his own house, he did something that no one else in the country would have done, or could have done, but him.

As his family was growing, his house needed to grow accordingly, so he decided he would build the new house on the exact same spot where his current house was standing. That was all grand, until Nicholas then decided he wanted to continue on living in the old house while the new one was being built. He was telling me about it one night, and I honestly couldn't get my head around it.

'How is that going to work?' I asked him. 'How can you build a house in the very same spot as the old one if you're not going to knock the old one first?'

'I can do it no problem,' he replied. 'I'll dig the foundation outside my old house; I'll start building the new house around it. We'll continue to live in the old house and when we've the new house built, I'll throw the old house out through the windows of the new one.'

I looked at him. 'You're joking me?'

'Am I in the habit of joking?' he said back to me, dead serious.

Nicholas is a right tough man, a very determined character altogether, so when he says he's going to do something, there's no question it will be done. Sure enough, he started building the new house around the old one. For a long time, when we'd go to visit him, we would have to climb up a ladder, go in through a window, and then down the stairs into the old house. We had to go through the new house to get to the old one. Confusing, but factual. While the construction of the new house was taking place around them, Nicholas and his family carried on living in the old house same as usual. Once the new build was complete, Nicholas went and did the one thing he said he would do. He quite literally threw the old house out through the windows of the new one. You can marvel at the construction of the American skyscrapers all you want, but you'd still be hard pushed to find a man who managed to build his house from the inside out only to then open the windows and start firing out the old house he didn't want.

I have always said that any individual is only as good as the people around them and I am very fortunate with the good people I have around me.

In finishing this book, I want to thank from the bottom of my heart the people that have stood with me through thick and thin; the people that have canvassed with me in the past, and those who will do so in the future.

I have purposely not named people from Kilgarvan who have worked so hard with me over the years canvassing, as to do so would take up another book! I would like these people to know, however that I appreciate every single one of them and the support they have always shown.

I'm telling you, money can't buy friends and neighbours like mine.

Gill Books
Hume Avenue
Park West
Dublin 12
www.gillbooks.ie
Gill Books is an imprint of M.H. Gill and Co.

© Michael Healy-Rae 2018

978 07171 8315 9

Designed by Carole Lynch
Edited by Tara King
Copy edit by Jane Rogers

Printed by ScandBook AB, Sweden
This book is typeset in Minion.

The paper used in this book comes from the wood pulp
of managed forests. For every tree felled, at least one tree
is planted, thereby renewing natural resources.

A CIP catalogue record for this book is available from
the British Library.

5 4 3 2 1